The Guns of
Dorking Hollow

OTHER SAGEBRUSH LARGE PRINT WESTERNS BY
MAX BRAND

The Abandoned Outlaw: A Western Trio
Bull Hunter's Romance
The City in the Sky
Crossroads
The Desert Pilot
Dust Across the Range
Farewell Thunder Moon
Fire Brain
Fugitives' Fire
The Legend of Thunder Moon
Luck
The Night Horseman
The Oath of Office
The One-Way Trail: A Western Trio
The Pride of Tyson
The Quest of Lee Garrison
Safety McTee: A Western Trio
Slumber Mountain: A Western Trio
Soft Metal: A Western Trio
Tales of the Wild West: A Western Trio
Thunder Moon and Red Wind
Thunder Moon and the Sky People
Two Sixes: A Western Trio
The Ghost Rides Tonight!
The Untamed
The Valley of Jewels

The Guns of Dorking Hollow

MAX BRAND™

Sagebrush
Large Print Westerns

Published in Large Print 2004 by ISIS Publishing Ltd,
7 Centremead, Osney Mead,
Oxford OX2 0ES, United Kingdom
by arrangement with
Golden West Literary Agency

British Library Cataloguing in Publication Data
Brand, Max, 1982–1944
    The guns of Dorking Hollow. – Large print ed. –
    (Sagebrush western series)
    1. Western stories
    2. Large type books
    I. Title
    813.5′2 [F]

ISBN 0–7531–7107–4 (hb)

Printed and bound by
Antony Rowe, Chippenham, United Kingdom

CHAPTER ONE

UNDER THE ARMS OF MOUNT CHESTER lay Dorking Hollow. On the opposite side of the valley, looking south, was Mount Crandall. When I first looked on the place, I told myself that I had made the long journey out from civilization in vain, because this valley was much too beautiful to make a mining camp. Much! I had been to California. I had dug silver in Mexico for five unlucky years. But I never before had seen metal taken out of ground in such surroundings as there. For behind Crandall and Chester, north and south, bigger ranges of white-headed peaks flocked away against the sky, and all the valley was covered with a great virgin forest.

A virgin forest is where the great trees have stood for a hundred thousand years, growing old, dying, and giving the decay of their bodies to the roots of some even more gigantic successor. And among such trees I have seen one the face of which was like the face of a man—the face of a wise man, and a hero.

But though I thought Dorking Hollow looked far too beautiful to have either gold or silver in it, I was wrong, and the first prospectors were right. In the hills of that valley there was enough virgin silver to break the price of that metal—in all the markets of the world, I think.

Here Joe Wayne looks over my shoulder and asks: "What are you doing, Paul?"

"Telling the story of King Stork," I reply.

"Then why don't you start at the right beginning?" asked he. "How much time did the King waste on scenery?"

That is true, of course, and I'll get to him in due time;

1

but I think it is best to give you, first of all an idea of the stage onto which King Stork stepped.

I was saying that Dorking Hollow looked much too good to be true. Usually, when you find gold or silver, it is ten thousands miles from the nearest town where one can get timber. It is either in the snows of the mountains, or the red-hot rocks of the desert, locked up in a place so hard to get at that bars and bolts are not needed to keep the stuff secure. But here was everything that one could dream of wishing for. The finest wood that ever felt an ax swarmed down the great slopes of the mountains. The waters of the Dorking River rolled smoothly down the center of the hollow; and, lest that should not be enough, or too inconvenient for any one, God striped the sides of the hollow with twenty creeks in silver flashing lines. The winter was never harsher than a brisk chill—not enough to let the hands of a miner grow numb when he held the drill. And the summer was never hotter than comfortable.

Dorking Valley was perfect. I have never seen anything like it. And no matter how much the newcomers spurred and raced to get across the hills to stake their claims, when they rounded the shoulder of Crandall, coming north, or Chester, coming south, they were almost sure to draw rein and gaze for a while.

Yes, Dorking Hollow was beautiful. And as the silver began to be taken from the earth in ores too rich for belief, and as the long mule trains began to pack it across the mountains—and floods of good dollars returned to camp in exchange—we stretched our hands to that cheerful fire of prosperity—we old-timers—and asked one another if it were a dream? It was simply too good to be true; certainly it was too good to last.

And it didn't last!

What is good for one is good for another. And those untracked forests which gave us such good hunting of deer gave other kinds of people good hunting of us! When we in turn hunted the hunters, we had a miserable job of it, for all the back country was checked and crossed and recrossed by deep ravines, clouded over with masses of brush. Ten thousand axes in ten thousand years could hardly have cleared that wilderness, and the robbers made their dens almost wherever they paused for the night. For there was sure to be perfect covert within half a mile.

We did everything that we could. We were not tenderfeet, those of us who had the real influence in the camp. We had representatives from all of the great mining rushes. And inside the camps we ruled with a vigilance committee which functioned perfectly. If a man so much as pulled a revolver and blew a few rounds into the air for the sake of celebrating a new strike, he was sure to be rounded up by a crowd of stern-faced men and asked what he meant. And usually the inquiry ended in his being packed right out of camp. There were a great many forced sales of claims, as a result of this method.

We had such perfect order that when some of the boys drank too deep of their good spirits and fell asleep in the street with their money belts loaded, they would wake up in the morning with all their wealth untouched. For the trials were short and brisk and to the point. And thieves were not given first warnings, or suspended sentences, or even terms in prison. They were simply strung up to some high branch and left to dangle there for a day or two by way of warning to kindred spirits.

There was never a more efficiently functioning machine than our vigilance committee at Dorking

Hollow; and, as I have said, inside the camp reigned perfect order and safety. The usual curses of mining camps were entirely absent. There were no rowdies running at large. There were no bullies. There were no man-killers. There were no thieves for long. There were no claim-jumpers.

But beyond the limits of the camp? Ah that was a different story. And I cannot help groaning and closing my eyes when I think of that other picture beyond Dorking Hollow itself.

What was the use of all the metal we took from the ground unless we could get it to a market? And how could we get it to a market unless we crossed the hills and valleys which rose and sank like the waves of the sea? No, there was no way! We had to send out our caravans of mules and horses. And every time they left camp, we shook hands gravely and bade good-by to the muleteers and the caravan guards, feeling that we were probably looking our last upon them—and the last upon our freight, also!

It was not such a great distance across the hills to the river, down which the boats carried our things securely and cheaply enough. It was not the mileage, but the nature of the country that gave us the trouble. And freight rates began to jump up at a dreadful speed. What else could the freighters do? As one of them said: "I have one chance in two of getting through with my mules and men. Perhaps one chance in three. Therefore, if you want me to carry your silver, pay me the price of my pack animals, and the wages of my men, and give me something in addition."

And even when we paid those prices, still we had no security. I saw three men in a single day give up rich claims and travel sadly back across the mountains. They had surrendered. And then a fresh difficulty arose: one could find no means of transport, at any price, for the simple reason that the supply of mules was giving out.

Those were miserable days!

You will say: "Why didn't the men in camp appoint one man to lead and command them and submit to any tyrant in order to catch the thieves?"

Ah, but that was exactly what we did! Avery Lucas was made king of the camp. Lucas was a man wise in mines and mining ways. He was an excellent shot; a man without fear; honest as the day is long; kind, just, and firm. He organized our posses. He led us across the mountains sometimes by day, and sometimes by night. He established a permanent committee of fighting men with the finest, fastest horses that could be bought; and these fellows, armed to the teeth, were continually ready to dash out of camp and take the trail of the miscreants.

And they caught a thief, now and then. But only now and then. The country was all in favor of the outlaws, and all against us. We were well-mounted, but so were they. And though we studied the country, we could not know it quite so well as they did. It was a matter of money to us; it was a matter of life or death to them. And such a spur makes men's minds active.

Sometimes people in the camp suggested other men to take the place of Avery Lucas. Twice he voluntarily resigned from his post and gave his place to another; and twice, after a reign of a few days, the new camp king slipped from the valley and disappeared, admitting that the task was too much for him!

Then we sent for that famous manslayer and man hunter, Oliver Masters. Masters came and looked wisely over the lay of the land, and carried on a ten-day campaign; but on the eleventh day his posse was

5

surprised, blown to bits, and Oliver Masters himself left on the ground for dead, filled full of lead. He recovered, but he recovered only with a desire to get away from the hollow at any price. And we had to let him go.

Matters constantly grew worse. We were running the mines at a terrible loss. It had become almost impossible to freight even provisions into the camp, because the robbers in the hills wanted our necessities for themselves. But in spite of our losses, we continued to moil and toil at the mines; because it was a huge provocation, of course, to know that that rich ore lay waiting to be dug out!

It was maddening. Our nerves were shot to pieces. Men went around with sad, dark faces. Friends quarreled with friends, and it was only the firm hand of King Avery Lucas that kept the camp from turning into a typical mining camp slaughterhouse.

No, we remained orderly perforce; but every day we grew poorer while working mines that were as rich as any in the world. And all of our toil was producing a current of silver which ran richly into the pockets of the scoundrels in the hills. Now and again, from a captured thief, we learned before we hanged him of the joyous, gay, careless life of the robbers, of the gangs into which they were formed. And we groaned and sighed, and prayed for help.

Then we began to send out caravans which we knew were not strong enough, but which we hoped could fight their way through—small groups of mules, attended by only a few fighting men. It was a very successful scheme, for a time. Those little groups started after dark, slipped out of the hollow in the dark of the moon and stole off through the forest making very little noise. If captured, the prize was not really huge. And each time, it would have to be fought for bitterly. Two or three sure shots, herding their mules across country, made a hard nut to crack; and many and many a group of the brigands paid richly in life blood for a small amount of treasure gained. But this good fortune did not last, for among the robbers there appeared an inspired young devil for whom this game was entirely suited. I shall never forget that day when we first heard about "a young gent with a yaller handkerchief around his kneck and a Mex sombrero on his head." The other bandits were apt to hunt in bands. But this was a solitary eagle who liked nothing better than finding a group of hawks and dropping on them out of the clear sky with a six-shooter in either hand.

A smiling young fiend, a battle-loving madman, he traced those little caravans, scattered the best of our fighters, and grew fat on the spoils. And the day of the small shipments ended abruptly.

CHAPTER TWO

EVERYTHING CAME AT LAST TO A STANDSTILL.

For three weeks not an ounce of metal left the camp. We were half starved. We were wholly desperate. And then young Chris Lagonda announced that he and two friends would take out a small mule train and try to slip through in spite of Mex, as we called him, because of his sombrero.

Lagonda and his two companions, after dark of that day, started out on the trail, and a dozen of us decided that we would follow softly behind him; not on horseback, because that might make too much noise, but on foot. We put Canada Harry at our head. He was half

Indian, possessed of wonderful craft and skill in following a forest trail, and behind him we went in single file. He set the example of soft walking through the trees, and we followed. If that mule train should be surprised, at least we would have an excellent chance of exacting vengeance. And there was a great deal of grim comfort in that thought.

I expected that the trail would carry us on for a long time before we had any trouble, but we were not a mile from the hollow, and the evening light had hardly died into utter darkness, when there was a chatter of guns before us, a scream that still darts through my ears in my dreams at night, and then silence.

Swiftly we of the rear guard sped forward, opening our formation, and coming on loosely abreast.

Then we came to the place where young Lagonda lay groaning and writhing on the ground; and, just ahead a single horseman was seen gathering up the leads of the four mules.

He heard us coming, but he could not judge of our numbers in the dark. He saw stealthy shadows, and opened fire. He shot twice from the back of his horse; and I heard two of our men curse and saw them fall. Then we poured in our volley, and the bandit disappeared.

No, he had not really disappeared. His horse had been shot through the head; and, when we came up, we found the outlaw pinned beneath the fallen poney. We moved the horse and took his rider out, unscathed, and tied him hand and foot. Then Canada Harry lighted a match and held it before the face of the robber.

We saw the flash of a yellow silk bandanna, richly spotted with blue, around his neck; we saw long, flowing, dark hair. And beneath the sombrero was as handsome a face as ever laughed at the world. And it was laughing now.

"Well, boys," he said, "it was a beautiful game while it lasted."

Canada Harry had lost a partner by the guns of this rascal. He leaned and struck him heavily in the face.

"I'm gunna fry you over a slow fire," said Canada.

"Do it," said the captive, "and I'll lay you ten thousand dollars to a dime that I give you no satisfaction. Not so much as a groan, Canada!"

"You know me?" asked Canada, more furious than ever.

"Certainly," said the other. "And I knew Louis Le Farge, too!"

That was the name of Canada's dead partner; he drew a knife and would have sliced the throat of our prisoner on the spot, but we held him back.

"This has to be legal," I told the boys. And though they were very excited, they listened to me. I was older than the others; and I had had more experience.

First, we built a fire, while two men watched our captive. By that firelight we brought in the wounded. By the grace of fortune, there were no dead. Lagonda was very sick from a bullet through the body, but I knew enough about medicine to tell that he had two chances out of three of living. For miners die hard.

Chadwick, one of Lagonda's companions, was shot through the shoulders; he was propped against a tree and cursed Mex, as the boys were calling the bandit, with a steady flow of venom. The third muleteer had fled from the deadly bullets of this fellow who seemed able to see in the dark.

Neither of the two who had fallen in the rear guard had been very badly hurt; just enough to put them out of

9

action, for both wounds were between the hip and the knee. We bandaged the hurts of the injured. Then we drew in a circle around Mex. Already a rope hung over a stout branch.

"We'd better rush this here business through," said Canada Harry. "This gent, he may have pals!"

"Many friends," said Mex. "But no pals!"

"Hold on," said I. "All of you bandits have your partners. I know that!"

"Not I, Mr. Loomis," said he.

It startled me.

"Do you know me, Mex?" said I.

"Why, sir," said he, "it's a foolish businessman who doesn't know his best patrons."

That insolence brought a growl from some of the boys with me, and Canada Harry was fingering his knife hungrily again, but I couldn't help smiling. Apparently the danger he was in meant nothing to this young scoundrel. I was immensely interested.

"Tell me, Mex," said I, "what we can do for you before we string you up?"

"Thank you," said he. "I'd like a cigarette and my hands tied in front of me so that I can smoke it."

"Damn him," said one behind him, "I'd see him in hell first!"

"Hold on," said I. "He only has a moment or two left. Let him have what he wants. We can't do more than kill him, boys."

For I had a slight hope that, by good treatment, we might be able to draw some most valuable information from this youth—information that would lead us to the haunts of others among the brigands. Therefore, I had his hands freed and then tied together in front of him so that he could manage the cigarette which I rolled for

10

him. With has back against a tree, seated comfortably on a stump, he smoked, and let his great, brown eyes wander lazily across our faces. He seemed mildly interested, quietly amused by this situation.

"Mex," I said, "I believe that a dying man has certain rights, and one of those is to send messages to those who are dear to him. You can safely confide any such messages to me."

"Thank you, Mr. Loomis," said he, "but why should I? I would have to give you my name; and my people would be greatly cut up. They would feel disgrace; sorrow; pity for me, and some pity for themselves—all disagreeable emotions, you'll admit. But as it is, I shall be to them simply a ship that sailed and never returned to port. My memory will be sweet with them. My father will keep his pride in me. My mother will keep her love. My brother will be told to grow up like me."

He paused and laughed softly, admiring the irony of life. As for me, my blood ran cold.

"I think you have very few regrets," said I.

"Not one—really," he admitted.

"Not for this sort of a life? When you've been raised for better things, and educated—"

"Stuff!" said he. "The vital part of my education didn't begin until I found a horse and a gun. And after that, I've done nothing to be ashamed of."

There was an angry growl from the men who formed our listening circle. They were as much interested as I; but their interest was based on a savage hatred.

"Be quiet," said Mex coldly to them. "You dogs have a wolf down this evening. But remember that you are still dogs!"

There was a general lurch toward him; but then they remembered that his hands were tied, and controlled

11

themselves. And I think, too, that their hatred of him was so intense that they were in no hurry to close this death scene. They were feasting their eyes on the man who was so soon to be hanged.

"Nothing to be ashamed of!" said I. "I don't want to think that there is a gap in your powers of logic, Mex."

"Not a bit," said he, blandly. "I wanted amusement; and I've had it. Every other man wants amusement; but most of them haven't the nerve to take what they want."

"Midnight murder has a black name in the world, my lad," said I.

"It has, hasn't it?" said he, very impersonally. "But, of course, I've never murdered a man in my life."

There was a general groan of disgust from the listeners. But Mex merely smiled, and running his dark eyes across their faces, he said: "Why don't you speak out? Which of you has ever heard of a man being shot from behind by me?"

There was silence, and he went on: "I've never drawn a gun on a lone man in my life."

"Is that a joke, Mex?" I asked him. "We haven't four wounded men with us tonight, I suppose?"

"Of course," he answered. "But there were three in the first party. I stepped out in front of them. I didn't even take them from the flank. I've never taken an advantage. Why, man, you don't think that I've been doing this work for the money I can make out of it, do you?"

There was such open disgust in his voice that I looked at him with a deeper interest than before, and a deeper amazement. And the silence of my companions told me that they were equally interested.

"Tell me, Mex," I said suddenly, "how you've come to know our faces so well?"

"By looking at them," he answered.

"Hello! And how could you manage that?"

"Why," said he, "when the streets are dark, the houses are lighted. And there you are."

"You mean to say that you've been wandering down into Dorking Hollow by night?"

"Certainly. It was perfectly safe—in such a well-governed community."

And he smiled at us again.

Suddenly Canada Harry broke in: "Ain't it time to try this gent, Mr. Loomis?"

"We'll try him, then, and have the thing over with," said I. "Who's judge?"

"You, Mr. Loomis."

"The rest of you are jurors, then. Pay attention, boys. Mex, you're now on trial for your life."

CHAPTER THREE

"LOOK HERE MY FRIENDS," said Mex. "I thank you for your kindness, but I'd as soon be hung without trimmings as with them. If you want to do me a great favor, leave the rope out of it, and finish me off with a gun. How about that, Mr. Loomis?"

There was a general shout of protest from the men of Dorking Hollow, and I, myself, felt that the request would not do. Because a great many of these reckless, gun-fighting outlaws cared nothing at all for death by powder and lead, with which they had familiarized themselves almost from birth; but the very thought of dangling and kicking at the end of a rope was horror to them.

Then Joe Wayne, who was usually one of the last to

13

speak, but who often had the most important items to contribute to a conversation, said quietly: "Let him buy a death by shooting. Why not, Paul?"

"Let him buy a death by shooting? How about that, boys?"

I turned to the crowd and continued: "Here's a man who doesn't care to be tried. He'd as soon take his death and call all quits. Do I understand you on that point, Mex?"

"Certainly," said he.

"Mr. Joe Wayne suggests that we allow you to buy a death by rifles."

"Thank you, Mr. Wayne," said the prisoner, smiling.

The thought seemed to attract a good deal of favorable comment from the rest of the men. I said briefly: "Has any one a good argument against selling this man such a privilege?"

"I have," said Canada Harry at once. "Choking is too good for him. And shooting would be heaven, to a skunk like that."

"Tut, tut!" said Mex. "How violent Canada is! You don't realize how kind I was to your partner, Harry, or I'm quite sure that you wouldn't talk like this."

"You was kind, was you?" said Canada, quivering with fury. "And how kind was you, might I be asking, you murdering swine, you!"

"When it came to the pinch, he was a little backward about settling the matter with guns in a square light, draw as you please. So I had to encourage him by dropping both my guns on the ground. Then he consented to go for his Colt. And that was how he died. You must admit that that's fair treatment, Canada."

"Ay," said Canada, "if it was true. But it's a lie, and a loud lie, because I'm asking all of you boys, how could

14

any man in the world have beat my partner when it come to a draw like that? A plain draw against a gun on the ground!"

"Very well," said Mex. "Since you say I'm a liar, let me demonstrate. A gun on the ground against the gun in your holster!"

Canada hesitated.

"And you to get a chance to break away?" he sneered. "A sweet job that would be!"

"Nonsense. The rest of the boys cover me with their guns. Their rifles, you understand. If I try to make a break for it, they fill me full of lead. But in the meantime, I have a chance to prove that I didn't lie. Do you like the idea, Canada?"

He leaned forward from his stump and stared at Harry with eyes that blazed with eagerness. Not anger, mind you, but a sort of feline, cruel delight in the fun which might come out of this. Harry was plainly abashed, and I didn't wonder. No matter what advantages might be given to me, I should have hated to stand up against this man of war. I cut the argument short.

"It can't happen, Mex," said I. "It's a good gaming proposition, and I admire your offer. But we're here to send you out of this world, not to see if you can send another man before you."

"Very well," said Mex with a sigh. "I only hoped that I might have a chance to shoot that lie out of his mouth. But I can't have that luck. But you were going to sell me a chance to buy a death by powder and lead. What about that?"

"Let's hear him talk, then," said Canada. "What'll you offer?"

"I'll offer—let me see—five thousand dollars. Does that sound all right to you?"

15

"Five thousand dollars?" I repeated, amazed to hear a man bid like this for the privilege of one form of death instead of another. "And where will you get that?"

"Why," said Mex, "of course one can't carry that much around with one. And so I have cached the money here and there, in convenient places. I can send you to find it."

"That's a pretty yarn," said Canada. "We blow you into hell and afterward we go on a wild-goose chase for the purpose of getting coin that ain't where you say it was."

"You can wait until you've found the stuff. There's five thousand within ten minutes' walk of here," replied Mex. He said it in such a way that I, for my part, had not the slightest doubt that he meant what he said. Neither did the others.

"Mex offers five thousand for a bullet through the head," said I. "Are there any objections?"

"Yes," said Joe Wayne, putting in his quiet word again. "It's not enough. Ten thousand would hardly do."

"Very well," said the prisoner. "I'll raise my offer to ten thousand and I call that a very fair offer. Do you agree?"

"I agree," said Wayne.

"Ten thousand is offered, gentlemen," said I. "Ten thousand dollars to be spent on Dorking Hollow in some public improvement. Does that meet with your approval?"

Some one grunted: "Why spend that money on Dorking Hollow? The town is dead as long as these rats stay here in the woods and cut off every ore shipment! Why throw away good money after bad? Dorking Hollow is sunk!"

There was a good deal of sense in this.

"How else can the money be spent?" I asked.

"You could have a very tidy monument raised," said Mex, "to the brave vigilantes who caught Mex and shot him."

"Monument? Hell!" exploded Canada.

"Well," suggested Mex, "if that doesn't please you, I suggest that you use the money for a widows and orphans fund—left relicts by the late Mex. Something to provide for the little dears. There must be quite a list of them by this time. Bullets have no conscience, you know, and dear papas go as well as bachelors."

It sent a chill swiftly up my spine to hear him talk in this fashion. And there was an angry murmur from the other men, but it subsided at once. They seemed more fascinated than infuriated by this fellow; and every moment increased his charm. He was like a beautiful dark panther, sitting there at his ease, so smiling, and so composed. And even with his hands and his feet tied, he still seemed so formidable that every moment guns were carefully trained upon him. We are all manifestly afraid of this young destroyer.

"Does that idea please?" inquired Mex, smiling at us still.

"Look at him grin at us and mock us!" cried Harry. "Hang him, I say; string him up!"

"Ah, gentlemen," said the robber, "think of the pleasure that you miss! To see me choke at a rope's end is nothing. But to drive a bullet through my heart or head—that would be a real satisfaction, I take it!"

"One moment," said Joe Wayne. "I think that we could drive a still better bargain with this man."

"For more money?" said the prisoner. "No. Mr. Wayne. Where is your sense of humor? Ten thousand dollars for a volley of bullets—that's enough. I won't

17

pay another penny for the privilege."

"Instead of ten thousand," said Wayne, "suppose that you simply tell us the locations of a few of the main strongholds of the thugs, your friends?"

"So that you could round up a few dozen of them?" asked Mex.

"Why not? After you are dead and gone, do you care how soon a few score of the others follow you to hell?"

"Excellent reasoning," said Mex; "and, as a matter of fact, when I think of the sport you could have hunting these fellows through the woods it fairly makes my heart ache to think that I am not on your side. But you all seem a little hard of hearing, and a little short of sight. You don't find the trails! I've been rocked to sleep in a treetop while fifty men hunted for me on the ground underneath. They seemed to think it possible that I could go into any gopher hole. But they wouldn't imagine that I really had hands for climbing."

I could remember such a hunt, and I felt my face growing hot. Mex was enjoying our confusion with another of his gentle smiles.

"But as for betraying them," said Mex, "if you offered me my life and a pension of a million a year, I would laugh at you. My word is a little bit better than a government bond!"

He said it not with flamboyant pride, but as a calm statement of fact, and I believed him. The terrible pride of this strange young man would have made it quite impossible for him to do a degrading thing. Many a wild and cruel thing, no doubt, but nothing mean or unmanly. His character was being revealed to me more and more, and though the strokes were exceedingly broad and heavy, I confess that I liked a great many of them. Ten good ordinary men could have been cut out of the

18

material that was in him.

Then Canada Harry suddenly cried: "*Mon Dieu! Mon Dieu! Mon Dieu!*"

"Hey, boys," cried one of his mates, "Harry's talking Frog. What's the matter with him? Maybe he has an idea!"

Canada Harry caught me by the shoulder and dragged me away from the circle. He broke into a flood of French patois, as he always did when he was greatly moved, speaking swiftly and softly.

"It has come to me from God, this great idea!" said Harry. "God said to me: 'Henri Bassompierre, this Mex is a tool with which much hard rock could be broken if he were on your side. Make him one of you, and he will drive the outlaws away like a forest fire!' "

It amazed me. And yet, when I thought back, I could see that the suggestion of this idea had been in the very words of Mex himself. An idea? It might be worse than useless. And, on the other hand, it might be the salvation of Dorking Hollow.

I went back and placed myself in the center of the circle.

"My friends," said I, "Dorking Hollow is done, isn't it?"

A groan answered me.

"We have to take violent steps to save the place?"

Another groan.

"Do you think that we could really trust the word of honor of Mex?"

There was a silence, but I could tell by their eyes that they really would trust him. I asked for no more from them, but turned to Mex.

"Mex, is there any real reason why you have not been able to get on with honest people?"

"The dull life, Mr. Loomis. That's all."

"Suppose that we asked you to come into Dorking Hollow and made you—well, I might call you our general? And gave you men to hunt the thieves out of the woods? What would you say to that, Mex?"

CHAPTER FOUR

SILENCE OF ASTONISHMENT FELL ON THAT CIRCLE.

"I almost think," said Mex, "that your Canada Harry made that suggestion. Did he?"

"Canada Harry is more likely to suggest burning you over a slow fire," said Joe Wayne.

"He hates me for one reason," said Mex. "But on the other hand, he loves that little claim of his and the silver which he's been taking out of it."

"Look here, Mr. Loomis," said one of the posse, "I know that you've plenty of sense. But I ask you if you ain't joking with us just now?"

"Joking?" I answered. "I was never farther from it."

"Then tell us what you mean?"

"Why," said I, "we have our hands on the worst of the rascals who have been robbing us and our mule trains. But he isn't the only one. It would be a good deal of satisfaction to string him up to the branch of that tree, or to send a bullet through his head. But unfortunately, that would not be an end to our troubles. He is one grain of dust, and there is a whole sandstorm blowing in our faces. But it occurred to Canada Harry, and it seems to me, also, that Mex should make a very good hunter. We know that he's been able to hunt us. And if it weren't for the bullet that went through the head of his horse— or for the accident that pinned him under the pony when

20

it fell—why, partners, Mex would be drifting among these trees trying to get in a few more shots. And we'd all be wishing that we were back in Dorking Hollow, I think!"

They could all see the point of that.

I went on, pursuing this stranger thought which Canada Harry had suggested: "Now, friends, when a man has a desperate disease, he sometimes has to adopt a desperate remedy, as you all know. It's better to risk a leg than to risk a life, isn't it?"

They had no answer for that. They were looking intently, first at me, and then at Mex. And Mex bore their glances with a magnificent indifference. I think that any one who had been looking on without being able to hear my words would have been sure that I was pleading for my own life, and not for the life of the man on the tree stump.

So I made my point as quickly as possible.

"It may be that Mex will simply take the life which we give him, slip away from us and go back to his robberies. But I really think he won't. Partly because he doesn't want to die. And partly because I'm sure that he really would enjoy the game of hunting the others. I say that this is a desperate remedy for you. But Mex knows us and our faces and names. Certainly he must also know the faces and the names of the robbers; and where they can be found, and their places of refuge, and all that. Now, then, if he can bring us that knowledge, and his own good hand at fighting, I say that we may have a chance to win our war, after all; and the mines which men have been giving away in Dorking Hollow will be worth millions, and we who have held out in spite of so many losses may have our reward for patience!"

You can see that I became more and more interested

in my cause as I progressed in the advocating of it. I was fairly warm on the subject before I finished, and my words made a good deal of a sensation. The boys talked the plan over noisily and earnestly; but there by firelight, in the middle of the night, it seemed like an inspiration.

"Hold on, though," said Joe Wayne. "What if we do agree to this? There is all of Dorking Hollow still to be persuaded."

"If we like the idea, the others will follow the leader," said Canada Harry. 'The boys in Dorking Hollow, they ain't no dashed debating society."

That was reasonably true, and it closed our argument with a laugh. I could say to Mex: "You've heard our talk. Your life goes scot-free, on condition that you give us your solemn oath, Mex, that you'll stay with us and our work. And not desert us and go back to your old trade."

He became very thoughtful.

"Well, man!" cried I, impatiently.

"And while I work there in Dorking Hollow," said he, "and fight for you fellows—and while I'm known as the reformed thief, and the crook who has gone straight—some one from the East comes through and recognizes me, and the news goes East—"

"That you are saving a mining town from crooks," said I.

"Tush!" said he. "No, the news goes out there that I have been a crook myself!" And he added suddenly: "No, Loomis, I won't do it. Rope or gun—I hardly care which finishes me. But my name is going to be clean when I die."

"You fool!" I exclaimed in annoyance. "What a complacent hypocrite you are! You shield your reputation from the knowledge of a few relatives, and in the meantime ten thousand men in the West know what you are!"

He blinked and looked up sharply at me.

"By heavens," said he, "I never quite looked at it in that light; but—why, man, it's really a species of cowardice, isn't it?"

"Unquestionably," I agreed.

He leaped up suddenly, his head thrown back.

"I'll give you my word, then, Loomis. By heavens, you fellows are wonderfully forbearing and generous! And I'll see that you don't have a chance to regret this. Give me free hands and feet, and I'm one with you!"

I waited no longer. I felt, really, as though I were about to turn a tiger out of a cage among a crowd of helpless children, but I set my teeth, and cut the bonds which held our prisoner. He yawned and stretched, and then: "Will you send a guard with me, Loomis, while I get my other horse? It isn't more than a mile from here, and her heart will break if she goes till morning without seeing me."

I felt that I had already made the decision. I determined to throw in the rod after the hook and line.

"Mex," said I, "we trust you perfectly. Go by yourself, and come on after us to Dorking Hollow."

I thought he hesitated for a single instant, with a curious light in his eyes, but then he moved away among the trees, and the shadows swallowed him.

The moment he was gone, there was a clamor from the men. This strange bargain now appeared ridiculous. The enemy had slipped through our fingers after we had at last caught him. The men rushed after him, but when they came to the darkness beyond the circle of the firelight, they stopped short, as though they had run into a wall. He was unarmed, yet so thoroughly had he impressed himself upon their imaginations that they dared not hunt him through the darkness.

"He'll come back!" I told them.

"Bah!" said one of the posse. "Do you believe it yourself?"

I said nothing; in fact I hardly did believe it; it seemed miraculous that the youngster who had been sitting on that tree trunk beside the fire had managed to avoid death at our hands—richly warranted death!

We had our wounded on our hands. We had to send back to Dorking Hollow for mule litters to carry the injured back to camp. And the litter that carried young Chris Lagonda went down the forest to the groans of the injured occupants. When the posse heard it, they turned gloomy eyes on me. I heard their comments, muttered just loud enough for them to be sure that they would reach my ear.

"There's some one that had better be back at his law desk than out here digging silver!"

"He could talk himself into a trance."

"He's made a fool of us and of all Dorking Hollow!" And much more, and many of the comments unprintable, but I was too downhearted to take up the insults. I felt that I had made a great fool of myself, particularly when Mex failed to show up. And then I realized that it was practically impossible that he *should* live up to his oath. He had scored such brilliant successes in his chosen profession; he had blazed such a name for himself across the mountains; he had made himself so thoroughly famous—or infamous—that it would be odd if he left that way of living for a new one. And the more I thought, the more entirely I agreed with the others that I had persuaded them into the rankest folly.

For instance, if Mex came down to Dorking Hollow, he would have around him a hundred enemies; men whose relatives, friends, bunkies, had been robbed or shot by this consummate master of guncraft and the mountain trail. His life would be momently in peril from their natural desire for revenge.

And if, as he had said, he was of good family, how could he afford to expose himself to identification by coming out into the broad light of day?

When we finally got down to the Hollow, I found that every one there agreed with my second thoughts, and none with my first ones. We were met by a large crowd, who escorted us up the winding, single street that followed the curving of the river, grumbling every step of the way at my folly.

Avery Lucas, king of the camp, met me, and said gravely: "If you had hung that fellow, Paul, you would have thrown a chill into the blood of every robber in the hills!"

That was all he said. He exercised a great deal of self-restraint; but nevertheless I went to bed the most miserable man in the world. This folly was a fitting close to my career as a miner. I had followed fortune to distant points of the frontier; and now, at the last, I had located a rich, a truly rich claim, but only to have the reward of my patience snatched away by lawlessness. I was without money. I would have to beat my way back East. But I swore that when I reach New York once more, I would never again leave the practice of law. The returns might be slow; but at least they were sure!

I wakened in the dawn. The sun was rosy in the east, but though it was very early, the whole camp seemed to be up. I heard voices, shouts; exclamations everywhere;

25

and I stumbled into my clothes and out of my shack, into the street.

There I saw a picture—

Well, I really cannot describe it. But I ask you to see for yourself the tall, rugged forms of Crandall and Chester, mountains leaping from the night shadows into the morning rose and gold of the upper sky; and in the hollow the ragged mining town pouring out its hundreds of rough men, while down the street the most gallant figure in the world was riding.

He rode a snowy-white mare, the most beautiful creature that I have ever seen; and on her back was a saddle of blanched leather, flashing with polished silver work. As the rider came through the crowd, the sombrero which he lifted here and there in acknowledgment of their attention, glittered with Mexican gold work.

I leaned back against my doorpost and rubbed my eyes and looked again.

Yes, it was Mex, come to keep his promise.

CHAPTER FIVE

Why, I have seen better and greater days, of course. But I think that never in my life did my heart so leap as it leaped that moment with relief, with self-justification, with trust in the eventual goodness of my fellow men, and with a vague, vast hope that all would eventually be well with Dorking Hollow! For here was the archrobber, come to keep his word to us all!

It made upon others an effect as great as it did upon me. And when Mex dismounted before me and shook hands and said: "I've come to report to you, General

Loomis. What are your orders?" a little crowd of the best men in town were already around us.

We held a conclave on the spot. On the inner circle were the leaders of Dorking Hollow. On the outer edges stood the rank and file. Avery Lucas, of course, presided.

"Now, young man," said Lucas, "you've had an odd proposal made to you by Mr. Loomis and his men last night. But I think the general opinion here is that we must fight fire with fire. Frankly, most of us never expected to see you ride into camp to keep your promise, but now that you are here, what do you propose to us?"

"You're the king of the camp, Mr. Lucas?" asked the robber.

"I'm the head of the vigilance committee; that's all," said Lucas quite modestly.

"You're the king of the camp, Mr. Lucas," repeated Mex. "And I know that you've done a very good job of it—keeping law and order inside the place. Well, sir, if I'm to work effectively, I'll have to have entire authority. I mean—I'll have to ask you to step down and resign your place."

"That can be easily done," said Lucas, smiling at the coolness of this demand. He raised his hand to hush the angry murmur which had been raised when the request was made. "But what do you purpose doing?"

"First," said Mex, "I give the fellows in the bush their chance to get away. I put out a proclamation in the woods in several places warning them that they have three days to clear out."

There was a chuckle at that. And young Mex laughed and nodded.

"It seems foolish, doesn't it?" he said. "But as a

matter of fact, I don't like to change sides without giving them the warning."

"You mean," put in Lucas, "that you will tell them you are coming, so that they will be sure not to be at home when your posse arrives from Dorking Hollow?"

The good nature of Mex was quite unshaken.

"They know," he said, "that I understand every trail, every by-path, every cave, every gully, every creek, every patch of brush, and every good covert in these mountains. I know them because I had to know them. Otherwise I should have had my neck stretched long before this. And when they hear that I'm coming after them, they'll be worried, and I think that a good many of them will simply move out. If not, at least we start with a clean slate, and the game will be played fairly on my part."

I don't know what would have been the answer, but there was an unexpected interruption at this point. The white mare suddenly reared and broke her reins. She had been tethered to a sapling by her master and now came at a gallop to find him, whinnying loudly.

Ears flattened, pawing and kicking, she was a veritable storm, and the men sprang from her path with curses. Straight up to Mex she came in her charge. I thought that she would trample him into the ground, and shouted a warning; but she stopped short; his arm went around her shining neck, and her ears were pricked again in perfect content.

The miners came back to their places, laughing, and in the highest good humor. One cannot help having a certain amount of respect for a man who is trusted by animals.

"Lou," said Mex, "you've spoiled those reins, and played the fool. You've absolutely played the fool,

28

confound you!"

But his voice was soft as silk, and there was love in his eyes. One could see that the mare was the greatest jewel in the world, in his eyes. And indeed she was an aristocratic beauty. The argument dissolved for a moment, and then came back weakly to the point at which it has been dropped.

"I think I understand you," said Avery Lucas. "You give them all a fair warning, and then you feel that you will have a chance to hunt them down?"

"Otherwise," said Mex, "it would be a slaughter, and no sport at all."

He said it so frankly and openly that there was no doubting him; but we, knowing how often we had rushed our horses through the woods and found shadows only, looked at one another and shook our heads.

"Very well," said Lucas. "I won't stop you at any point until you've outlined your entire plan. First, you want me to step down and put you in the chair as head of the committee—"

"Not in a thousand years," interrupted the other hurriedly. "I wouldn't be at the hanging of a man for a million dollars' worth of glory."

Mex closed his eyes with a shudder of horror. And the white mare, as though in sympathy, flattened her ears and snorted. A little laugh ran around the circle again. The horse was arguing for her master better than he could argue for himself, for she was drawing all sympathy upon his side.

"I don't want the chairmanship of that committee," said Mex; "but you're the man who says how many men shall be detailed to act as the escort for a caravan; and which newcomers shall be allowed in the camp, and which shall be turned out because they're rough characters. Well, sir, what we need here in Dorking Hollow is a few more rough characters. I see a lot of good miners, here, but I fail to see many good gunmen. And gunmen we must have!"

He was not insulting. He was simply stating facts, and he ran his eyes quietly over our faces.

"I'll have the passing of those rules," said Mex. "I'll be the camp king, or else I can't work effectively for you. Let me have the authority, and I'll have a batch of man hunters here who will get results for you! It takes a genius or a fool to make a persistent outlaw. Most of those fellows in the woods are a bad lot. But there are a good few who know that they're following a fool's way. They would be glad enough to have a chance to leave that road and come under the wing of the law. Very well. I'll give them that chance."

"Name it in your proclamation?" suggested Lucas with a smile.

"After all," said Mex, "I won't need to make any proclamation, because now I see here among you fellows who belong to the gang in the woods. And they'll carry the news everywhere."

There was an uncertain stirring here and there, and every man looked at his neighbor with suspicion.

"Point out the spies to us!" cried Lucas, in an honest fury, "and we'll put an end to them!"

"Betray them?" said Mex, smiling. "Not I! Let them have their three days, together with the rest of the gunmen in the woods. During those three days, I'll recruit my band of hunters. I'll offer them five dollars a day and food. That isn't big pay, but the work will be amusing for them."

He paused. There was no comment, for every one was

thinking profoundly over these singular proposals.

"Then," said Mex, "when the three days are over, I start on the warpath. And seven days after that, you can plan to send out your first mule train—without an escort!"

He set his teeth as he said it, and looked around at us with blazing eyes. I saw a few incredulous smiles dawn. But they faded at once. Mex was serious. Yes, in most deadly earnest; and as he stood there, beside his mare, he looked quite capable of running to earth any creature incapable of flight through the air. Then many heads turned anxiously to Avery Lucas.

He stood up and said in his usual grave manner: "For my part, I think that there's a risk in this. Mex may fill the camp with ruffians. Are you going to bring in a crowd of scoundrels who will turn the camp into a hell?" he asked the new leader.

"The camp will have to be a bit brisker," admitted Mex. "But as for murder—no, there'll be none of that."

"Are you sure?"

"I give you my word of honor," said Mex. "Will that do? Every gun that's drawn in this camp and fired at a man is drawn and fired at me."

And who would care to undertake that responsibility?

"If that's the case," said Lucas, "I suggest that we vote him the power that he wants. Does anybody want to speak on the question?"

"I say," put in a big fellow, round-shouldered from work, "that I ain't gunna vote for no gun-fighting hound!"

"Nor me!" shouted another.

"Any other objections?"

Then Lucas added: "Let's have a show of hands. Who is in favor of having Mex for camp king?" Up went nearly every hand.

"Contrary?"

Hardly more than a scattering half dozen were raised. "Mex," said Lucas quietly, "you're elected. I now step down. You are in the chair."

And he waved Mex to an imaginary throne.

There was utter silence. We all felt that we had taken a perilously long stride into the dark. God alone could tell what would happen to us. We waited, too, for the first act of the king. He acted instantly.

Stepping into the center of the open space, he called: "Has every man here worked his load of silver for that mule train? It starts in ten days—every mule in the camp! Are they going to have empty pack saddles?"

Why, that brought a cheer from them! A loud, ringing cheer. My own confidence leaped up to boiling point; and I walked down the street with Mex, the white mare behind us, the flood of miners hurrying this way and that about us. Voices had broken into loud, good-natured raillery and chatter. There was slapping of shoulders and much hearty comment. And the noise was welcome; for silence had become the curse of that camp.

Then I saw that the current of men before us was splitting away from a broad-built man who stood in the middle of the street with a double-barreled shotgun in his hands. And the moment I spotted him, he jumped the shotgun to his shoulder, crying: *"Take this for the sake of Jack Sloan!"*

He did not fire. There was a spurt of fire from the hand of Mex—from his hand, for it hardly seemed possible that he could have conjured a revolver into his grasp—and the man with the shotgun dropped to the ground.

"Get a doctor," said Mex calmly. "He's only drilled through the legs."

CHAPTER SIX

THERE WAS ALMOST A RIOT ON THE SPOT. The grumblers and the doubters would have mobbed any other man than Mex, then and there. But he was not a convenient subject for mobbing. They scowled at him; they cursed him behind his back; but they did not like to confront that dark, active eye. And so Chuck McGinnis was carried straightway into my shack; Mex and I attended him in person. When the bandaging was finished for it was merely a double flesh wound—Mex said: "Now I can tell you that I didn't kill Sloan, Chuck."

McGinnis glowered at him, but said nothing.

"Very well," said Mex. "I was on the spot and saw the shooting done; but I've told you the truth. I didn't kill Sloan."

"Then who did?"

"If I bag the man who did it, I'll make him confess before we string him up. But I can't betray old secrets which I learned when I was on the other side of the fence."

"By heaven," said McGinnis suddenly, "I believe you!"

He held out his hand; Mex took it; and that little feud was nipped in the bud. Afterward, loitering for a moment in front of my house, Mex thanked me for standing by him during the crisis.

"The first day or two will be the hardest," said he. "After that, when I begin to get results, they'll think

33

better of me.

I could agree with that. Results were what we wanted. And results we began to get, results of the oddest sort. Before that day was over, three rough, unshaven fellows rode into the camp. They looked as though they had not a penny in the world. Everything about them was in tatters. But they were mounted on magnificent horses, and they were armed to the teeth with the finest weapons that money could buy. The first glance was sufficient to tell us that these were men from the mountains. They asked for Mex; and when they found him, they disappeared into the hut which had been consigned to him as headquarters.

Two of them presently came out and rode away, looking very black. But the third man remained. Was he the first recruit for the man hunt?

During the night, half a dozen others came and went. In the morning, it was reported that Mex had retained only two men. The following morning—which was the second day of his sojourn in the camp—he sent out a summons to a dozen of the miners. When they came, he had them go through their paces with revolver and rifle, shooting from a rest, at a walk, and on horseback. There was a continual roar of guns from behind his shack. But of the dozen he retained only two! He retained the men, but not any of their horses.

They must be better mounted, he declared. And he went among the horses which we could produce and selected four. They were to be turned over to the hunters until our war was ended, to be fed and maintained at the public expense, and their owners compensated from the public purse if any of the animals were maimed.

Other wild riders from the mountains continued to drift into the camp during the second and third day.

Fifty or sixty men came to be examined by Mex; and of them he retained only nine. He had two from the camp; and he himself made the twelfth man.

In the meantime, we had other news. A fifteen-year-old boy, a roustabout at one of the mines, was caught by bandits while squirrel-hunting among the trees. He was released by them and sent in with a message to Mex. The message declared that Mex was a low, traitorous, sneaking hound, and that the moment he showed his head out of camp it would be fairly blown off his shoulders. The story ran instantly through the camp, and I think most of us believed that the threat would be executed. We had tried our hands with those wild men of the woods, and we had been beaten time after time.

On the evening of the third day, with a soft trampling of hoofs down the dusty street, the horsemen of Mex passed out of camp. Their going was not announced. Almost before we knew it, they had slipped from among us.

I went to see Avery Lucas.

"What will Mex do, Avery?" I asked.

"Why," said Avery, "did it never occur to you that he was recruiting the most promising band of robbers that ever, mounted horses?"

"We'll know by the morning!" said I.

But when the morning came, there was no sign of Mex. And by noon of that day, he and his party had not returned. The afternoon and evening went by. There was then no doubt as to what he had done. He had taken his band into the woods and, swearing them to fidelity to himself, he had resumed his old life. This time not as a single marauder, but as chief of a gang!

The night passed. In the morning of the second day, a draggled band of men came down the mountainside,

35

driving before them a string of thirty mules, and every mule carried a pack saddle. With the riders came five men whose hands were tied to the pommels of their saddles.

It was a stirring reception that Mex received that day, you may be sure.

We could guess what wild work had been up. Not a single one of the posse was astride the same horse that he rode out; but a small herd of horses accompanied them—as fine a looking bunch of remounts as any man could ask to see! And in that herd were the horses from the camp. Next, we counted the posse itself. It had gone out numbering twelve. It came back, numbering nine!

The second thing was the examining of the packs, to which we were invited by Mex. The contents were what you have probably already guessed. Mex had performed with his first stroke such a miracle as not one of us had really dared to expect. He had slipped up on a band of nearly thirty of the brigands, surprised them completely, and shot them to pieces. One of the posse fell dead; a second was wounded, and a third remained in the woods to take care of him until relief was sent from the camp. Two more men remained at the site of the battle to hunt for the buried silver which Mex suspected must be near that spot. Mex, with the others, pushed ahead on the trail of the fugitives. He knew their habits of thought; he knew the refuges to which they would take; and in twelve hours of pursuit he and his party killed six, and brought back these five prisoners.

Altogether, it was a vastly successful stroke.

It sounded like a fairy tale to us, but the two men of the camp were the ones who told the story.

"How shall we reward your men, Mex?" Avery Lucas asked the leader.

"They have the best half of their reward already," said Mex.

"And what's that?"

"They've had the fun," said Mex, his eyes glittering. "Royal fun, man! What was the old game compared with this? And as for cash—why, I've given them a thousand dollars a man."

A thousand dollars a man!

Well, Lucas said nothing. What could have been said at the moment—seeing that one of the mule packs of silver had already been distributed to the posse? But Lucas came back and gathered some of the rest of us to hear what he had learned.

While we were gathering, high festival began in the shack of Mex. A liberal quantity of whisky was bought, and some musicians were brought over from the dance hall, which for the last few weeks had been almost deserted. Noise of great rejoicing immediately poured forth from the shack, and from time to time gunshots boomed and whooping voices pealed across Dorking Hollow.

The rest of the town lay strangely silent for a little time; and then it, too, began to run wild. And it was not odd that it should have done so. Yonder, in Mex's shack, was the shining example. Mirth rang in the ears of every careless, freedom-loving, laughter-seeking miner. They were tired of the strict rule of Avery Lucas. They had been wearied by the long weeks of penury and suffering which they had endured while the robbers in the forest enjoyed an unchecked reign. Now it seemed that that reign was ended—or at least that it had received a serious setback. A portion of the stolen silver had been returned. And the people of the town were quite willing to celebrate the change.

A crowd flocked to the saloon and into the dance hall. Music began to sound. And presently, whooping, yelling, laughing, cheering groups went up and down the long, winding street of Dorking Hollow.

Lucas and the rest of us looked on, half smiling and half serious. We were a little too old for such boyish excesses, but we smiled because we could appreciate this promise of plenty after the lean years. We could appreciate this desire to celebrate the great victory and all that might be held in store for us.

There were things to make us grave, however, and I may as well give them in the words of Avery Lucas.

"Gentlemen," said he, "Mex has voted a thousand dollars apiece to his men."

"Not half enough!" said one of the group. "I'll add another thousand a head to them out of my own pocket."

"One moment," said Lucas. "The important point here is not how much was given, but the fact that Mex had the power to give it—and took it with his own hand and made the distribution to his men. So far as we know, three mules' loads may have been distributed by Mex. And hereafter a larger and a larger percentage may go that way."

This brought silence. We began to feel gloomier and gloomier, seeing that we might have exchanged one evil for another.

And then Lucas asked, "Do you know the story of King Log and King Stork?" No one answered him, and he went on:

"The frogs wanted a king. Jupiter threw down a log into their pond. For a time they were very happy with it. They admired its size and its solidity and its roundness. But when they grew accustomed to it, they despised it for its quiet, and for the green slime that began to gather along its edges. They called again to Jupiter and demanded a more powerful ruler. Then Jupiter sent them a stork. And as soon as the stork arrived, he showed his power by beginning to eat the frogs as fast as he could reach them!"

Lucas said no more. There was no need of explaining his little fable from Æsop. Lucas had been King Log. And Mex King Stork.

How long would it be before King Stork began to devour us?

CHAPTER SEVEN

PARTLY GLOOMY AND PARTLY JOYOUS, therefore, we remained in my house and looked on at the celebration. All of us in that shack were owners of very considerable properties in the region. The combined holdings of the eight of us were greater by half than the mines of all the other owners in Dorking Hollow. We had held on while less optimistic spirits sold out and went packing. And we had snapped up their claims for a song. But, as one of the men said: "What are we to do? Without King Stork, we'll be eaten by the robbers. And, so far, King Stork has made a great deal of noise, but he has only pecked at one man!"

That was referring, of course; to Chuck McGinnis. And in that case, Mex had apparently not been to blame.

That evening, while we were still watching, we heard a new note come into the celebration: big Dan Sedgwick came down the street, half drunk and wholly dangerous with a Colt in either hand, shouting out the name of Alabama Charlie and challenging Alabama to come out

39

and fight like a man.

We in the house looked at one another, and Avery Lucas stirred uncomfortably. During his reign, no man had dared to conduct himself in this fashion. But now King Stork was on the throne, and violence would be the rule of the day.

"When Charlie and Dan meet," said Lucas, "we'll hear of the death of one of them. They both have their records in the past."

That was plain enough. And in our exasperation, I determined that I would take a hand in this affair. Mex was running the camp. There was no reason why this affair should not be put up to him, so that we could see at once where he stood in such cases.

I went straight to his shack. It was bursting with music, laughter, jeers—a veritable pandemonium. When I opened the door, a whirl of tobacco smoke and the strong reek of whisky greeted me. On the farther side of the room I saw Mex standing, playing a violin, which he had taken from one of the musicians; and, though I was no judge of such matters, it seemed to me that he fiddled extremely well. The bow flashed back and forth in his long, slender fingers far less jerkily than it usually did in the grip of an ordinary camp musician. Keeping time with that music, two giants, wild with whisky, were performing a buck-and-wing, their rhythm broken now and then by a stagger which brought whoops of glee from the rest of that party.

I took this in at a glance and then pushed toward Mex.

I was within a step of him when a mighty hand caught my shoulder and whirled me back and around.

"Keep out, you fool!" a big chap was saying to me. "This ain't your party. Keep out—and get, quick!"

A perfect invitation to a gun play, you will say, but I was not there to use a gun. Besides, I would have had no chance at all confronting any one of these experts, half drunk, or wholly drunk as they were.

The voice of Mex broke in on my behalf:

"Back up, Jerry!"

Jerry threw a scowl at his leader, but he obediently stepped away.

"Wait a minute, boys," said Mex. "Now, what's wrong, Loomis?"

"You're the camp king, Mex," said I.

"You're right, he is," answered one of the others. "And on the throne he's sure gunna stay!"

"Shut up," said Mex, coming slowly and uncertainly toward me. "What's up? Noise bothering somebody, perhaps?"

"Never mind the noise," said I. "We didn't have such scenes while Lucas was running the camp. But what I've come to tell you is that Alabama Charlie and Dan Sedgwick are looking for each other with guns in their hands."

"Hello!" said Mex. "Looking for each other? And isn't there any one to bring them together? Wait a minute! Let's go and see the meeting, boys!"

"Hold on," said I. "You promised that there would be no gun fighting in this camp."

Mex paused, blinking.

"Ah-ah-ah!" said he. "So I did. No gun fighting! I forgot that I'd come to a peace meeting! Hey, you, back up!"

Two or three wild men were already bursting through the doorway; but, drunk with liquor and excitement though they were, they instantly returned and waited. It was a miraculous thing—this control which Mex

41

exercised over the crowd. He had hand-picked these fellows, and as I looked them over I could tell that he had not selected them for docility. A wilder, more wicked-looking crew I never laid eyes upon. But Mex held them in the hollow of his hand. In their midst, he looked more slender and childish than the least stripling in the camp.

"And what do you suggest, Mr. Loomis?" asked he. "What's to be done about the two boys who want to stage a little party of their own? Why don't you send them home?"

"Come outside, and I'll explain," said I.

He followed me out into the night, saying: "Stay back, boys. Let the party go on!"

And with a wave of his arm, he bared the way to the others and then slammed the door in their faces. There was a fierce growl of protest; but then a drum began to beat, a flute began to whistle, and in another moment the celebration was under way again.

Under the stars, King Stork leaned on my arm, saying: "Now, old fellow—wha's masser? Wha's up?"

"Look!" I exclaimed, and pointed to the lights which blazed over the town. "Listen to the yells and the shouting. Do you hear those guns? Perhaps two of those shots are fired by Dan and Charlie at one another. God knows how many dead there will be before the morning! And every dead man in this camp will be laid at your door. We had no murders before you came. Are you a murderer, Mex?"

He stiffened and glared at me, standing as proudly as he could, though he still wavered. His arms were folded, but the hands were thrust into the bosom of his coat, and I knew that he was grasping the butts of two revolvers.

But I was fairly desperate, and I went on: "You've

42

started hell in Dorking Hollow, Mex. Are you man enough to stop it?"

"Man enough?" said Mex. "Man enough? I?"

He spoke haltingly. Then he steadied himself by grasping my shoulder.

"Wait li'le minute," said he.

With his head thrown back, and his eyes closed, he remained in that position for a moment. And by the starlight I saw a strain of purpose in his pale face.

"Now," he said in a low, hoarse voice, "I'm better. You be the guide. Bring me to Charlie and Dan."

Down the hill he walked with me—for his shack was built a hundred yards back from the street. Twice he stopped and demanded: "Where we goin', partner?" Then he remembered, and pushed ahead again. But I wondered how he could possibly be of use to quell an incipient riot. However, he grew steadier on his feet as he walked down the single street of Dorking Hollow. We had turned a sharp corner when my companion jerked himself suddenly from my arm and whirled about. At the same instant a gun barked and a bullet sang close to my head. It was instantly answered from the hand of Mex; and looking back, I saw a man rise from a bush between two shacks, stagger out into the roadway, and fall upon his face in the dust.

How had Mex been warned? I had seen nothing. Nothing whatever, though I was certainly alive and alert, whereas this decidedly confused man had detected the subtle shift of a shadow behind a shadow, and wheeled about with lightning speed. That quick movement had doubtless saved his life. And before a second bullet could be fired, the would-be assassin had received his death.

For he was fast dying when we got to him.

43

We turned him on his back, and a savage, unshaven face was revealed to us by the shaft of lamplight in which the man had fallen.

"Hello, Turk," said Mex, dropping on his knees. "What made you try that trick on me?"

"Didn't want to do it kid," said the dying man. "But I drew the first black jack. Am I a goner?"

For Mex was rapidly opening the coat and shirt of his victim.

"You're a dead man, Turk," said Mex, with a wonderful tone of gentleness.

Turk blinked his eyes, and then set his teeth and nodded.

"Sure," said he. "I am. I got a hand at my throat, now. Where am I goin', kid?"

"It's only falling to sleep, Turk. You'll wake up in a better place than this," said King Stork.

"Will I? You know a lot, kid. But do you know that?"

"Of course I know it."

"I never done a dog's trick before tonight," said Turk feebly. "And I got what was coming to me. I—"

He choked and stopped, then added faintly: "So long, kid."

"So long!" said Mex, and gripped the hand of Turk.

Presently, he laid that hand back on the dead man's breast.

"It's over," said Mex again, with that wonderful gentleness. "And I'm glad that there was no more pain. Poor Turk!"

I helped Mex carry the dead body to the side of the road. "Shall we get help and bury him now, Mex?" I asked.

"No," said he, gravely. "Let him lie there while we finish the other job."

And he set off straight down the street.

44

CHAPTER EIGHT

I SHALL NEVER FORGET that walk. Mex was sober enough to walk unassisted by this time, but now and again he would stumble. Before us, noise raged, and on each side. And as we approached Jackson's big saloon and gaming hall, the flare of the strong lamps outside the door made the starlight ineffectual and dim.

We came there in the very nick of time. Out of the door came a tall figure, shouting: "Walk out here, you skunk! Walk out here and say it again!"

It was Alabama Charlie, and behind him plunged Dan Sedgwick.

"I'll say it anywhere in the world!" bellowed Dan. "They don't raise nothing but hounds in Alabama."

Then two guns flashed, but before they could speak, a bullet cut the dust at their feet. The men turned with a start and a volley of curses to see Mex walking up on them out of the night, a gun balanced in either hand.

"Put up those gats, my friends," said Mex, coldly. "Put them away, and march on ahead of me!"

"Who'll make me put up my gun?" asked Dan Sedgwick. "Ain't I got a right—"

"You have no rights at all," said Mex dangerously. "I have all the rights in this camp, and I intend to use them. Put up those guns, and put them up carefully; for if one of them happens to point my way—why, I'll salt the pair of you down in lead!"

Their brains had cleared enough by this time for them to realize with whom they were contending. The guns were shoved back into the well-worn holsters.

"Now, march!" came the command.

"Where, Mex?" they inquired. "And what have we done?"

"You've bothered me in the middle of a party," said King Stork arrogantly. "That's enough for you to know, I guess."

"Where'll I take them?" asked Mex of me, as the pair walked out before us, down the street.

"Where do you want to take them?"

"I don't know. Haven't you got a jail here?"

"No. There was never any need for one—before—"

"Before I came, eh? That's all right. I've taken a good deal from you, Loomis, and I suppose that I'll be ready to take still more, because I haven't forgotten that it was you who spoke for me the other night in the woods."

It was the first acknowledgment he had made of that intercession, and I thought that he must have forgotten. I began to see that there was a little more moral nature in this fellow than I had suspected.

Presently, as we reached the spot where the dead man lay, Mex stopped with a little cry.

"I've got it!" he said. And he forced the pair to go to where Turk lay.

"Right here," he ordered, "you'll dig a grave eight feet deep. You'll have it finished before the morning comes. And you'll have this fellow buried in the hole. And over the grave you'll stick a board, with the words written on it: 'Here lies Turk, because he missed his shot.' Understand, I'm not going to stay here to watch you; but if you try to run off from this place, I'll trail you. Remember that! I'll trail you if I have to go a thousand miles, and when I catch you, I'll feed you to the buzzards."

He turned his back on the pair, and walked off with me. There was no chance that the pair of would-be fighters would try to escape. For the woods around us, as every one knew, were alive with the banditry who would like nothing better than a chance to cut out one or two of the miners from Dorking Hollow.

He turned his back on them, but he did not go toward his shack. Instead, he went straight back to Jackson's saloon.

"What now, Mex?" I asked.

"You'll see," said he.

When he got to the saloon doors, he kicked them wide with violence, and strode in. The door guard swung the great muzzle of a sawed-off shotgun and covered him.

"No rough stuff here, kid," he began.

And then he recognized the intruder and gaped with fear, while the shotgun sagged down in his hands. There was no doubt that Mex had made an impression in this camp.

"Where's Jackson?" asked Mex. "Send him, and send him running!"

Beyond, we looked through the haze of tobacco smoke at the long, narrow bar; and opposite it, through other doorways, we could peer into the big gaming chambers, where on the earthen floor scores of men sat in to lose the money which fortune and Mex had saved for them on that day of battle in the woods.

There was a cheerful murmur running everywhere through the place. From one of the doorways presently came Jackson, a tall, dark-faced man, with sunken eyes surrounded by great purple patches, and a pair of sagging, black mustaches drooping past the corners of his mouth. He wore a wide black hat. And behind him came four stealthy-footed fellows—his professional bouncers who maintained order in his house.

It was plain that Jackson intended to maintain his dignity in his own place. He stalked up to Mex and said coldly: "You want me, Mr.—what's your name?"

"My name is Arthur Holles," said Mex. "And I want to speak to you about a little matter, Mr. Jackson."

His voice was so soft and gentle that I thought Jackson would laugh in his face, and the four bouncers looked on with broad sneers. Let Mex be a lion in the woods, but this was their own private domain where they would tolerate no lions save themselves.

"You've called me away from an important piece of business," said Mr. Jackson. "What's your excuse, sir?"

For Jackson was fond of putting on a stern formality in his speech.

"The fact is, Mr. Jackson," said Mex—or Arthur Holles, as he called himself—"the fact is that I have to make an embarrassing request of you—"

"Make it quick and short, then," said Jackson. "What is it?"

Some of the men at the bar had heard some of the words, and now they began to drift closer, gaping when they saw Mex apparently singing small to the proprietor of the gaming hall.

"You see, sir," said Mex, in that soft, soothing voice of his, "Dan Sedgwick and Alabama Charlie started to fight in this place—"

"That's a lie," said Jackson. "They were shown to the door before they could start fighting."

"Exactly!" said Mex. "You showed them to the door, but I think it would have been a great deal more thoughtful on your part if you had locked them up in a spare room and kept them under guard until they sobered up."

"You think," began Jackson, wild with anger, "and

why the devil should I pay any attention to what you think? Answer me that!"

"You seem to be very angry!" said Mex, spreading out his hands in a deprecatory gesture.

"You've been talking like a fool, young man," said Jackson, his arrogance growing, as the arrogance of every bully is sure to grow when it feels itself triumphant. And the four bouncers behind him cast sneering glances on Mex and shouldered closer.

"You've done very well in your way," said Jackson. "But that gives you no authority inside these doors. Are you through talking nonsense to me?"

"I'm sorry," said Mex, "but I have one more thing to ask, Mr. Jackson."

"Well? Well?"

"And that is that you close up your place at once; and stop all the games; and tomorrow make a public apology for having allowed two men to get drunk in your place and then allow them to go out to murder one another and—"

He got this far, when he was interrupted by a stifled cry of rage from Jackson.

"By heaven, this man's mad!" cried Jackson. "Boys, throw him out—and throw him out on his head!"

And he stepped back to give his four hired bullies way.

They made one lunging stride forward, devilish pleasure in their faces. But that step halted them. They were looking into a pair of the brightest, coldest eyes that ever flashed at mortal man.

"Keep away from me!" said Arthur Holles. "Keep away from me. Back farther! If I have to draw my guns, I'll—"

At that, the rearmost of the four made a movement to
49

get his Colt, but his arm was stopped in mid-gesture. For a six-shooter had flashed out of the bosom of the coat of King Stork, and the moment it glittered in his hand it exploded. The bouncer, with a gasp, clutched a broken arm through which the leaden slug had passed; his own weapon, which he had barely touched, dropped, from, his nerveless hand.

The other three leaped back; and they leaped with their hands held high above their heads. No doubt they were brave and practiced fighters, but they wished to have naught to do with one who carried charmed lightning in the tips of his fingers.

"The three of you—out!" ordered Mex, and they leaped through the doorway and into the street as if strong hands had thrown them there.

"Now, you!" said Mex, advancing.

Mr. Jackson had not raised his hands, but he had turned very white.

"You didn't quite understand, Jackson?" said Mex.

"No," said Jackson huskily, "I didn't quite understand, Mr. Holles."

"You understand now. Get every one out of this place, and lock the doors. And tomorrow, at twelve-thirty, you'll make a speech in front of these doors, explaining what you did that was wrong—explaining it in detail, and showing how much you regret it. Give orders for the place to be closed. I'll expect you back at this door in thirty seconds."

He took a watch out of his vest pocket.

In less than the half minute, white and sweating with alarm, Jackson was back with us, and gasped: "And now, Mr. Holles?"

"Now walk ahead of us down that street."

He marched Jackson down the street to the spot

50

where he had left Sedgwick and Alabama Charlie. They, in the meanwhile, had got picks and shovels, and were rapidly sinking a deep trench.

"I've brought you a bit of help," said Mex. "Mr. Jackson needs a little of that same exercise! Jackson, jump in there and get to work."

Jackson jumped in.

"You'll see that he does his share, boys?" called Mex as he turned away.

Their broad, malicious grins proved that they would see that the gambler, at least, performed his part of the job.

"But," said Mex, "if any one comes to bother you while you're working here, send them to me!"

And he turned away into the night.

CHAPTER NINE

"DO YOU KNOW," said I to this terrible young man, "that you've made Jackson your deadly enemy for life?"

"I know it perfectly. I'd like to have all the men in the world of that kind as enemies, Mr. Loomis."

"Aye, and such as Sedgwick and Alabama Charlie?"

"Not a bit!" said he. "They realize now—or they will by the time they've worked up a good sweat digging that grave—that they were fools to try to fight each other, and they'll be fast friends before the morning comes. Then they'll be grateful to me because I stopped them. And if they're what I think, there'll be no malice in them. There are some fellows like that. The evil in them is never more than skin deep—and you can sweat it out of 'em. Why, Mr. Loomis, I've seen fellows commit the most horrible murders, fellows who in their

51

hearts were the best in the world. But they're not the sort that should be allowed to have guns in their hands. Charlie and Dan will get over this, and be thankful that they got off so easily. But Jackson? Yes, it's hell for him. It shames him, and there's nothing so proud as a hound such as Jackson. He hates me, of course, and I'm glad of it. But he'll have to watch himself from this time onward. For if he makes a foolish move, his house will be shut and remain shut! I'll run him right out of the camp!"

I said good night to Mex and thanked him for what he'd done.

"It's all right," said Mex. "If that's the sort of a camp that you fellows want, I suppose I'll have to give it to you. I prefer another kind, myself, where every step you take is over thin ice, and where you always feel as if you were half a second away from hell. But every one to his own taste. I have no complaint to make!"

He waved to me cheerfully and walked up the hill, and before he was out of sight, I heard him whistling.

I watched him, still, until the door of his shack opened, and he entered in a burst of light, and was greeted by a vast, drunken cheer.

The door closed. The hills were dark again, but the ringing voices poured down, sounding hollow and far through the thin air of the mountain night.

It seemed to me rather fitting that this man should have been greeted by a burst of glory—even if it was glory which came from no more than a drunken little scene of carnival. For certainly he was not like the rest of humanity. He was apart and aloof from them all.

I went back to my own house, where I found my friends still waiting for my report. I told them briefly and clearly everything that had happened. A little

52

silence followed my résumé.

"This is all very well," said Lucas, at last. "God knows I hope that King Stork can manage his affairs as well every day as he's managed them tonight! But, mark this: One man has been killed; another has been shamed in public and will be a dangerous element in the camp from this moment forward. After all, it isn't a particularly auspicious beginning—but we beggars can't be choosers."

That summed the matter up well enough. Except that there was something else which defied any words. And that was what I had learned about young Arthur Holles. For I felt I had been out walking with a spirit rather than a man—a dark spirit, if you will, but one with certain marks and touches of the divine about him, too. I thought that the death scene of poor Turk would linger with me in all my dreams.

One night wipes out a great deal in a Western mining town. When the morning dawned, the miners went to their work as cheerfully as though nothing had happened, except what was for the best. It was long since I had heard them singing in the street as they marched off in the dawning toward their claims. But now they went joyously toward their labor of the day. Many weeks had passed since they had been able to work for themselves. Their toil had been expended for the unseen taskmasters in the woods, but now they had a chance to use their drills for their own profit and they naturally appreciated the change.

And what of Mex?

In the middle of the morning, his shack became the center of great activity. Men were seen bringing quantities of boards from other shacks through the camp which were vacant at the time. And when I inquired, I learned that Holles had impressed a number of men who were idle for the day, and set them to work tearing down the unused quarters and rebuilding them again as additions to his own shack.

"For," he had said, "my lads need a bit of elbow room. You have to put race horses in box stalls, my friends!"

That was rather a neat way of putting it, but I bit my lip with worry when I heard the tale. Then I went off to supervise the work at my own claims.

I was busy there until the beginning of the evening; about sunset time, just as my men were laying down their tools, Mex came flashing up the hillside on his beautiful white mare, and drew rein beside me.

"Look here, Mr. Loomis," said he, "would you like to be in on this wolf hunt?"

"Wolf hunt? You mean to say that you're riding on the trail again?"

"Aye," he said. "There's still plenty of work to be done. It seems that the boys in the woods have taken things in the wrong way. Instead of having their spirits broken by the last little fight, they feel that they were taken at a disadvantage. And now they want to even up the account with me. You understand how it is. Some people learn quickly. But dull fellows can't be expected to learn a new language in one lesson."

I can't say that his manner was boastful, no matter how his words may look on paper. He rather seemed in the highest of good spirits, and perfectly enchanted with the grim prospect which lay before him.

He said in addition: "I have four new men. Four beauties. About twenty of the rascals came in today. Some of them were the weaklings who had been scared out because they knew that I was on the warpath, but

54

some of the rest were just the stuff I want. The first little job showed them that I meant what I had said. And they want to be in on the fun. What do you say, Loomis? Will you come along?"

Perhaps you have guessed before this that I am not a fighting man, and never have been. I am willing enough to strike when I have to, and several times in the rough life I've led I've had my back against the wall and have had to cut my way through difficulties. However, I've made it a principle never to go in search of danger; for danger in the West, in those days, was sure to come and seek you of its own accord. But I thought that this was a game too rare to miss. I accepted the invitation, and felt, moreover, rather honored. So far, I was the only man in the camp who had been asked to join the campaign, except the two recruits whom he had regularly enrolled in his forces. So I accepted the invitation on the spot after a moment of considering.

"But you know, King," said I, "that I'm not a hero, and I'm not a great shot with a rifle, and nothing at all with a revolver!"

"You're to be a spectator, not on the stage," said he with a grin. "Come along, and let me do the worrying. Only—you have a fast horse, I hope?"

I had. A hardy little mustang, not a great deal for looks, but a miracle of endurance. And as the darkness of that day began, I found myself with the group of the King's riders winding down the long street and out of the camp.

That name was fixed on him, now. It does not take long for a nickname to stick in the West. And besides, it was apt. One could not look at the graceful, proud figure of Mex without feeling that there was something regal about him—certainly something far beyond ordinary

55

men and their understanding.

Now, at the head of the procession, a figure flashing through the night on account of the whiteness of the mare Lou, he seemed to me the ideal leader for such an excursion. Yes, and my fancy carried me back to other times when skill with weapons and dauntless courage gave a man something more than physical reputation. What were the Richard Lion-hearts, and the English buccaneers, and the viking marauders other than just such hearts as that which beat in the breast of Holles? But in those days the talents could make them more than mere marauders. They became kings and lords. The commoner, more timid souls, looked up to them from a vast distance.

Who can say that the change to modern manners is all for the better? Society has been made a place where the commonplace virtues may succeed. Honesty, laboriousness, patience now reap a golden harvest. But we miss something which the iron ages possessed. And while we have many talented and clever and wise men, we have few, few of the great burning souls of those times who throw a light even into our own day and still seem like blinding suns compared with our crowded but faintly shining stars. As I rode out of Dorking Hollow behind young Holles, I knew that society considered me far the more valuable member. I was valued here in this rough camp; and in the East I had a value, too. I would build, in time, a fairly secure fortune. I would educate my children well if God gave me any. I would be a respectable and respected member of any community in which I finally settled. But at the same time, on that night I knew that society was wrong, and that I was not worthy of brushing the dust from the shoes of Mex.

I had not his vices. No, I was not marred by his great

and glaring faults. But neither did I have his heroic virtues. I felt that he was as far removed from me, as infinitely superior to me, in actuality as he was now in fact, riding at the head of the procession, while I brought up its rear—a mere observer!

We wandered out of the town, the lights scattered behind us, then grew together, grew small and finally clustered together. Then the forest received us, and closed around us, with a chill night mist which damped my ardor at once. I looked at those great trees bearded with fog, and wondered how we could find our way through the wilderness. And all around us, what danger of fighting men, more savage than wolves, as Mex had called them!

I wanted with all my heart to turn around and go back, but shame kept me in my place. Presently a word was relayed down the line that the leader wanted me. I pushed reluctantly forward to the side of Mex.

I found him to my astonishment in the highest spirits.

"Nothing could be more perfect!" he said. "They'll never suspect that we'll go hunting through this mist, and unless I miss my guess completely, we're going to catch them in their hives—catch a whole swarm of those hornets and smoke 'em to death!"

CHAPTER TEN

DID YOU EVER SMOKE A NEST OF HORNETS? Real hornets, an inch long, with a lance of poison half the length of their body? The shock of their sting is enough to stagger a grown man. But what of smoking out brigands, tried and true in their defense of one another, practiced with weapons, and now on the alert because of

57

the preceding attack?

I listened to young Arthur Holles and said nothing for a moment. Then I had to exclaim: "Why, Mex, if the thing goes through, I hope it won't cost the lives of more than half of your party!"

He smiled at me and my concern.

"I'll tell you, Loomis," said he. "This is not regular warfare. In regular war, between regular troops, you have great losses of life. This is only guerrilla stuff. You know the Indians fought a whacking lot of battles, but they didn't lose many men at a time. One famine winter was worse to them than twenty wars. And these bushwhackers are a good deal like the Indians. Take them man by man, and they're great fighters, very clever, and brave enough to try anything. But take them all together, and it's a different story. Now, man by man, it wouldn't be very hard to find twelve of them as good as the twelve that I have to follow me. But they're not closely knit together. They have a chief who makes the general plans, but he's only obeyed by those who feel like obeying. Well, it's not so with my party. They looked rough and ragged enough, but I'm already getting them into a spirit of discipline.

"They obey orders because they think I won't make very many mistakes, but still more because I dole out the rations and pay them their salaries and give them their bonuses. Without me, they'd be nothing. They'd never be accepted among the honest men of Dorking Hollow, or any other mining camp. And they've cut their own throats, of course, so far as the robbers they've left are concerned. I have them between the devil and the deep blue sea the instant I get them away from the bandits and into my ranks. They've got to stand by me. And if I can show them not only a way out but a way to a little glory, money, and a good time, they'll be the happiest men in the world, and they'll think that I'm the best of all possible leaders. You see, I'm going into details, but I know you're a bit nervous and I want you to be at ease tonight. I hope that we'll find a large bunch of the crooks, and when we do, I'll show you how my little band of fellows will smash straight through them. They may stand for a few minutes, but they'll scatter when the work gets hot."

He chatted away in the most cheerful manner imaginable. And I listened to him and tried to believe what he was saying. But, after all, it was rather hard to think that this mere handful could rout one of the small armies of robbers which infested those woods. As many as five score of them had been known to attack one of our big mule trains, in the days when we had the ore turning out in quantity. However, it was pleasant to have Mex talking, and he continued fluently, keeping my spirits up.

He said that he hoped he could strike at McGregor's main band that night. And if he could ever bag Johnnie McGregor himself, he hoped that he would throw such a chill into the hearts of all the other lawless that they would break up and scatter from the woods.

"I've heard a good deal about this Johnnie McGregor," I told Mex. "But as a matter of fact, isn't he more or less of a myth?"

"A myth?"

And Mex laughed at me.

"There are six and a half feet of that myth," said Mex. "If you once see him, you'll never forget, and I'll promise you that."

"Hold on," said I. "Is there any real truth, then, in that story about the giant that held up Cruickshank and

59

Evers and Ransom, and beat them all in a hand-to-hand fight?"

"And broke the rifle of Cruickshank?"

"No—bent it almost double."

"Yes," said Mex. "Every word of that is true."

"Including the bending of the rifle?"

"Yes."

I laughed a little.

"Come, come, Mex," said I. "Don't ask me to believe that yarn!"

"Listen, then," said he. "I saw him take that same rifle, and unbend it! Oh, he's a rare fellow, is McGregor. I don't think that even he knows the strength that's in his huge paws. He could take a man and break him open like nothing at all. I saw him do that, once. Break a man's back—whew! It was not a nice thing to see, my friend!"

"Break a man's back!" I gasped.

"Not over his knee," said Mex. "No, he didn't have to do that. Just with his arms and his hands, you know."

"Come, come, Mex! How is that possible?"

We had entered, just then, a lofty avenue which opened naturally into the heart of the woods. There was clean footing for a time under the hoofs of our horses and the cracking and stamping and snorting with which we had hitherto gone ahead now ended. The silence fell pleasantly and mysteriously about us. The mist was thinner, here, but still we were like a procession of ghosts winding through that night, and on either hand the trees like standing spirits watched us pass.

Mex continued his description of Johnnie McGregor. He spoke softly, as though he feared the giant might be listening, and yet he spoke with an unconcealed fervor.

"With his arms and hands, Mex?" I repeated. "Tell

60

me, really, how could he actually break the back of a man like that?"

Mex was silent for a moment.

"Do you know," he asked, "that McGregor doesn't ride a horse?"

"Well, I've heard that."

"That's the reason," said he, "that he can't leave the mountains. Across rough country, he can leave a horse behind him—I mean, across country that's sufficiently broken by cliff and ravines and thickets, you know. And through dense brush the man's a marvel. He forces himself through where even a porcupine would have to turn back. I want you to understand that McGregor is simply queer. He's a freak."

"I thought he was just a word in a song," said I. "I didn't even dream that he was up here in the woods!"

"I know what you mean," said Mex. "When men are of a certain kind, they excite odd talk, and pretty soon they disappear, because people can't believe in them. A light that's too intense is no light at all! And of course people *do* sing songs about Johnnie McGregor. I sing a lot of them myself. Nevertheless, Johnnie McGregor is a fact, and they've never said about him things that he can't do."

"Such as pulling up trees by the roots, eh?"

"Oh, I know what you mean. There's the story about how Johnnie McGregor tore up the forest and threw it on the village where his dog had been poisoned, and buried the village alive."

"Yes, that's the one. That's true, is it?"

"You want to make it out rather ridiculous. And of course some of the stories *are* just yarns. But most of the stories about his battles are true. For instance—well, you name one."

61

"Why, a long time ago," said I, "Johnnie McGregor was attacked in a mountain pass by seven Mexicans. He killed three of them and captured the other four and tied them together and drove them ahead of his horse until they died of exhaustion, one by one."

I laughed a little as I said that.

"I chanced to follow that trail the next day," said Mex thoughtfully. "It didn't happen a long time ago. As soon as Johnnie does something, people make yarns and songs about it, and in six months the entire range believes that the thing hardly happened at all. But I followed that trail through the mountain pass the day after Johnnie went through."

He hesitated, and then added: "The plan was that the Mexicans were simply to turn him back with their numbers and their rifles. And when he turned back, he would run into me, and there I could have my chance to finish him."

I listened, breathless. For this was really like tearing down a picture from the wall and turning it into flesh and blood—this vivifying of the legend of Johnnie McGregor. And now, on either side, from time to time, I began to see a giant form waiting in the mist ready to stretch out for me an arm as big as the limb of a tree, not swift, but inescapable. For mere strength paralyzes resistance, as the eye of the snake is fabled to do.

"You met McGregor, then?" I whispered, quite overcome by this story.

"As I went up the trail," said Mex, not to be diverted from the regular course of his tale, "I found the three dead men, and then the four of them, one by one. Horrible-looking picture! I saw that our plan had failed, but still I hoped that I could overtake McGregor if I hurried. I let Lou have her head, and she fairly flew."

The mare, hearing her name, turned her head and cocked her ears, but her master merely laughed and waved her on. I felt a little thrill at this byplay. It was like a flash of dialogue between two human beings rather than the obedience of a brute to a man.

"I came up with McGregor at the farther mouth of the pass, where he'd killed a deer and stopped to eat it."

"Good Lord, man, eat a deer?"

"No, no," laughed Mex. "But still, I think that he really eats enough for six ordinary men. I've never seen such poundage of meat disappear!"

"You stopped and watched him eat?"

"Oh, yes! I had managed to get the drop on him."

"You had the drop on Johnnie McGregor!"

"Yes, I was lucky. And he said he would finish eating before he died. A calm brute, you see!"

I tried to picture that scene, but my mind failed me. It was like a tale out of some semi-fabulous legend of the Norse.

"We talked while he ate," said Mex. "And afterward, it didn't seem to me that I could shoot him. Not in cold blood. I offered him a chance to fight fairly. He suggested hand to hand, and of course I laughed at the monster. Then he suggested knives, and I agreed. So we had it out, knife to knife."

"Wait a moment, Mex! With that prodigious length of arm against you it was—"

"But I was faster than he on my feet," said Mex. "And I managed to slip away from his rushes. And I tagged him a couple of times with my knife. It was like slicing at a side of beef! It merely stirred him up. Finally, he began to grow a little winded, and so he tried another trick that was worth two of mine. He picked up a thirty-pound rock and shied it at me as you'd throw a pebble at a quail. And when I woke up, afterward, McGregor was gone!"

CHAPTER ELEVEN

"YOU COULDN'T DODGE THAT ROCK, MEX?" I asked him, feverish with interest.

"My foot slipped on a pebble as I was dodging. And then the stone hit me and knocked me into a trance. When I woke up, Johnnie had left me for dead and gone off with Lou. But she managed to pull away from him, and half an hour after my wits were back she came to me. She's a faithful thing. Eh, Lou?"

She tossed her head as though in agreement, and Mex laughed joyously.

"I kept on the trail of McGregor for two months, and then a friend of his came to me and we patched up a truce, because we'd heard that there was plenty of plunder and excitement up here at Dorking Hollow, and we both wanted to have our hands free to join the fun. That's why I'd like to find McGregor tonight. And if I can run him off, I think that a good many of the others will scatter, too."

"Do you think that you can find him, Mex?"

"I hope so. Because, you see, he won't move from his old quarters. He's too proud to do that! It would show that he's a little afraid of us. And he won't want to show fear. He'll simply be laughing at me and my work."

My heart turned to stone. I had my hopes high that the encounter with this dreadful and half-fabulous giant would not take place that night, but it seemed fairly certain that Mex would reach his goal, after all. After a time, we entered a region of broken, sharp-sided hills,

64

with the mist thicker around us, where the trees became a dense growth.

Then Mex dismounted us and leaving the horses behind with two men who were to bring them on very gradually, the rest pushed ahead. Mex himself presently left us and disappeared silently into the fog. We drew close together after he had gone. It seemed as if he had carried away with him half our vitality. The men moved on very slowly, pausing now and again to listen, and looking at one another with gloomy mutterings. It was plain that their hearts were not in this work since Holles had left us.

But Holles came back again in a moment. He called us around him in a close circle and told us his news. He had ventured up to the old quarters of Johnnie McGregor, and had found, just as he suspected would be the case, that McGregor had been too proud to shift to a new lodging in the woods.

"Some of you have been here before," said Mex. "But I'll explain the lie of the land to those who haven't been. Johnnie and his men have put up three big lean-tos in front of a cave that runs back into the hillside. In that cave the horses are kept. If there's an alarm from in front, the robbers can bolt through the cave, take their horses and push out of the rear entrance, which is big enough for a horse to walk through. Beyond that rear entrance there's a long slope of easy ground, and once out, they're pretty sure to be able to ride away from us. Shoreham and Skinner, go back and guard the rear of the cave. When you get there, you'll find a big rock beside the entrance. Topple that rock across the gap. And when we hear the sound of the falling stone, we'll attack from this end and—"

"Plumb easy and simple," broke in Shoreham,

"except that Johnnie always keeps a good man on guard at that rear door! He'll spot us when we come up!"

"You'll find no one there tonight," said Mex. "I called around there and made sure of him. That entrance has no guard, now!"

It should have raised our spirits to hear of this daring exploit of our chief; but, for my part, I was more depressed than ever thinking of Holles gliding like a hunting cat through the mist and bringing with him a swift and silent death for the sentinel. Shoreham and Skinner waited for no more, however, but went off at once, swearing that they would do their part.

The rest of us pushed softly ahead, and, after a time, we saw the dim glow of a great fire before us. Great sections of trees had been flung on the blaze, and, when we came nearer still, we could see that the main fire had died down and left only a gigantic bed of coals which still threw a sufficient heat to keep the three clumsy lean-tos that surrounded it fairly comfortable.

A man came out of one of the shacks and started to drag more fuel and throw it on the fire, whereat a great voice roared: "Not so damned much noise!"

Mex, in the meantime, brought us all close together and whispered his orders. The horses had been tethered in the distance, and the two who conducted them were now with us, so that all available force was at hand. I could not help yearning for the presence of fifty of the honest men of Dorking Hollow to polish off this important piece of work. But still I suppose that Mex was right, and that if we had had too great an army, we should never have been able to approach the camp stealthily enough to take them so by surprise. We were to spread out in a semicircle, each man taking good cover, and then when we heard the sound of the falling rock—and he promised us that it would be clear enough for us to make out a hollow, booming sound—we were to open fire on the lean-tos.

As I write it down, I realize that the plan was murderous enough, but at the time it seemed perfectly right and logical. These devils had too often burst out of ambush and shot down the guards of our mule trains for us to show them the slightest mercy now that we had our chance.

We began to scatter, accordingly. But the maneuver had not gone very far when a clear and ringing neigh burst out from the woods behind us, and was instantly taken up and repeated by half a dozen other horses.

I was just behind a great log, and I sank into the shelter of it as four or five men poured out of the lean-tos to listen. And then the great voice which I had heard before called: "Jimmy and Burgess—take three or four more and scatter out through the trees. It may be Beecham coming in—or it may be that young fool Holles coming to wake us up. I hope it is. Because I'm gunna eat him!"

Two or three of the men who had issued from the lean-tos at once started across the clearing, and I gripped my rifle hard. Then I was amazed by the voice of Holles calling: "Get back to cover, boy. I count three and then we start firing."

Fair play, you say? I thought that it was suicide when I heard that voice, and the rest of our party felt the same, because a great groan came from them. As for the robbers, they whirled without asking questions of the voice that had sounded out of the white wall of the fog.

"It's Holles!" they yelled, and dived for cover. All save one were out of sight before Holles cried: "Fire!" and the dilatory bandit screeched and leaped into the air as at least half a dozen well-aimed rifles poured their fire into him.

The lean-tos became a scene of wild confusion. They shuddered with the rushing of their inmates to and fro; then hoarse cries of rage and pain began to issue from them, as the repeating rifles were turned on them, the men firing knee-high to make sure of any who might be crawling on the floors. There was not ten seconds of that work before a sudden flood of men burst from the shelters and darted for the great mouth of the cave. I counted wrong, because of the dimness which the fog cast over everything, but I thought that at least two score of those leaping shadows gained the cave. No, not all gained it. For three of them fell before they reached the entrance, though one of these crawled on and got out of sight.

After that, from the cave issued shouting, terrible curses, and the snorting of the frightened horses within.

"Hughie!" called our commander sharply. "Run for the back of the cave and help out the other two. They may have their hands full—and they haven't yet been able to roll the big stone."

But just as he spoke, there was a shock, and a heavy booming noise, very like an explosion. Instantly there followed a wild outburst of rage and fear from the interior of the cavern. The bandits found that their last resource had been blocked up and that they could not leave the cave except in the face of the sweeping fire of our rifles, with the firelight to show them as perfect targets to us as they came out. They would charge nevertheless, I was sure; otherwise their case was desperate.

Then half a dozen riders rushed out of the shadows of the cave. I had my rifle ready, but I had hardly pulled my trigger when every one of those horses was down. Shooting? I've never heard of such quick work, and it was apparent that Mex had not hand picked his men in vain. Each of them was working now like a Gatling gun.

Of the six riders on that frantic charge, two dropped to the ground and lay there without moving, and two more crawled back wounded into the cave. The remaining pair seemed unhurt, so far as we could tell by their actions.

A shadow stirred behind me; it was Mex, slipping into place beside me with the log for a bulwark. He began to load his empty rifle-magazine with deft fingers, whistling softly the while.

"How is the sport, Loomis?" he asked me. "Better than quail hunting, eh?"

"A thousand times," said I. "But they'll all come out in a mass! Then what?"

"Two or three might break through if they did," said he, "but I don't think they will. Johnnie is too wise for that; he'll wait."

"Not unless he's mad!" I broke in. "We can have two hundred rifles up here in the morning to make a sure job of it!"

"He'll have help long before that time," said Mex cheerfully. "And it wouldn't be so comfortable if twenty of Mc Gregor's friends should take us from behind just now, would it?"

I shuddered at the thought.

"Then we've done enough, my boy!" I insisted. "And let's get out of this! We've all apt to be murdered before the morning comes!"

"Maybe not, though," said he. "We still have a few minutes. And I have a specially fast way of negotiating with 'em. There's a wind rising. Bless that wind, I say!"

In fact, the mist was rapidly thinning as the breeze rose, and already we could look up through loopholes in the sailing clouds and see the stars.

"Partridge!" called Mex.

"Aye!"

"Start a fire in that brush above the cave, and begin to throw down some of the green brush before the mouth of the cave. You understand?"

"To smoke 'em out?" cried the voice of Partridge. "Aye, we'll hear howls, now!"

CHAPTER TWELVE

UNMERCIFUL! I SAY TO MYSELF, as I think of this proceeding. But it didn't strike me that way just then, when I was wondering how soon some of the companions of Johnnie McGregor might hear the noise of the rifles and sweep up through the brush to take us in the rear. No, I was only anxious to see that smoking process advanced as quickly as possible.

Partridge ran around the edge of the clearing, climbed up the side of the hill, and soon was slashing down the brush with his hatchet, and had a roaring little bonfire on the top of the hill above the cave entrance. When it was of considerable size, he pushed off half of it; and as it dropped to the ground before the cave, he threw more dry fuel on top of the blaze. Then, on top of this, he dropped down green stuff which made a thick smoke that in part wandered back up the hill, but in part was blown into the cave. For the wind was rising every moment and blowing from exactly the right quarter to favor this cruel work.

From within the cave there was a wild outcry of fear

and anger, and presently buckets of water were dashed into the fire before it. Instantly, however, we began to comb the darkness behind the bonfire with a steady rifle fire, raking the cave on all sides. Screeches of pain, and howls of execration answered us, as our bullets stung those within, and they gave us an answering fire directed at the flashes of our guns. I heard two or three exclamations from our boys, but I guessed that no serious damage had been done them.

The first of Partridge's fires was finally extinguished by the water which was thrown upon it by the valiant bucket line of the brigands—for of course there was a store of water running somewhere within the cave to supply them. But when it was put out, it still fumed more terribly than ever, and the wind blew banks of the stifling smoke into the cave.

Finally all of this smoking ended, also, and the fire was reduced to a few wet, glistening cinders. The bandits greeted their victory with a wild cheer, but that cheer had hardly ended when Partridge thrust over the lip of the hill a second conflagration three times the size of the first one; and, while we shouted with joyous excitement, the leaping flames from this fire showed us the shadowy shapes of the brigands far back in the darkness of the cave. We gave them a few hearty volleys, and sent them into corners. We could see that the whole interior of the cave was now misted with white smoke, and filled with confusion as the horses reared and plunged and whinnied in a panic. Twice one or two of their mounts broke away and bounded across the clearing, but we let them go willingly enough. We had no care for empty saddles. Filled ones were what we were looking for.

The second fire at their threshold broke their nerve,

and presently we heard the already familiar roar of the giant calling: "Holles! Holles"

"Hello, Johnnie."

"How far you gunna push this foolishness?"

"I just wanted to warm you up a little, Johnnie."

"You've done that, dog-gone you! You've plumb spoiled my sleep for tonight. Now tell me what you want, old boy?"

"What can you offer, Johnnie?"

"Enough silver to dam a whole river!"

"You mean that you could promise us that?"

"Well, no! We got it here in the cave—"

He was apparently stopped by a fierce protest from a companion and he added hastily: "It ain't here, Holles. I wouldn't be fool enough to keep the stuff right where we camp. But I can lead you to it!"

Holles merely laughed.

"We want you, Johnnie," said he. "We want you and all the rest. Walk out here with your hands over your heads, and we'll do you no harm. But if you make us waste any more time, we'll smoke you out of that place and then kill you as you come!"

"My Lord, Holles, give a man a decent chance!"

"A better chance than you've given many a poor devil!"

"Remember that I let you go when I had you, kid!"

"You left me because you figured I was dead."

"And your head would have been busted to flinders if you'd been like other folk. Holles, will you be reasonable?"

"I want to be reasonable."

"Then talk sense. Don't talk surrender to us. You know that we can't surrender!"

"I don't know that."

"Why shouldn't we die here as well as in Dorking Hollow?"

"That's up to you," said Holles. "Besides, there may be some of you that won't have anything proved against you. You'll get some sort of justice in Dorking Hollow, I think."

"You think! You think!" cried Johnnie McGregor. "But your thinking it ain't good enough for us. We want your word of honor, Holles. We know that you'd keep that snow white."

"I'll never give you my word of honor, Johnnie. I'll see you all hanged first. If the boys in Dorking Hollow feel like stringing you up without a trial—why, that's their privilege! But in the meantime, you're wasting our time. We'll give you one minute to decide with your men. Then we'll line the mouth of that cave with a wall of fire and stifle you, or burn you to death. Take your choice."

There was no answer from within the cave except a loud groan and then voluminous cursing.

"They'll charge us now!" I said to Holles.

He merely laughed. He did not even have his rifle pointed at the mouth of the cave.

"They'll never rush us, now," said he. "They've had too much of their blood let already, and their eyes are filled with smoke. They're afraid, Mr. Loomis, and Johnnie is one of the most scared!"

And behold, before that minute was up, there was a loud call in the voice of the giant: "Holles!"

"Yes, Johnnie!"

"Here I come!"

"Hands up?"

"Yes."

"Then you can come safely."

73

"Your word of honor on that?"

"Yes. I'll shoot the man that fires at you."

With this for his warrant, out came striding the most monstrous figure of a man that it has ever been my fortune to see. There were all manner of guesses made about the size of Johnnie McGregor. Some said that he was hardly seven feet. Others said he was much more. But his actual inches and his bulk were never determined. That was the desire of Johnnie himself, who saw that his feats and his actual physical magnitude were constantly exaggerated by the legends which were springing up about him.

He wore three cartridge belts around his waist and two more slung over his shoulder; but what would have been a crushing weight and a clumsy burden to any other man appeared on Johnnie McGregor as the most normal and natural sort of equipment. He had an enormous hat, too, placed on the back of his head which surrounded his huge red, square face with a black halo. His shirt was open at his hairy neck. His trousers were homemade sacks of canvas which swelled like half-deflated sails. His feet were shod in vast, shapeless moccasins.

It hardly mattered what came behind Johnnie McGregor, but as a fact, twenty-four men came in single file behind him, each man with his arms stretched high over his head.

As they passed out of the cave, each one was searched, and his hands securely tied behind him.

"Is that all?" asked Holles finally.

"Except for the dead ones," said Johnnie brutally, "and them that are groaning back yonder in the dirty smoke."

We went into the cave. There were eight wounded

74

men there. Eleven had been killed outright. Which made the total of choice ruffians we had attacked that night amount to forty-four. Twenty-five remained untouched, and from the capacious deeps of that cave we took out no fewer than seventy-four head of horses and mules. It was robbery on a grand scale, and as I walked through that cave, flashing a lantern into the far corners and coughing as the smoke filled my lungs, I felt that the backbone of lawlessness had been broken. Hereafter we would have comparative peace around Dorking Hollow. For if Johnnie McGregor and his legion could not resist us, who could expect to do so?

The price that we paid for this astonishing victory was exactly one dead man—Tommy Wentworth—and two slightly wounded. Firing out of a bank of fog at a fire-lit target, we had been quite safe. But still it seemed a miracle to me. The great thing, of course, was the nerve that our leader had showed in bringing up such a handful against such an army. The smallness of our numbers enabled us to steal up softly and effect the surprise, and after that the fog and every detail of the fight had favored us.

Well, one can explain such a thing. Explanations before the fact, however, are the ones that really count; and I know that I, for one, had no hope of anything but a miserable death as we trailed through the thick fog and the dripping trees toward the camp of Johnnie McGregor.

Our spoils were not all human prisoners, however. We had another sort of trophy to show. For from the floor of that cave we dug up enough silver—following the directions of some of the band who hoped to curry valuable favor by assisting us now—to load every one of our animals to staggering.

"And," said Holles, "you boys can take as much as you can carry!"

A very generous reward, you may think, considering silver at twenty dollars the pound, but it seemed to us at the time nothing extraordinary. The rest of that great pack train was to go to the pockets of the men who had remained safely sleeping in Dorking Hollow.

And so we began the homeward march. Two were left behind to guard the wounded and fortify themselves in the cave against any attempted rescue on the part of other bandits, until we could send up reinforcements from Dorking Hollow. The rest of us marched with the train toward the town.

Dawn was barely breaking when we came from the woods for the first time, and saw the river flowing like tarnished metal down the valley. Dorking Hollow still slept. Not a man was stirring. And Holles said to me with a laugh: "They only have to sleep and dream. We make their dreams come true!"

CHAPTER THIRTEEN

I SUPPOSE THIS MIGHT BE CALLED THE GREATEST DAY in the entire history of Dorking Hollow. Even that day when the rich silver was first found there was not so important, for of what use was the discovered richness when it had to pass into the pockets of the robbers of the forest? And even the first coming of the great Arthur Holles was not so important, for when he came he promised to help us; and his first attack on the robbers had proved that he could do much. Though it still seemed impossible that he could really clear the woods of our secret enemies. But the capture of the giant

Johnnie McGregor and his men made us positive that our woes were at an end. After that, a few more days would sweep away the great bulk of the brigands, we were confident.

Half the townsfolk were busied not at the mines, that next day, but in celebrating their deliverance and in arranging a place of safe-keeping for the prisoners. Some advocated putting them to death en masse and so getting rid of our problem at a stroke. But others felt that we must follow some form of justice; and I think that of this method Avery Lucas was the greatest advocate.

So we labored with might and main to get the place ready. We put up four mighty walls of solid logs, and divided the interior into cells which were composed not of iron bars—we had no such iron to spare or on hand— but of big saplings. There were four of these cells, and the prisoners were divided into four groups and distributed.

Young Holles, living up to his word, would have nothing to do with the trial of the prisoners. He and his men had a twenty-four-hour carouse to celebrate their deeds, and spend a portion of their prize money. Then once again they rode out of the town in the dusk of the day and were gone until the second morning following. They came back with a handful of prisoners to show for all their long raid, and with only a few mules loaded with the recovered silver. It would have been a great victory a few days before, but Holles had already familiarized us with much greater triumphs.

His report was now more interesting than his deed, however. He declared that they had scoured the woods far and wide, and had gone to a score of the old haunts of the brigands; but everywhere they found traces of rifled stores of buried treasure, and there were hosts of outward tracks of men and horses, showing that the multitude of the robbers who had been living on our mined silver had taken warning at last and had pushed away across the mountains. The capture of Johnnie McGregor had been warning enough to them. Thereafter they were concerned not so much with taking fresh booty as with preserving their threatened lives, and they had carried away their treasure with all the haste they could. One small band had been pursued and overtaken, and from them these prisoners and this silver had been taken.

The woods were now free!

That same day we got together a caravan and dispatched it with high hopes. It pushed straight across the hills and reached the river and the waiting boat without the slightest difficulty. A flying rider came back to appraise us of the success of the journey, and the whole town went wild with rejoicing.

When that news came to us, we prepared another and far larger freight train, and while it was in preparation, Holles came to Lucas and to me. He told us he felt that his work had been accomplished, and that hereafter, having seen how the nut was to be cracked, we could keep out of trouble.

I did not like this idea. Lucas paused to consider, but I told Holles straightway that we still had need of him. If it were known that he had gone, the bandits would swarm back to their hunting grounds. And that very evening, we had ample proof of what I said. For the second freight train was taken by surprise, vigorously attacked by at least thirty brigands, and nearly routed that same day. The defenders barely made their stand and brought the train through, but it had been a close call. Yes, there was still police work needed, and no one could do it but Arthur Holles.

I put the thing to him on those grounds, and he agreed with a sigh, saying that he had promised us to stand by us, but that he hoped we would not keep him longer than was absolutely necessary.

"But why, Holles?" I asked him.

"Because," said he, "I've started a good deal of trouble here and there. You might say that there are half a dozen tidal waves chasing me across the world, and if I stay long enough in one spot, one of them is sure to overtake me and wipe me out."

"Look here, Arthur," said I. "Here you are at the edge of the world, so to speak. No matter what bad you've done the good is a great deal greater, as all of Dorking Hollow would freely testify. Now, one day or other, you will want to settle down. You can't be a boy all your life. Neither can you be a robber or a hunter of robbers. This is your grand chance to give yourself a great reputation. You can so fortify yourself now that in a few years you will have thousands of friends, men who believe in you heartily. Isn't it true that this is the time for you to start writing on the credit side of the ledger? You can't continue a debtor to society forever."

He listened to me seriously enough, but when I had finished, a smile came up in his brown eyes. He was a wonderfully handsome rascal, and so filled with life that a smile was always coming or going on his face and one could hardly be sure whether he were smiling with one or at one. Which made him an awkward fellow to talk with, except for the telling of a joke. I saw that electric smile fighting at the corners of his mouth now.

"Laugh at me if you wish to, Arthur," said I. "I don't really mind a great deal."

79

"No, no," he cried. "All that you say is wonderfully kind. I can't laugh at it. But as for settling down—" He stopped and whistled.

"You couldn't do it?"

He shook his head.

"You realize that all the time you're running wild, you're running along the edge of a cliff—"

"Certainly," said he, "and that one false step will drop me into perdition, and all the rest—"

"No, I'm not preaching to you, Arthur. I've been young and fairly wild myself."

"I don't believe it," said the grinning Holles. "You think you've been young and gay, but you really haven't, you know! You've had a glass of beer too much, now and again, and you've slapped a friend on the shoulder a little too hard, and laughed a little too loud. But really wild? No, not you!"

And he laughed openly and joyously. It was an infectious laugh. When it began ringing and pealing, one could not help joining in. So I laughed heartily, with myself and my serious advice for a subject.

"However," said he at last, "I'm going to think it over. I'm going to think about becoming a steady man. But they would never let me!"

"Who?"

"Why," said he, "you took a walk with me one night!" I remembered, of course, and the flash of the gun from the bush.

"But they'll never keep on after you," I told him. "Besides, they're afraid of you! They're mortally afraid."

"Every man that I've ever fired a shot at," said he, "has a brother or a friend that would like to down me. And there are other things. There are men in this town of Dorking Hollow, for instance, who would like to get me under. We make too much noise in my shack to suit them!"

"It isn't the noise, Arthur. It's the way your cavaliers walk abroad and bully the rest of the men. They're not accustomed to such manners in Dorking Hollow. King Log used to keep better order."

You see, the fable was known far and wide by that time, and laughed at.

"King Log is a useful sort of a man," said he. "I wouldn't deny that for a moment. And of course he kept good order. But I can't keep that kind of order."

"Why?" said I. "You can rule those rough fellows by merely lifting your hand."

"Because I'm one of 'em," he replied instantly.

"Nonsense!" said I. "Between you and them there's the difference that lies between night and day."

"That's kind, but not true. They like trouble, excitement, danger. So do I. They like a free-swinging way of walking through the world. So do I. In short, we're the same stuff. They know it. They like violence; so do I. Let me begin to talk down to them, and they'd be at my throat like so many tiger cats."

"But suppose," said I, "that you took a new way of life, and formed your posse of law-abiding citizens?"

"Because I can't abide the law-abiders," said he. "I can't abide their self-satisfaction, and their smugness. Besides, show me the law-abiding citizens who can shoot as straight as any of those rascals? A man has to be used to risking his life before he can learn how to handle a gun. All of those fellows have been riding on the edge of adventure for so many years that they've forgotten what a quiet life could be like. Besides, while I'm with them, they guard my back. I don't have to worry."

"Not worry?" said I. "Why, every time they're deep in liquor, they're apt to sink a knife in you or pull a gun on you!"

"No," he said. He paused for a moment's thought, and he repeated more decisively: "No, they wouldn't. Not while I can make this life attractive to them. They know that I give them their fun, and that I foot the bills. And besides, they like the queer position that they're in—which is a sort of licensed brigandage. No, old fellow, don't think that they'll ever turn on me."

I couldn't help thinking that he was probably right. "There's no use arguing with you, Arthur?" I asked him.

"Not a bit," said he. "I'll never have better sense until it's beaten into my head by a strength greater than my own. I suppose, after all, that what I need is a master."

"The very thing," said I. "You need a master—with a whip."

We laughed at this, together, but underneath the laughter I think each of us realized that the other was more than half serious, and each was sorry.

I wanted to save this youngster from himself. But I knew that I hadn't the strength to do it. What he had suggested was right. He needed a master. But where could he possibly find one?

CHAPTER FOURTEEN

NOW, DURING THESE DAYS a serious business had been going on in Dorking Hollow, namely, the trial of the miscreants who had been taken with Johnnie McGregor.

Johnnie was held to the last, from a rather shameful motive, I'm afraid. We were very much amused by this great giant, his huge voice, and his apparent good humor. There was no doubt about his guilt. Half a dozen murders could be fastened on his head. It was only necessary to bring him before the vigilance committee of Avery Lucas to condemn him. But in the meantime there were all the others, and their trials were dull and trying work, because we were all keenly bent upon achieving real justice in these trials, and we did not wish to string up by the neck any even partly innocent men. It was a favorite trick with these fellows to declare that they had not wished to join, and that they had been bullied into working in the ranks with the others. If we had had a regular law court, no doubt two or three of the scoundrels would have been permitted to give evidence against the others, and in that case we would have been able to make short work of the entire crew. But we had a scruple about taking the word of one villain against another. To the best of our ability, we sifted the evidence, entangled the prisoners in their own lies, and when it was fairly certain that a man was a willing freebooter, we hanged him up to a tree and left him dangling for a day or two as a warning to others of his ilk.

In this manner we got through the entire list. There were twenty-four with Johnnie McGregor, and there were twenty-nine others who had been rounded up by the wonderful skill of young Arthur Holles and his pack. That made fifty-three prisoners, all told, and of the fifty-three we felt that there was indisputable evidence against at least eighteen. The eighteen were hanged, which seemed heavy enough vengeance. Of the remaining thirty-five every one was flogged like a dog at a whipping post in the center of the town, his name and description recorded, and a promise given him that if he were ever caught again there would be no trial at all.

Some of these fellows, as they went off, murmured together and swore that one brave night they would burn down Dorking Hollow around our ears. But we paid no attention to these threats, feeling fairly sure that their braggings would be greater than their accomplishment. But now that we had disposed of the lesser criminals, we came to the last and the greatest of them all— Johnnie McGregor. And I think that a great many of the men who gathered on that Sunday morning felt they were committing a sort of sin against the Western legends in accusing this man who had been for so long such a great hero in all the stories.

However, on that beautiful and quiet morning, we gathered under the great trees which stood in the center of the village. Why they had not been cut down like their brothers to make houses I never could understand, unless it were that their big trunks looked too hugely unwieldy to suit the impetuous loggers who were building the cabins.

Now they gave us fine shade and supplied us with a sort of council hall, large enough to admit all. It was an extremely cheerful time in the town. The mines were working full blast; a steady stream of mule trains was pushing across the hills, carrying treasure to the river, and freighting back to us necessities and luxuries at so cheap a rate that a man could have all he desired without feeling robbed. There were no monopolies. King Stork had seen to that, and it was the one valuable measure which he had contributed toward our domestic economy. Jackson's gaming hall was now rivaled by an equally prosperous institution run by one Brick Lewis, who had responded cheerfully to the invitation which

King Stork sent out. There were two stores, dispensing everything from needles and clothes to picks and chewing tobacco.

"Competition is the spice of life," said Arthur Holles, and as a result of these measures we were buying at rates fifty per cent lower than we had ever been able to buy at before.

What could have been better, then, than our situation at this exact moment of our career? Behind us lay the shadow of a dreadful danger from which we had barely emerged. Around us lay treasure heaped up by our own hands, and we had apparently inexhaustible opportunity to gather more from the same source. The only thing that could trouble our minds was the turbulence of the men in the shack of our partisan leader, Arthur Holles. Hitherto, however, his reign had been one of unmixed blessing. He ruled his wild followers with a hand of iron. And all went well in Dorking Hollow.

We were to signalize this splendid condition of affairs, then, by doing justice upon the greatest marauder who had ever stamped his way through a Western forest and taken for his own the product of the labor of honest men. Every man in the town had ceased labor, not in honor of the Sabbath, but in honor of the trial of so important a personage. And in a great circle we stood about and eyed the jury the vigilance committee—seated comfortably upon cracker boxes in the shadow of one of the trees. From the jury we turned our attention to great Johnnie McGregor, who sat on a log, quite at ease, with his hands free, but with his feet chained together to keep the lion from charging suddenly into our midst. And though it was an inch chain, by which a two-ton wagon could have been drawn, more than once we examined that chain with anxious eyes, fearful lest the giant should snap it and leap into our midst.

Avery Lucas made the opening address.

He simply said: "In the absence of a court of justice, with many dangers to our lives and our property around us, we have been forced to establish our own court. Its working is bound to be often based on error. We can only do our best, and promise to every prisoner accused here the best chance that we can give. No private grudges are heard here, if we can detect them. Now our duty is to try a man who is well known by reputation to all of us. We have heard of many great things he has done. But I point out to you that nearly all of them are crimes.

"McGregor, you are on trial for your life. We accuse you of having established yourself in the woods near Dorking Hollow, and we declare that from a central headquarters you have issued forth and taken the lives and the property of the honest men of Dorking Hollow. This is our general accusation. Before we proceed to particulars, we wish to know if you have any general defense to offer?"

"Gents," said McGregor, "and ladies, too!"

There were a dozen in a single little group, staring wide-eyed at these proceedings.

"Ladies and gents," began McGregor again. "This here trial ain't unpleasant. But it's sort of foolish. I could spin a fine yarn here. But who would believe me? Or if I wanted to be low and mean, I could give you the names of them in the camp that have kept me posted about the treasure that was being sent out and the routes that would be followed—"

Here he was interrupted by a great groaning. We long ago had suspected that there must be traitors among us, but we had never been able to locate any of the sources

86

through which information passed to the hands of the marauders.

And some one called: "Let's have those names, Lucas. Let's have those names, if you please. It's better to get the hounds who have been working safely from the inside than to simply snag the gents who took their lives in their hands when they were robbing us in the hills!"

A chorus of assent followed this. I looked straight at the gambler Jackson, and saw him turn pale. But I had long ago suspected that this scoundrel was a tool in the hands of the robbers. Or perhaps it would be better to say that they were merely tools in his hands. Because it would have been hard to manipulate that shifty rascal for any profit except his own.

But here big McGregor broke in:

"It ain't any use, boys. I ain't going to tell tales out of school. It ain't right and it ain't fitting. Why, they would be ashamed of me in hell when I got down there! No, I've had my fun, and now I'll pay for it. Only—you better take your biggest rope for me!"

I couldn't help feeling a warming of the heart toward the giant when I listened to this speech. There was a general murmur of applause.

Lucas said quietly: "Do we take this simply that you plead guilty?"

"Guilty to what?" asked the giant carelessly.

"Robbery," said Lucas, "and foul murder."

"I don't like that word murder," said the giant. "Robbery? Sure! I've taken a few handfuls, here and there. And it takes a good deal to fill my hands." He held them out with a prodigious laugh. "But as for murder—I dunno about that. I never sneaked up and bashed a man over the head when he wasn't looking!"

"Did you never shoot down—" began Lucas.

"Nobody that didn't have a gun in his hands."

"You plead guilty to robbery, therefore, but not guilty to the charge of murder?"

"Aw, I don't know," answered McGregor. "What's the use? You boys want your fun, and you're gunna have it. If it makes things any easier for you, go right ahead and have your party. I won't say no. Guilty? Sure, I'll say that I'm guilty, and you can write it down."

It dawned on me that life, after all, made no great difference to this man. Life or death—he hardly cared. Better death than life in a prison—which was his alternative.

Lucas turned to the jury.

"This man McGregor," said he, "has pleaded guilty, with what qualifications you've heard. Is it your pleasure, gentlemen, that I should proceed to pronounce sentence upon him?"

"Damn my heart," said an admiring man near me, "if old Avery Lucas ain't just as good as a regular judge!"

He was, at that, and better than a good many.

The jury declared that it *was* their pleasure that the judge should proceed to sentence, and he pronounced it gravely: "I sentence you, Johnnie McGregor, to be hanged by the neck until you are dead. And may God have mercy on your soul!"

We had heard those words often enough recently, but not often enough to wear off the sense of awe which attached to them. The giant stood up and yawned. And he deliberately unbuttoned his shirt at the throat! It turned my blood cold. Then we heard a familiar, ringing voice of authority calling: "One moment, friends!"

It was Arthur Holles hurrying to the place of judgment and execution.

CHAPTER FIFTEEN

WE HAVE READ HOW PRINCE RUPERT dashed and crashed through the ranks of the Puritans, and how they stood by, gaping in amazement, when the man, like a pillar of fire, rose up before them; but I think that he inspired no more awe than the awe with which we regarded smiling Arthur Holles. As he came up to us this day we saw that his step was a little fumbling, his eye a little too bright, and he walked fast and slow alternately. A stranger who did not know the man would have felt that the least jar might throw him off balance. But we knew him better, and we would rather have nudged a granite moutain than run against that slender, supple form.

As he came into our circle, he walked up to Johnnie McGregor and, dropping his hands on his hips, swayed a little back and forth as though he were balancing against a high wind.

"You've come to see the last of me, lad, eh?" said Johnnie, with the most perfect good humor. "Well, I'll promise you that there ain't going to be much kicking and squirming in the air. The dance that I do will be short, lad! I'm heavy enough to break my own neck, I guess!"

And he broke into a roar at this ghastly witticism. Holles nodded and smiled at the prisoner.

Then he turned to Avery Lucas: "Mr. Lucas," said he, "I've been thinking about Johnnie McGregor, and I've come to the conclusion that I could use him."

"To feed to the buzzards, Arthur?" asked Lucas.

"No," said Holles, "but to keep the buzzards away!"

"Ah, yes," said Lucas, "as a scarecrow?"

"Wrong again."

"Wrong?"

"I don't want him dead. I want him living."

"To kill by inches, then?" asked Lucas, frowning. "No, Holles. We give you a good many privileges in this camp, but there is going to be only one way of putting criminals to death—and that must be the most legal and merciful one. You yourself turned these matters over to the vigilance committee."

"Spoken as though you were reading a book, old fellow," said Mex, smiling as usual. He went uncertainly toward Lucas and laid a hand on his shoulder.

"I've give you fellows the right to condemn," said he, "and to hang, too, at times. But I never took away my right to pardon. Eh?"

"Pardon, man? Pardon?" gasped Lucas. And we were all completely at sea. We could not understand what might be passing through the mind of King Stork.

"All rulers," said Holles, "have the right to pardon. These parliaments and juries and congresses and what not can always condemn, but the king or the president can always pardon. And what better thing can a man do? Good for the soul, Lucas, to pardon a crime, now and then."

"Man, man!" cried Lucas, "what are you talking about now? This McGregor has been the rallying point of the robbers, and the chief stone in our road. Are you going to throw him in our path again?"

"Perhaps," said King Stork. "I want to make no more trouble than has to be made. I want to avoid that. But at the same time if I let Johnnie be hanged up by the nape of the neck to swing and die, I've robbed myself of the greatest pleasure that life can offer to me!"

"Will you tell me what you mean, Arthur?" asked Lucas, frowning.

"I'll tell you, of course. You see, in the old days there was a bit of trouble between Johnnie and myself. We started to fight it out, and we were interrupted. But now we have a chance to fight it out freely again. And I intend that we shall."

"Tomorrow, then," said Lucas. "You can fight it out tomorrow, Arthur, but not today."

"Why not today?"

"Because you're a bit under the weather."

"It's only a fair handicap," said Arthur Holles. "You wouldn't ask Johnnie to stand up to me with guns. He hasn't quite the speed that he needs. And you wouldn't ask him to face me with a knife. Because I'm faster than he is, as a rule. But now I'm a little off color, and I think that there's just enough of a handicap to make it a good race. Well, now, what do you say, big boy?"

"I say," said McGregor, "that for the pleasure of busting you in two and throwin' the two parts away, I'd double my time in hell. Holles, I'm sure gunna kill you!"

"Listen!" said Mex, pointing and laughing. "You hear him? He's not afraid!"

"Because he sees that you're helpless, lad," said Lucas.

"Then he's a fool," declared Mex. "No, he doesn't think I'm helpless. He only thinks that he has a slight edge."

"Drunk or sober, day or night," said the giant, "there ain't a time when I can't manage you, kid. I can tie you into knots, and press you into a pulp. You hear?"

But Mex merely shook his head in wondering admiration, as one might at a child.

91

"How brave we are!" said Mex. "Turn him loose, Lucas. Free him from that chain, and a couple of you come along to see fair play."

"Not I," said Lucas. "I'll never let you endanger your life like this, my boy. You've meant too much to us, Arthur. You've saved Dorking Hollow, and now we're not going to let you throw yourself away."

"There's kindness!" Mex smiled. "But I tell you that I want him and that I'll have him."

"Suppose he gets away from you? Have you the right to endanger the safety of the entire community, man?"

I wondered what answer Holles could make to this, but he was never in the slightest doubt. He merely raised his hand and pointed mockingly to the sky.

"Kings," said he, "rule by divine right! Don't question my judgment, Lucas. Give me that man!"

Mex said it so loudly and clearly that Lucas made a sudden gesture of despair. He turned and faced the jurors.

"What's to be done, boys?" he asked.

There were twelve of those jurors, and they were tried and true men. They had a revolver, each of them; and there was not an unarmed man in the crowd. And yet we were all in doubt. To resist the will of Holles meant gun fighting, of course, for none of us doubted that that tigerish spirit, in spite of the odds, would drive straight forward to the execution of his will. And if he drew his guns—though there were enough of us to riddle him with bullets—he would die shooting, and shooting straight. Who would go down before those guns? Avery Lucas, first of all, and then others, the best and the bravest men in the camp.

It may seem strange to you that we gave way, but considering what priceless service had been rendered to

92

us by this man, perhaps you can understand.

We struck off the chain from Johnnie McGregor and saw him stand up to his full, great height.

"Who'll come along to be witness?" asked Mex cheerfully. "Because I don't want any one to accuse me afterward of tricking the big fellow or knifing him in the back. Loomis, will you come along? And you, Brick?"

The gambler and I want forward side by side to follow this pair to the scene of the battle. There was a general movement on the part of the entire crowd to come after us, but Mex simply said: "Stay where you are. Suppose that the big boy downs us, then what will happen? Some of you will out with your guns and fill him full of lead. Loomis, you and Brick leave your guns behind. Thanks!"

We did as he instructed us, and the others, like so many sheep who hear the voice of the shepherd, remained in their places, murmuring hoarsely, and grumbling loudly, but none daring to follow.

And as I walked on, I felt that we were truly following a king. Change the century, and Mex would not have been wearing an imitation crown in a mining camp, but a crown of gold, with noble peers to follow him and support him in battle.

Ahead of us strode the giant McGregor, and at his side walked Mex. What a vast deal of difference between the pair of them, and yet they walked toward a death fight with the utmost friendliness!

Said Brick to me: "The poor kid has bitten off more than he can chew, this time! Think of that McGregor with a knife in his hand! Worse than a grizzly, I'd say. A lot worse!"

"I'm not so sure, Brick," said I. "I'd lay a bet with you, if I felt like betting."

"I'll give you three to one," said Brick.

"I won't take you. I'm not in the mood for betting."

"No," said Brick. "Nor me. But if Johnnie McGregor carves him up, I'll camp on Johnnie's trail until I get him! I'll camp on his trail and see how fast and straight he can shoot. Why, the kid brought me up here! I never done him no good in all my days, but he brought me here and gave me my start. 'You go in and clean up, Brick,' says he to me.

" 'And what do you want out of it?' says I to him.

" 'Nothing,' says he. 'I simply don't want Jackson to get rich by a crooked game.'

" All right, old fellow,' says I, 'but you'll sure let me hand you something for protection. Jackson would have me run out in half an hour if you wasn't behind me.'

" 'I'll protect you for nothing,' says he, 'so long as you run a straight game. But if I hear of a brake on the wheel or any queer dealing in your house, I'll go down there and wreck you. Is that fair?'

" 'Fair as can be,' says I. And from that day to this he's never asked me for a penny! I call him a white man, Loomis!"

I couldn't quarrel with that judgment. My heart was racing with excitement as we came down to the edge of the river just outside of Dorking Hollow. There, on a smooth stretch of grass, the pair halted and looked about them, and nodded. And I knew that this was to be the scene of the duel. I was shaking like a frightened girl!

CHAPTER SIXTEEN

THEY THREW OFF THEIR COATS. They kicked off their shoes and pulled off socks and shirts. Stripped to the waist and with bared feet for griping the grass more securely, they now glared at one another with intent eyes.

I saw that the giant was flushed with excitement and he was brandishing a great knife which his enemy had given him—Johnnie's own knife, carefully saved from the spoils at the time of his capture. That weapon had been carefully made, it was said, of an old cutlass. It had been ground down to the proper size; in temper and edge it was all that heart could ask, and the blade was fifty per cent longer than the blade of any bowie knife that I had ever seen. Such a knife was necessary to balance the bulk of the giant and the weight and the length of his arm.

"Kid," said he to Mex, "you're game, and you're square. I got to say that. And I wouldn't be for killing you today, except that I sure got to do myself right in the eyes of other folks. You see how it is? You've challenged me to a fight, and so we've got to have it out. But when I've stuck you, I'm gunna plant you with a monument over you, kid, and on the monument I'm gunna have some poetry carved about you."

"Thanks." Mex smiled, feeling the edge of his knife, and, advancing a little toward the big man, after throwing his Colt to a distance. "Thanks, Johnnie. I know that you'll do what you can for me. And that makes me anxious to tell you what I'll do for you."

"Lemme hear, kid!"

"In the first place," said Mex, "I don't want to take you by surprise, Johnnie. So I'll tag you twice in the fight, before I stab you to the heart."

"Hello!" said Johnnie. "It's to be through the heart, is it?"

"So you'll feel no pain," said the youngster. "But I'll tag you first on the left arm, between the elbow and the shoulder."

"All right," and Johnnie grinned.

"And after that I'll prick you in the hollow of the throat. I've thought of making that the final cut. But, after all, it's an ugly thing to see a man floundering and gasping on the ground with a cut throat. I've seen it only once, and I don't want it to happen again. I hate blood, Johnnie."

The giant laughed good-naturedly.

"Why, kid," said he, "I'm just the opposite, and when I begin I'm gunna lay your throat open from ear to ear."

"Good!" chuckled Mex, and he nodded briskly to his foe. "Are you ready now, big fellow?"

"Ready as can be."

"What's fair and what's foul?"

"Everything's fair," said the big man. "That goes, then."

"Wait a minute!" cried Johnnie McGregor. "There's some damned wet, slippery places on this grass. Suppose that one of us should slide and fall—why, then, it only stands to reason that the other gent should let him up!"

"Make it like boxing, then. No hitting when the other man's down, McGregor!"

"I'd like that better. I don't mind granting you that, kid."

"You grant me nothing. I want no favors of you,

Johnnie. It's your dunderheaded feet that will slip, and not mine! I could run all day without tripping over worse grass than this."

"You're talking too much," said the giant. "Are you ready?"

"As ready as can be."

"Then, here goes!"

And Johnnie McGregor threw himself suddenly at Mex. It appalled me, and Brick shouted aloud in amazement and fear. One would never have expected such tigerish activity and speed in such a hulk of a man. But McGregor came with an irresistible rush, and a mighty lunge at Mex.

He struck. The flash of his knife was like the flash of a broadsword. We could hear it whistle through the air—hand and knife. But Mex had dodged away. Again, and again the thrust; and again and again that wonderfully agile fellow avoided the knife blade. Not with leaps and bounds forward or backward or to the side, but with smoothly gliding steps that were wonderful to watch, making the lunges of the giant miss him by the fraction of an inch each time.

McGregor sprang back with an oath as Mex, in turn, threatened him, and with uplifted knife.

"You damn shadow!" gasped Johnnie.

"But you've improved a great deal, Johnnie," said Mex, perfectly himself, and not breathing in the slightest degree hard. "You're ten times better than you were the last time we had it out."

"I'll carve you in two!" gasped Johnnie, and leaped in again. I thought that the sweep of his knife would fairly cut the slender boy in two. But there was a gleam of the knife of Mex in turn, and then a hoarse shout from the giant.

He sprang away again, staggering and cursing as he almost fell on the slippery grass.

On his left arm, between elbow and shoulder, there was a little red smudge.

"You rat! You rat!" he shouted.

"The first nibble, Johnnie," said Mex. "And the second nibble is coming right away!"

"You lie!" thundered McGregor, and, rushing in again, he slipped, lost balance, and fell with a thundering roar prone on his face. Mex sprang in as lightly as a leaf spinning in the wind, and I thought that he would be guilty of foul play and stab the fellow in the back. But instead he merely slapped Johnnie between the shoulders with his open hand.

"That's for a warning, old fellow," said he. "The next rush I'll touch you in the throat, and then you can give up, if you wish!"

Johnnie McGregor, pouring out a torrent of curses, as rage and shame and perhaps a little fear worked in him, lunged to his feet and at this will-o'-the-wisp. Thrust, slash and cut, he hurled himself at Mex, and every moment I felt as though the very wind of his blows would flatten Mex to the ground.

No, he still survived, and stepping in like lightning— and out again—he had touched McGregor again with the knife. I shall never forget Mex at that moment, his face half serious and half smiling, intent on his deadly work.

McGregor went backward, clutching at his throat, his eyes starting from his head. Fear seemed to benumb his nerves. He dropped to his knee and, bracing himself on his left hand, he panted and gasped; for, though the work had been brief it had been terribly violent on his part, at least. Holles? He was as cool and self-possessed as an idler out for a stroll.

"Not a quarter of an inch deep, old fellow," said he to McGregor, examining the end of his knife.

I could stand it no longer, and I called out: "Mex, you've got to end it. He can't stand up to you! You have him in the hollow of your hand."

There was no protest from McGregor, but Holles said cruelly: "Then you can have your choice, Johnnie. Go back with me to Dorking Hollow and there let them string you up to the first tree that's strong enough to bear the weight of a great beef like you, or else, fight it out here!"

"I'll fight it out here," said the big man, "even if you've got a devil inside of you, helping you. Because I swear that I've drove my knife ten times right through your body, but the devil came and snatched you away. You could never have moved that fast by yourself!"

"Are you sure?" said Mex. "Then come and start the dance again, Johnnie. I'll be waiting for you as long as you want. Only—the next time it's the heart, McGregor."

He raised his voice a little as he said this, and a ring came into the words, so that I was half sickened. I saw big McGregor get unwillingly upon his feet again, his legs braced.

"That's right," said Holles, laughing wickedly. "Stand up straight and stiff and still, and I'll come and put my mark on you, Johnnie!"

And he advanced carelessly toward his enemy. All this work and excitement had not completely sobered him, and there was the little awkward fumble in his walk as he went over the grass. Yes, and he went laughing.

Half a hundred times in the last ten minutes,

McGregor had been able to test this semi-drunken state in which young Holles appeared. And half a hundred times he had found that Holles became as agile as a whirling spark the instant a critical need presented itself. I felt that I could understand the invincible nature of the fighting qualities of Holles. The secret lay in his complete relaxation up to the moment of impact. When he was not actually fighting, he was always resting perfectly.

Yet, though McGregor had been able to test the steel-spring swiftness of Holles these many times, once more that laughing, careless, triumphant approach seemed to madden him into a new hope. He darted forward with a hoarse bellow, most like the roaring of a bull, and Holles, still laughing, sprang backward. He raised his knife, he seemed hovering to strike the fatal blow as he drifted light as thistledown before the charge of the monster, and then his feet slipped from under him, and he rolled on the ground

I was paralyzed with horror. That instant, I suddenly knew that McGregor would never keep the contract of fair play which he had made, and which Holles had allowed to bind him so honorably during the fight.

Now, with a wild yell of delight and bewildered surprise, McGregor hurled himself on the fallen man. And I saw those monstrous hands grasp Holles and lift him, and beat his head against the ground.

Blackness swam for an instant before my eyes. When I recovered myself, I ran toward the gun which Holles had thrown so carelessly from him at the beginning of this battle.

I was much too late. Brick had stood still, as though enchanted with horror. And, by one long bound, McGregor threw himself on the Colt and scooped it up an instant before me.

He was master of the field, as I recoiled before him, and threw my glance toward the spot where Holles lay motionless and crumpled on the grass.

CHAPTER SEVENTEEN

I COULD NOT BELIEVE WHAT MY EYES TOLD ME.

Have you seen that desperate pirate of the upper air, the frigate bird, balancing deftly around some heavy-winged, strong-taloned fish hawk, eluding every attack, swift as flashing light and dangerous as sharp steel, so that it seems utterly impossible that the marauder can ever be brought under by the far larger and heavier bird? Then you imagine the frigate bird met, crushed, and hurtling downward through the air.

So I looked on Mex. He had seemed to me the very spirit and essence of invincibility. I had thought that no hand in the world could touch him if he did not care to be touched. He seemed literally to think himself out of the way of danger, when he returned dexterously to the attack. But there lay the great Arthur Holles on the green grass, limp and helpless, and looking hardly larger than a child!

He was all spirit; little substance.

I never saw a man so entirely vengeful as big McGregor. And I never saw a man so stunned with joy and bewilderment, as though he could not believe the great victory which chance and treachery had placed in his hands.

He bounded back to the fallen form of Holles and kneeled beside it, fumbling at it—with one hand, and guarding us off with his gun.

"Touch him again—do him another harm, McGregor, you brute and traitor," I shouted at him, "and I'll have your life. I'll hunt you with a thousand men!"

"Bah!" snarled McGregor. "You talk like a fool. And what are you and a thousand like you—compared with one like him?"

I gripped the fallen man; there was no movement from Holles. I could stand it no longer. I hurried up, crying out: "Let him be, McGregor. Let me take care of the boy! He's dead already!"

"You lie," said McGregor. "There's too much hell in him to die at one grip of the hands. You lie! But dead he's gunna be or else I'll never live out the month!"

There was good sense in that. If Holles ever came back to his senses and to his life, there would be no long shrift for McGregor. Straight as an eagle through the air, this dreadful young destroyer of men would fly for the giant and end him.

And I saw the great hand of McGregor fumble again at the throat of his victim.

"Stop it, McGregor!" I shouted. "Brick, back me up!"

But the gambler, though brave enough, answered: "He's got a gun on us, and what are the pair of us compared with one of him, if we managed to close with him?"

"Johnnie McGregor," I said solemnly, "if you murder him now, after he took you away from the hangman's rope, after he gave you a fair chance for your life, and fought fair against you, you'll be a byword and a scorn through the whole range of the mountains. You're throwing yourself away, if you do this detestable thing!"

He hesitated, and then his hand left that slender throat. He scowled at me, as a man might scowl at the voice of his conscience.

102

"It's him or me!" said McGregor. "He chased me and hounded me. Now I got him where I want him."

"You've got him where a slip of his foot placed him," said I. "And not any fighting on your part. Twice he could have rammed his knife into your heart, and you know it. And a third time he could have stabbed you in the back as you lay floundering on your face."

"There's two of you and no more that have seen this here fight," said the great Johnnie. "And suppose that I fire a couple of times, suppose that there was no witnesses left at all—"

"You can't do it, Johnnie," I told him, though I really had no such assurance as I pretended. "You can't do murder, old fellow! There's too much decency in you. You'll give us that man to carry back to Dorking Hollow!"

He glared at me, his face convulsed, as good and evil fought in it.

Suddenly he said: "The kid was game."

I leaped at that concession.

"Aye, Johnnie. It would take the gamest man in the world to dare to face you like that!"

He swallowed that raw flattery with a mere nod of the head.

"Game," he repeated, "and square!"

"All of that, Johnnie!"

"I'll take him home myself!" said McGregor, and he started up with the senseless form of Holles thrown over his shoulder. To stay near Dorking Hollow was, of course, the vastest peril for McGregor. Already the noose had been around his neck that very day. And yet the giant seemed impervious to fear.

I followed him, Brick beside me. Straight up the hill strode McGregor, who apparently knew perfectly well

103

the shack in which young Holles and his crew were lodged. And as he drew nearer to the place, I saw a flying-squadron of half a dozen riders swing out from the farther end of the town. They were swept off toward the river bank where the fight had taken place, then they spotted us going up the hill and turned and rode toward us.

I knew what it meant. After we departed from the place of council, there must have been a serious debate, some of the wise men holding that we must maintain our faith and let Holles take the prisoner off; and others declaring that Holles had no right to imperil the safety and the wellbeing of the entire community by allowing such a person as big Johnnie McGregor a chance to escape.

And, finally the advocates of action had predominated. This was the vanguard of the resolutes, hurrying out to make sure that McGregor, if he managed to escape from the knife of Holles, should not escape from their avenging guns.

Behind them came yet other riders, streaming out of Dorking Hollow in hot haste. Once a man begins to act, all his doubts about the moral phases of a question disappear. The way to be sure of one's right in an argument is to strike a blow.

I saw the vanguard of the avengers, then, spot us on the hillside, and turn and spur their horses after us. At the same time, big Johnnie McGregor saw them also, and with a shout of excitement and fear, he leaped ahead for the shack.

I suppose that to him that shack was filled with greater enemies than even the wild riders who were approaching us. But he could handle numbers at close quarters, whereas in the open he would simply be shot

104

to pieces by many accurate guns. It was amazing to see the speed with which he ran. But what surprised me more was that he did not abandon his burden the instant that this danger threatened. He kept young Holles slung limp across his shoulder and rushed up the hill to the door of the shack, beat that door open with his hand, and stamped into the interior of the house.

What happened then and thereafter I know not by eyewitness, but by the reports of many others who told me all that occurred.

When McGregor strode into the house, he found half a dozen of the chosen men of Holles sleeping; two or three idling, or cleaning their guns, and several others playing a game of poker which rarely ended, night or day, in that house. The players changed, but the game went on until the next call to arms and the next ride into the wilderness broke up the sport and gave the players a new occupation and furnished them with fresh supplies of money.

Players, idlers, and sleepers, however, started to their feet when the great hand of Johnnie McGregor thundered at their door and beat it in with a crash. Every man had his gun out, but they were bewildered at seeing McGregor's shoulder supporting the body of their chief. They saw Johnnie whirl about and slam the door shut, and at the same instant that door was punctured by three bullets fired by the riders. One of those bullets dashed a pipe from the teeth of Christy Munn of the Holles band.

"Hold 'em back," cried the giant, placing Holles gently on a bunk and scooping up a shotgun as he turned toward the door. "Hold 'em back, boys!"

Hold them back? Hold who back?

The men of Holles did not stop to consider. They merely knew that McGregor, though a presumed enemy, had brought to them the helpless body of their chief, and that their house was being attacked.

They threw wide the door which McGregor had closed, and four or five of them, fearless of gunfire, rushed outdoors.

There they encountered the head of the pursuit. On foaming horses, grasping from the race up the hill, and standing now with hanging heads, sat the furious riders.

"We want McGregor!" demanded Canada Harry, at the head of these men. "We want him quick!"

Christy Munn, the broken pipestem still in his mouth, said through his teeth: "I hate to be rushed, Canada. Why in hell should we give you McGregor or anybody else? And who in hell shot a bullet through that door?"

A dozen fresh riders had come up, all keen for action. Some of them swirled around to the rear of the shack, to make sure that McGregor did not slip away in that direction. And Holles' posse men retreated toward the door of the house, their guns ready for use.

"McGregor beat up Holles," said Canada Harry, seeing that there would have to be some sort of an explanation. "And now we're here to get McGregor. Why, Christy, we're on your side. We ain't against you!"

"I asked a question," repeated Christy. "I says: 'Who fired through that door?' Am I gunna get an answer?"

"Hold on," began Canada. "The fact is, Christy, that there was shooting to get McGregor, and that was all!"

"Firin' into a plumb peaceful house—that was all, was it?" said Christy fiercely. "Well, and that was enough! I ask you again, who fired them shots? I got a personal reason for wanting to know—plumb personal!"

There was no answer to this aggressive demand, and Christy backed into the house, his companions with

106

him, and slammed the punctured door in the faces of the riders.

McGregor had not showed himself. And he had been wise in not doing so.

"Thank you, boys," said he. "I knew that I wouldn't do a good turn for Arthur without you backing me up. Would have been easy for me to leave him to die. But, instead of that, I carried him here!"

"What happened?" asked Christy Munn.

There was a fierce clamor outside the door, and Munn stepped to it and roared: "Get out of here! We got nothing for you. Nothing but the same kind of bullets that you fired through this here door. Now, get!"

And the riders scattered hastily from before the house and withdrew from vicinity in order to confer. Others were coming up rapidly from the town, and the numbers were growing in size to the dimensions of a little army.

CHAPTER EIGHTEEN

IN THE MEANTIME, WITHIN THE HOUSE, Christy Munn was demanding again; "What happened?"

McGregor saw at once that all that had happened at the trial was unknown to these men. They had little to do with the townsfolk.

Between them and the good people of Dorking Hollow there was no sympathy whatever, and there were enough of these ex-brigands to afford one another society. Above all, they would have found trials of their old companions most annoying. So they purposely remained at home while justice was taking its even way in the town.

And now McGregor said: "The boys were going to

string me up. But then Holles broke in and took me away from them. He said that he didn't want to see me pass out with a rope around my neck. A square gent is Mex, boys!"

There was hearty agreement to this.

"There had been a little argument between me and Mex in the old days," went on McGregor, "and now Mex said that him and me was to fight that argument out, man to man, with knives. With guns, he was too fast for me, maybe. And with bare hands, I was too big, of course!"

There was a general nodding. Interest was growing in this tale. And from the bunk where two or three were working over the unconscious form of Holles, there came a groan, to tell that their work was receiving its reward.

"That's good," said McGregor. "The kid is coming to! He'll soon be all right. Because I didn't bear down on him any too hard!"

"Hold on!" broke in Bill Dodge, long famous on the border of Mexico for deeds celebrated and doughty. "Hold on, boys! Do you mean to say that you beat the kid in a fair fight, Johnnie?"

"With knives," nodded McGregor. "No, I didn't beat him by plain fighting, either. Look here—and here!"

He pointed to the red smudges upon his left arm and at the base of his throat, and he laughed.

"The little devil," said he, "made a game of me. You know how fast he is?"

"Don't I?" groaned Bill Dodge. "Yes, I know well enough!"

"Well, he promised me that he'd tag me twice and then kill me. I fought as hard as I could. I learned knife play in old Mexico, where they know how, but I couldn't reach him. He was like a ghost. Turned into air when I made a pass at him!"

This praise of their hero filled the faces of the gang with perfect contentment.

"He nicked me in these two places, and he was coming at me the third time, to finish me—and he sure would have done it—when his foot slipped on the grass and he fell flat!"

There was a groan of excitement.

"I was near to driving my own knife through his heart when he lay there," said McGregor. "It was sort of a temptation. But, somehow, I couldn't knife a gent that was down—not such a fine, upstanding, hell-raising gent as young Holles. But I had to do something—in the flash of a eye he'd— be up and at me, and then he'd finish me off sure. So you can see where I caught hold of him and bashed him a couple of times against the ground to keep him quiet!"

They turned from him to the injured leader and nodded. Holles was slowly recovering, but very, very gradually. His face was purple and white in patches; his lips were pale, his eyes sunken, and his body flaccid, to show what he had been through.

"He ain't got a fractured skull," said one who was tending the fallen hero. "But he's sure been slammed hard. You might have bore down a little more easy on him, Johnnie!"

"I did, boys!" said Johnnie. "I hardly touched him. But he ain't very strong, y'understand? Just fast! I forgot that. I handled him like he was one of you tough nuts that would need a lot of quieting!"

This explanation was received with a burst of harsh laughter. They enjoyed that way of putting the matter. It was at once a subtle compliment to the mighty hand of

McGregor and to their own qualities.

At this very moment there was a thundering knock at the door of the shack. The boys opened the door, and outside they saw fifty men, with Avery Lucas at their head.

They hated Avery Lucas with all their hearts. He was the head of the vigilance committee which had disposed of so many of their old companions, and they had nothing but the profoundest loathing for this man of all others.

He had come now with much force behind him. Together with all the other men of the town, he had decided that Johnnie McGregor must be brought to quick justice. It was bad enough to have him given a chance to escape, even when they expected that Arthur Holles would remain to shield them against any danger which the famous bandit might bring upon them. But now it was reported that Holles was half dead, or dying, and that in addition, McGregor was at large.

The whole town was desperate, and the townsmen had determined to take McGregor at once and give him the hanging which he so richly deserved. So they had come up the hill, with Lucas at their head, and now he quickly said: "Gentlemen, I think that you have Johnnie McGregor inside?"

It was Christy Munn who stood first in the doorway. He was still very, very angry because his favorite pipe had been blown out of his mouth.

He looked at the speaker, but his words in answer were for the men behind him.

"He's promoted us to gentlemen," said Christy Munn. "Thanks very much, Lucas."

This rough sarcasm brought a chuckle from the ruffians in the shack. Lucas grew very angry. He had

110

endured a great deal lately. And since he had been deposed as king of Dorking Hollow, he had frequently heard men say that he had never really shown sufficient strength to rule a mining camp. This very day he had seen King Stork take McGregor from their midst—take McGregor from the vigilance committee of which he was still the head!

And now he decided that he would take a strong stand. He cast one glance behind him, and saw the numbers of resolute faces among his followers.

"I'm not here to make speeches," said Lucas. "I'm here to take McGregor away, give him up at once."

"My, my!" said Christy Munn in mock wonder. "Ain't he cross, though? He ain't here to make speeches, boys!"

And he eyed Avery with open contempt.

It must have been terribly trying to Avery Lucas to endure such language, but he controlled himself as well as he could.

"Munn," he said, "I want no disagreeable scene with you. You see that I have numbers on my side!"

"Numbers?" said Munn. "Numbers of what, Mr. Lucas?"

That brought a confused roar of rage from the men behind Lucas. Of course, they felt that insult, and there were some of them almost as brave and rough and ready with their guns as the selected rascals whom Holles had banded together for the policing of the woods.

Munn, however, did not shrink before that sound of fury. He said: "I want to tell you something, Lucas."

"You're laying up trouble for yourself—and for all your friends," said Lucas. "But I'll hear you out."

"Thanks," sneered Munn. "I wanted to tell you about a pipe. It was a real brier. Dog-gone me if it wasn't a rare good one! I had it for eight years. I got it off of a gent down in Mexico. He was terrible fond of that pipe, but I gave him a fifty-dollar pony for it. I've kept that pipe ever since. It was so dog-gone sweet that gents to the windward of it used to always ask me where I got the high-priced tobacco. It was *that* good. Now, Lucas, that there pipe was shot out of my teeth a minute ago by one of your lions. Lemme see that lion, I ask you. Let that there lion that fired through this here door step out and take what's comin' to him! And after that's settled, then maybe we can get down to talking about McGregor!"

"Munn," said Lucas, "if you insist on wasting time like this, I'll have to give you my preemptory command to surrender McGregor to us at once!"

And here McGregor broke in cleverly, saying: "All right, boys. I know you want to stand by me against those skunks out there that have hung so many of our pals. They sent Sam Josephs and Ollie McGuire to kingdom come this morning. I know that you want to stand by me against them, but I ain't going to be the means of getting all of you into trouble. Clear the door, there, and lemme at 'em. Lemme see how they'll handle a real man!"

And he started to move toward the door, gun in hand, but several hands pushed him instantly back.

"Shut up, Johnnie," said Munn. "I'm running this deal, and if the setup ain't what you like, you can deal for yourself later. I say that until they settle with me for that pipe, they ain't going to settle with us for McGregor! That goes for me. That goes for all of us!"

"Do you mean that?" asked Lucas, white with indignation.

There was a general shout from the men of the shack.

112

They would not back down. It was not a matter of where right or wrong lay. It was merely a question of which side they would take. And there could never be a doubt that they would side with Christy Munn against the chairman of the vigilance committee.

Lucas decided to try another string in his bow.

"Is Arthur Holles still alive?" he asked.

"Thanks to McGregor, yes."

"Thanks to McGregor?" echoed Lucas. "Thanks to the man who promised Holles to fight fair; no striking a man who was down—and who was spared when he himself went down—and then who seized the first slip of Holles to grapple with him! Thanks to McGregor?"

"Hello, Johnnie!" said Munn. "They're slandering you, here!"

"I hear them!" said McGregor. "Lemme get at that fellow, boys!"

He made a rush forward, but the men of the shack were thoroughly enlisted upon his side now, and they would not let him expose himself to the overwhelming gunfire of the men beyond the door.

If he had wished, he could have burst through them like a bull through reeds. But he chose to allow himself to be thrust back from the doorway again.

"I have your answer then?" said Lucas, growing stiffer and angrier every minute.

"You got our answer, Lucas. How does it sit on you?"

"Men," said Lucas, trembling with fury, "I'll have to order our rifles into action against your house!"

CHAPTER NINETEEN

AFTER ALL, IT WAS RIDICULOUS to threaten these fellows by declaring that rifles would open on that shack.

In the first place, it was five hundred yards from any covert, except brush, which guns from the house would search through and through; and, besides that, when young Holles had the shack enlarged and rebuilt, he had arranged it so that it could withstand a siege. Outside the walls there was a low, thick bank of packed earth. Inside the walls, there was a shallow trench. And the defenders of this improvised fort could lie down as if in rifle trenches and fire through convenient loopholes.

So the threat of Lucas was received with a roar of mirth. Munn crowded back the men who were behind him and slammed the door in the face of Lucas, shouting: "We'll give you ten seconds to get off the face of this here hill, Lucas!"

Those ten seconds were not used. The instant that door was closed, rifles were thrust out of the cracks and loopholes of the shack, and at the sight of them the whole band of hunters for McGregor threw themselves on their horses and raced for covert.

They reached it, with a few random balls singing about their heads to speed them on their way. And then they drew together for a parley. I was at that parley—though I was so thoroughly out of breath from having sprinted on foot a quarter of a mile that I couldn't make any speeches at the conference.

We were thoroughly angry—angry with Holles for having brought us indirectly into this predicament;

114

angry with big McGregor for having turned the Holles men against us; angry with those men for having turned on us; angry with ourselves because we had been shamed and driven like sheep before that handful of resolute fellows in their little fort; and, above all, angered with Avery Lucas because he had carried on the negotiations in such a foolishly dictatorial tone. Lucas himself had no ideas, and simply walked up and down, listening to the others.

For one thing, we were even more thoroughly dismayed than we were angered. And, as the first speaker pointed out, once news of this dissension and the crippling of Holles spread through the woods, we would have the bandits back at their old work, thicker in numbers than ever before, and with their work given a new zest because they would want vengeance for the things that Holles had done to them.

We were instantly in need of a new Holles. And where would we find him? No doubt, there were many of the robbers still in the woods, simply lying low and watching the development of affairs, and hoping against hope that they would have a chance to resume the old practices.

But where to get a successor for Holles? That was the bitter question on which we split. He alone had been able to hold together those ruffians out of whom he had formed his posse. He alone knew the woods perfectly and had been able to unearth the robbers from their dens.

Aye, we needed him most urgently.

Some one proposed that we should select from among ourselves the best shots and mount them on the best horses that remained to us, and appoint our best man as leader—then go out to range the woods in the night, exactly as Holles had done. But the idea met with no enthusiastic reception.

I said: "Where shall we get a man who really knows the woods? Where shall we get a man who really knows the robbers and their hiding places? And above all, where shall we get a man who knows how to take a handful of fighting fellows and accomplish miracles with them? We can go out with a small army and search those woods. But there are ten thousand square miles of mountains and forest and thickets for us to comb. And the noise we make in coming will announce us while we're still a half mile away. No, I think that we've come to our last resource. We've got to have Holles back. If we can't have his posse, let's have him. He can form a new posse, but we can't form a new Holles."

I meant what I said, and they all agreed with me, of course. Every man of us felt the same way about the thing. I had stated the manifest necessity, but how were we to go about what we needed?

Then one of the men remembered that I had always been a friend of Holles, and, in a way, a confidant of his. So it was suggested that I should go up to the shack and try to open a parley with the garrison.

If possible, I was to get Holles away from them. They would probably be willing enough to get rid of a helplessly injured man, and as soon as he was gone, we would set to work nursing him back to perfect health. It might take a few weeks, but the wait would be infinitely worth while.

At any rate, it was decided that we should get together as large a mule train as possible and push it across the hills that very night to get to the river before the brigands might hear of the new troubles in Dorking Hollow and waylay our trade routes.

That idea was too patently sensible to be opposed. We flocked down to the town and began to do the necessary work; equipped and armed a large body of guards, and under the leadership of Avery Lucas in person—strange that we continued to trust that honest but inefficient man!—we sent the train away before the evening came.

We sent it away, and settled down to a gloomy time of waiting. In the morning we had news of our cargo, and news that was bad enough. For in the dawn, back came a wounded, weary man, on foot. He reported that he had walked in fifteen miles from the place where the night before the mule train had been suddenly rushed by a host of robbers. The rear end of the train had been cut away. Avery Lucas, with the forward section, had apparently retreated through the woods, fighting every step of the way. But the survivor saw the rear portion of the train taken, saw three of his fellows killed and others wounded in the attack, and he himself had barely managed to crawl away to cover, tie up his wounds, and then drag himself to Dorking Hollow.

Our messenger fainted before he had quite completed his tale. But he had said enough. The devil which we had feared had descended upon us instantly. And I remember that one man cried in a voice that was a groan: "God, give back Arthur Holles to Dorking Hollow! We need him!"

This advice was so to the point and sounded so feasible that I accepted the mission at once and started instantly for the shack. When I came out of the brush, I shouted, and there was a call from the shack to give warning that I was seen. So I advanced slowly, straight for the front door. And at every step of the way prickles of fear ran up and down my spine. A rifle had been thrust out of a loophole, and it looked me in the eye all the way.

When I was close to the door, I said: "I want to learn how Holles is."

The door was opened at once.

"May I come in?" said I.

"Certainly," said Christy Munn, who appeared to be the chief power in the shack.

I went in and gave a casual glance around the big main room. The men were all there, a formidable group, seen rather dimly through the wreaths of tobacco smoke. And, particularly, I saw that the giant McGregor had not fled from the house during the night. He was still there, peaceably occupied in braiding horsehair of various colors into a long rope which would be at last manufactured into a bridle, I supposed.

Some of the group had been yarning. Some had been sleeping. And the eternal poker game went on at the corner table, with the floor strewn with matches; cigarette butts that had been ground to splotches under heel; two or three fragments of broken glass; some crumpled papers, while the whole place breathed an air of confusion much worse than it had worn during the headship of Holles.

The men greeted me in a fashion friendly enough, though Christy Munn said as I came in: "Look around and take your time, old man. Maybe you can find out something that would be useful to the rest of the gents in town."

I thought it best to overlook his sarcasm, and to offer no protests of innocence. He who speaks least in the presence of such men as these is apt to be the person who gets on with them with the least friction. At any rate, as I entered this room, I spoke quietly and nodded

118

to the men that I found there. Then I asked the way to Holles. I was told that he was in the next room.

"I'll show you the way," said Christy Munn.

I would gladly have gone alone, but I could not refuse this escort. So we passed out of the big ramshackle general room and entered a smaller and even flimsier chamber, where I found Holles lying on a bunk, his eyes closed, his face pale, a seal of suffering stamped upon his mouth.

He looked up at us in startled fashion when Munn said with brutal loudness: "Here's one of your little playmates come up from town to talk to you, Mex!"

"Thank you," said Holles. "Hello, Loomis, I'm glad that you came to see me. Sit down there. Have you any thing to smoke?"

"If he hasn't," said Munn with sullen earnestness, "I guess that I ain't got a pipe to offer him."

That infernal pipe! It alone, it seemed, had wrecked our hopes and brought us to this gloomy condition in Dorking Hollow!

CHAPTER TWENTY

I LOOKED EARNESTLY AT HOLLES. I had liked him before, as I think I've said. And now, moreover, it seemed that the actual fate of the Hollow once more depended upon the leadership of this youngster. If he lived and grew well and strong to fight for us, we could continue the mines with prosperity. If he failed us, all our labors would be in vain, for we could not ship the metal across the hills in the teeth of the banditry.

I said: "You look pale and weak, Arthur."

"I'm a bit down," he replied. "Johnnie McGregor

hasn't the lightest touch in the world. But I'll be about in no time. McGregor is kindness itself. He's laid hold of an Indian doctor. A wise old devil, he is. Knows all about herbs. He's working to get me in shape again!"

I was rather surprised at this, but now as I turned my head, I saw standing in the doorway a tall, thin figure, a little bowed with years, so that the face was ever bent toward the ground as though in serious thought. The Indian glanced quickly up at me, and I thought that I could read suspicion and something like fear in his eyes.

Why should he be afraid of me? Why should he be suspicious? Feeling that there was no reason, I dismissed the thing from my mind at once.

"What does he do for you?" I asked young Holles.

"He mixes up the most horrible concoction you ever have tasted in your life," said Holles, smiling, "but after I drink it, I feel nearly fit enough to get up and fight the whole world. Afterward, however, I realize that I'm still not quite up to myself and have to take things easy. I really think that big McGregor must have knocked something loose in my head, I have such a buzzing and humming there: darkness whirling across my eyes, and sickness, and a devilish feeling all over, Loomis."

I didn't like this, and I told him so. I asked him more in detail for the bad symptoms, and he explained to me that they were not always with him, but that at times he had a terrible sense of depression, and a great weight seemed to be pressing on the back of his brain. Then the Indian doctor would give him the potion which had such qualities that it removed all signs of his distress and made him feel quite well again.

"I'll tell you, Loomis," said Holles, "if I didn't have the medicine of that fellow, I think that I'd sink and keep sinking until I died. The power goes out of my brain, and the power goes out of my heart. I'm quite done for. No nerve left. Like a child afraid of the dark. Confounded feeling, old fellow."

He smiled at the idea of it, but at the same time the recollection of what he had suffered brought great beads of perspiration on his forehead. It alarmed me.

"I want to get a good doctor here for you, Holles," said I. "I've heard that there's a man in camp who used to be a practicing physician. And if I can find him, I'll bring him here to you. You won't object to that, Munn?"

"Why, man," said Christy Munn, "what do any of us want more than to see old Mex on his feet again? Of course, you can bring a doctor. Bring all the doctors you want."

The glance of Holles flashed from me to Munn and back again, and I thought that a faint smile appeared on his lips. It puzzled me to know why he should have smiled in just that way at just that time.

"In the meantime, Arthur," said I, "do you know that the robbers are at our throats again?"

"Ah? They're up once more, are they?" said Holles, and a flash of fire came back in his eyes again.

"Yes. They've broken in two the big train that we sent out. I hate to guess how many thousands of dollars we've lost!"

"The hounds," said Holles, "learned that I was sick. But I'll tell you what I'll do, old fellow. Christy knows the trails through the woods almost as well as I know them. And I'll have him take out the rest of the boys and find what he can find. He'll soon show them that Dorking Hollow isn't dead, even if I'm not up to lead the boys. What do you say to that, Christy?"

"Why not?" said Christy. "I think that we could warm

121

them up a bit even without you, Mex!"

"Talk it over with the boys," said Holles. "Work out a plan, and then I'll tell where you had better ride, as it seems to me. Do they know who was leading the gang that tackled the train?"

"Not sure. Only one man has come in so far. He says that he thinks a chap by the name of Leveret had the leadership of the gang."

"Andy Levered" murmured Holles. "He's holding his head up with the rest of them, is he? I've seen the day when he would hardly have been used as a roustabout in one of their camps. They've fallen off a great deal, Christy, if they let a rat like that lead them!"

"Leveret ain't such a fool," said Munn. "No whirlwind at a fight, but he's got a head on his shoulders and he knows how to use it better than he knows how to use his hands. When it comes to sitting and planning, he's apt to do a lot."

"Let him sit and let him plan," said Holles fiercely. "I would give a year of life to be able to sit in a saddle for six hours. I would find Andy Leveret and break his back for him. We'd have back the stolen stuff, too."

"Ah, lad," said I, "it would be a great thing for Dorking Hollow if you had that same six hours of life in you. And we'll get you fit again," I went on with enthusiasm. "Why, no matter how strong that devil of a McGregor is, he couldn't have used you up so badly. It's a mystery to me, Holles, that he could have damaged you in such a way as to give you these symptoms now—what could he have done with his brute violence except to break a bone or strain or batter a muscle?"

"He might have jarred the brain in some way—I don't know," said Holles thoughtfully. "Ask the Indian. He could say something, I think, if he would."

I turned to put the question, but the "doctor," after peering in at me and at his patient, disappeared again at once. I can't say that the Indian had made a very favorable impression upon me.

I said: "I'm going to get you a *real* doctor, Holles, and I'll bring him back here at once."

So I said good-by to him, and he was smiling as I left. Outside, in the warmth and the brightness of the sun, I wanted to turn back and speak to him again, but I hesitated to do so when I had no definite reason. I merely felt, blindly, that all was not well within that house. And the smile which McGregor gave me as I passed through the living room was entirely too bland and innocent.

I set off straightway to get the doctor. He was not to be found at his claim. I went to the gaming houses and he was not there; but I heard that he had ventured off into the woods to do some hunting.

"I hope that the fool isn't cut off by the bandits," said I to myself, and went to Avery Lucas to tell what I had found out. There were several other mine owners with Lucas when I arrived. They greeted me with the sharpest attention, listened to every word that I had to report, and when I had finished, Lucas said: "It seems to me that all the welfare of Dorking Hollow rests on Holles. If he recovers, we'll be able to make these mines pay. If he doesn't recover, we'll have to close them up. And then what will happen? They may be jumped by the robbers themselves and worked by them. These veins are rich and they're probably shallow. We return in a year and find that Dorking Hollow had been gutted of all its silver. No, we've got to get Holles back on his feet—unless, indeed, Christy Munn and the rest of them

123

will serve us!"

I said I felt that that was a great possibility. Christy Munn, we could all testify, was a man of force, and if he put his heart into the work, he would make the woods hot for the robbers. Perhaps!

Old Charles Henderson, the senior of our assembly, said quietly: "Well, lads, it has seemed easy enough for Holles to ride into the hills and spot the robbers. But when another man tries to perform the same job, I think that you'll discover it's not half so easy! Not half! Everything that a genius does seems to be done easily. But when an ordinary man attempts the same thing, you see the difference. I tell you, Holles is a genius; and a perfect fighting machine as well. That combination will be hard to duplicate, even if Johnnie McGregor himself would stand on our side and fight for us!"

We all thought afterward that Henderson, in the light of what was to happen, was a good deal of a prophet. I mean, in what he said about McGregor. I supposed that he simply reached out for an impossibility and hit upon McGregor as the first handy one. However, all that remains to be told in its due place.

In the meantime, I had to find the doctor. His name was Cochrane, and I forgot the nickname that he bore in the camp. He had come out to locate a claim, and had found a rather spotty one. However, he was too much a good-natured idler to make the claim prosper greatly, and he spent more hours in the woods shooting than in his mine laboring.

I started on the search for Cochrane again, and luckily I located him within the next hour, just returned to his shack, and unlimbering a string of birds from his shoulder, for he had had a successful outing. He started to tell me about his adventures, but I cut him short and

124

explained in detail the predicament of Dorking Hollow. Being one of us, he could appreciate at once how important it was to put Holles back on his feet; so he simply washed his hands, took up a small kit of instruments and drugs which he had with him, and accompanied me up the hill toward the shack where the gang was located, and where Holles was lying sick.

"But," said the doctor, as I reached the end of my story, "is there any reason why that band of thugs should wish to keep Holles sick on that bunk?"

I paused with an exclamation, but then I shook my head.

"What reason could there be, Cochrane?"

"I don't know! I don't know!" said he. "Only—from what you say, it seems extremely odd. However, there's no use trying to diagnose a case before we've had a chance to see the patient. Let's hurry on. I'm growing interested!"

But before I get to the door of the shack, I have to explain what had been happening inside it, as we all learned afterward from many witnesses.

CHAPTER TWENTY-ONE

AFTER I LEFT THE SHACK, having visited the sick man, Christy Munn went back into the living room and sat down by the stove, whittling a stick and frowning at the floor.

He said, finally: "Boys, I want you to listen to me!"

He spoke rather softly, which instantly brought the full attention of the whole crowd upon him.

Munn, he went on: "You know that Loomis has just been here. He says that the boys in the hills have jumped that big caravan and cut it in two, and grabbed the best half of it."

There was a groan from half the audience.

"Aye," said Munn, "it would have been sweet to have our own hands on some of that stuff. But Loomis came to talk to Holles, and Holles wants me to lead out some of you fellows to try to trail the gents that got the stuff. Now, what do you say?"

This abrupt question left them gloomy and silent for a moment, until some one said: "We've just held them off with our guns when they threatened to rush the shack. Now they come whining and wanting favors!"

"I know," and Munn nodded: "They're a bunch of quitters. Well, none of us would ever have been here, if it hadn't been for Holles. But what do you say? Ain't we able to do a thing except with Holles to lead us?"

The answer came quick as thought: "Mex is a good man, but he ain't the only man in the world. You could do a good job yourself, Christy!"

"Thanks," said Munn, "but I ain't here to set up in the place of Holles." He added with a grin: "I only pack one gat, and he's a two-gun man! But, just the same, he ain't done such miracles as the tenderfeet down here in Dorking Hollow think. I say, let's have a whirl at his job, and show the world that Holles ain't the only he-man in the Rockies! It would be fun, besides! And I got an idea that I know where Andy Leveret would be hanging out after making a haul like that one of yesterday!"

On this proposal the ideas varied; some taking one side, and some taking the other, but on the whole, opinion favored Munn. For these were men of action, and being so, they preferred almost any sort of life in the open to a life of idleness. At about the time when the question would have been carried by a unanimous vote the big voice of Johnnie McGregor rumbled: "Boys, I got no right to speak up, here—"

"Sure you have, Johnnie," said Munn. "What's in your head?"

"I'll tell you," said McGregor. "I've been sort of on the other side of the fence, and up to now it used to sort of make me laugh when you went ahead and made fools of yourselves. But since you've been so damned square to me, and herded away the gents from the Hollow when they wanted to mob me, I've got to tell you something—if you'll listen to me!"

When was there a time when Westerners would not listen to Johnnie McGregor? Of course they all sat mute with attention.

"You been up here like hired laborers," said McGregor. "Or you might put it worse than that even. You've been up here like soldiers in an army. Only you get precious little glory, and not much pay."

"Hold on, Johnnie," interrupted one. "We've had our pockets filled a good many times, since we joined up with Holles here."

"Sure you have," said McGregor. "After you saved a couple of hundred thousand dollars for the miners, they were willing to throw you a handful. Why, when a dog pulls down a deer, you'd give him a mouthful of the meat, wouldn't you?"

He paused, and the gun fighters looked one to another, sullen, surprised, their brows darkening. They were not serious students. They were not trained thinkers. And this suggestion from Johnnie McGregor bewildered them a little. However, all men like to think that their services to others have not been fully recognized. They waited eagerly for the explanation. It

127

came quickly.

"You've got what?" said McGregor. "Think it over. How much have you really got?"

He paused for them to estimate, and then Munn said: "For my share, I've pulled down about three thousand dollars and keep. Which ain't so bad for a few days, when you come to think about it."

McGregor merely smiled. There is nothing quite so mysterious and maddening as the smile of superior knowledge.

"Partners," said he, "I ain't gunna laugh, though I'm pretty tempted to! But I want to ask you, what does even an insurance company charge? Why, about six or seven per cent for protection, a lot of the time, I guess. And on risky things, they might run the protection up to twenty or thirty per cent. Now I ask you: is the business that's done in Dorking Hollow risky? Is carting the silver across the hills to the river risky?"

He paused. The answer was so obvious that it was not put into words.

"All right," said McGregor, "you know that risky is hardly the word for it. Out of every ten dollars that left the camp, hardly one got to the river. The rest went to the boys in the woods. Then along comes you gents and what do you do? Why, you police them hills so that a two-year-old baby could walk across them with his pockets filled with diamonds, and nobody would dare to rob him. He would come in safe at the river. All right. Have I told the truth?"

"It's all true, Johnnie," said Munn. "We sure threw a scare into 'em!"

"It was a fine job," said McGregor. "There ain't any doubt but that it was a very extra fine job. Nobody could find any fault with the way that you done it. But after

128

you come back from the hills maybe you got noisy and obnoxious here in town? Maybe you started in shooting things up? No, you didn't do nothing of the kind. You sat down inside of your shack and you took things dead quiet and easy! Never made a peep. None of the townsfolk was hurt by you. You would have thought that this here shack had a Sunday school or something like that in it!"

There was a murmur of agreement.

"Well," said McGregor, "I want to ask you: What did the gents of Dorking Hollow do? They seen that instead of losing nine dollars out of ten and having to close down their mines, they were delivering ten dollars out of ten, and working their mines right wide open. What did they do? Did they say: 'We been saved by those gents, and we're gunna pay them according—say a dollar for every four that we send out?' No, sir, they didn't say that. They didn't have to. Because they seen that they had a bunch of simps to handle. And they handled 'em. Yes, sir, I've had to laugh when I thought about it—it was so dog-gone foolish, the bargain that you made!"

"By your line of talk, we've been fools, Johnnie," said Christy Munn.

"Well, look for yourselves," said McGregor. "One day these gents think that their troubles are over, and that they're gunna fire into the shack here and clean you out without no trail. They figure that they don't need you no more, and that's their way of getting rid of the whole bunch of you. But the next day they've lost a big mule train loaded down with silver and all at once they say: 'We need protection. Well, we'll send out the bloodhounds to clear the trail for us again, and when everything is safe, we'll shoot the pack, because they

129

cost too much!' That's the way that they figure, and it seems that they figure right, because here I see that you're all aiming to do just what they want you to do! They're clever. I got to admit that for 'em. Mean and low, they are, but clever! They never spend two dollars when two bits will do just as good!"

By the time McGregor had finished this speech that little crowd of gunmen was red-hot. They were hot enough to tear out of the shack and start shooting up the town. Every one of them felt that McGregor had spoken as a sort of neutral.

But Christy Munn said soberly: "All right, boys. I'm with you as much as any of you are. I see that McGregor is right and that we ain't been paid what we should have been paid. But then, the job that we done with Holles to lead us was a pretty clean job. Are we gunna scare out the robbers so well when he's in his bed like this?"

"Hold on," said McGregor. "You all know what I think of Holles. I risked my neck to carry him up here to you. He's a good, clean kid. But, after all, he don't know everything that's to be knowed: Might there be others that know the hanging-out places of the robbers in the hills?"

"Who, McGregor, outside of yourself, say?"

"Well, leave it at that. I'd say that I know their places as well as Holles ever did."

"Aye, McGregor. There's no use in denying that. But, at the same time, you ain't on our side of the fence."

"And what's to keep me from getting there? Can't I jump over a fence as well as the next man?"

"Why, Johnnie," exclaimed several, "they want to hang you, if they can get a chance!"

"Bah!' said McGregor. "They want their pockets

130

filled, and that's all that they care about. As long as I was on the other side of the fence they were keen to kill me. But if they could use me, they would do it quick!"

It put another face upon matters.

"Only," said McGregor, "I would rather have my neck stretched by a rope than to waste my time working for them at the rate that they've been paying you boys. They couldn't drive a bargain like that with me."

Suddenly Christy Munn said: "I'll tell you what we'll do, Johnnie. We'll make another offer to them. We'll offer to do business with them, but only in case that they'll let you be at our head while the kid is sick!"

"All right," said McGregor. "I don't mind running things for a while till Holles is back on his feet. Then him and me will have to finish our fight. And after that, the one that's left will be head of the gang. That looks pretty logical!"

It was agreed on all hands that the most intelligent and entirely satisfying speech that had ever been heard by any of those present was the speech which had just been concluded by the big man. And almost instantly he had a chance to act as their spokesman, for just then I rapped at the door of the shack, and it was the great voice of McGregor that bade me enter.

CHAPTER TWENTY-TWO

WHEN I OPENED THE DOOR, I said simply: "I've got Doctor Cochrane with me. Can he see Holles?"

"Wait a minute," said McGregor. "If the lad ain't asleep, you can see him."

He left the room, and presently returned with a nod to us, and then a sharp glance at the doctor.

131

"You can see him," said McGregor, "if you know your business. You a practicin' doctor, Cochrane?"

"I have been," said the doctor. "It's nearly five years now, since I had an office. But I have done a good deal of tinkering in a medical way around camps, you understand, during the last years. I have my hand fairly in, I think."

"Mind that you have," said McGregor. "Because you ain't going to take care of no ordinary gent today. Mex is the upstandingest gent in the mountains, bar none. And if anything should happen to him, or if anything should go wrong with him, I'll tell you what—there would be hell popping for you, my friend. We would come to get you! I can tell you particular that I've fought twice with Holles. He come off worst each time, but maybe the next time he would win. And he's my friend. He's my friend because he's the first man in the world that's been able to fight with me twice."

And he roared with laughter at his own remark, half jest and half boast.

He himself led the way into the room where Holles lay, and I noticed as we passed through the living room that the glances of the other men no longer fell upon me in such a friendly fashion as they had before.

But I had other and more important things on my mind, and I paid small heed to this symptom. I was interested in Holles, and I was shocked as we reached the door of the room, and found the Indian doctor bending over the bunk on which the sick man lay, for there was not the slightest doubt that Holles was sick. He had seemed a little done up when I had seen him earlier in the day; but, now, he was a mere ghost of a man, his cheeks and his eyes sunken, and his face of a dull, sickening pallor. I caught my breath and looked at

132

Cochrane, and he frowned instantly. His practiced eye had seen even more than mine, of course.

The Indian was holding a glass to Holles, and the latter raised himself upon one elbow with difficulty and drank off half the greenish potion.

He made a wry face afterward, and then nodded cheerfully to us.

"You can look him over, doc," said McGregor. "I'll be back in a minute."

And he left the room with the Indian doctor.

Cochrane went instantly to the patient and shook hands with him.

"I didn't expect to see you looking as bad as this," said he.

"Do I look bad? I've been feeling like the devil," said Holles. "But now I'm bracing up again. That Indian is a handy fellow, Cochrane. There's something in that medicine of his that braces me at once. After I've finished that glass, I'll feel almost like my old self."

"All right, then," said the doctor. "Let me have a look at you, though."

And, dropping on one knee beside the bed, he felt the pulse, leaned lower, and listened for a moment to the heartbeat of Holles. Standing up again, he flashed at me a glance which said as plainly as words: This is serious indeed!

"You were not a sick man when you fought with McGregor?" Cochrane asked.

"Never better in my life than on that day."

"Well," said the doctor, "you're sick now! What's this that you've been taking?"

He raised the glass of greenish fluid and sniffed it.

"It tastes like hell, doc, but it works wonders! Look here, I'm almost back to normal again!"

133

In fact, the color had returned suddenly to his face and his eyes were brighter.

The doctor suddenly took an empty flask from his kit and poured the contents of the glass into it.

Then he winked at the patient.

"Just keep your mouth shut about that, old fellow?"

"What the devil do you suspect?" asked Holles, frowning. "Because, you understand, there is really not the slightest doubt that the Indian is doing his very best for me—"

But here the Indian doctor slipped back into the room again and cut short that conversation.

Cochrane continued his examination, going over the whole body of the sick man, listening again to his heart.

Finally he stood up, looking at the thermometer which he had just used.

"It beats me," said Cochrane under his breath.

And he turned around and looked hard at the Indian, and then at McGregor, who had entered the room behind the native medicine man.

After that, he seemed in haste to leave, so I went out with him. Passing through the living room, I said to Christy Munn: "Well, Christy, are the boys going to ride out with you?"

He smiled at me—a grim, mirthless smile.

"We've been talking things over, Loomis," said he. "And we figger that we need somebody better than me to take the place of Holles. What you think about McGregor?"

I turned and stared at the giant. He was leaning against the wall, smiling in his turn.

"The boot's on the other foot," said McGregor. "Want to hang me today—have to hire me tomorrow. I know that it's a tight fit, Loomis!"

However, my reaction was not what the giant had expected. I knew that McGregor understood the robbers and their habitations and their ways as well as any man, and I could not help exclaiming: "Why, boys, this seems to me a plain inspiration. For my part, I hold no special grudge against McGregor. If we can have safety with McGregor working for us, well and good. If not, then let's try to hire him if we can't get on without him."

"Thanks," said Johnnie. "I like the way you say that. Now it only remains to settle the terms."

"What terms, Johnnie?"

"The terms of the hiring."

"Why, Johnnie," said I, "I presume that we could treat you just as handsomely as we treated Holles."

"Handsomely?" queried the giant with a grin at his companions.

I saw by that smile that there was a secret understanding among them, and I was instantly on the defensive.

"What do you want?" I asked him.

"Reason, that's all," said he. "We want only what our work is worth. You got any way of figuring what it's worth, old-timer?"

"Certainly," said I. "That work is worth the time you put in, plus the danger that you run while you're ranging the woods. But I don't think that that danger will be very great. Holles has already broken the back of the robbers' strength, you know."

"They seem to be thick enough, at that!" said McGregor. "Now, I'd like to suggest another way of looking at the deal. You fellows that have mines can't send out a pound just now. You're afraid to. You'll keep on being afraid, unless me and the rest of the boys fight your battles for you. We could claim fifty per cent

135

maybe."

"Fifty per cent!" I shouted.

"But we ain't hogs," said McGregor. "Twenty-five per cent will do for us."

"Twenty-five per cent of the output of the mines?" I asked, outraged and amazed.

"I've made the proposition," said he. "And you can take it or leave it. I'm tired of seeing these boys made fools of so's some of you that don't take no risks can be made rich!"

I looked helplessly about the room, and everywhere I encountered the same grin, half mocking, and half delighted.

"You say this seriously then?" I asked.

"Nothing but serious, old-timer."

"Take care," I warned them, "that you don't kill the goose that laid the golden egg. I'll go down to the rest and tell them the wild idea that you have. It's my duty to tell them but I can give you their answer beforehand."

"What will it be, then?" asked McGregor.

"They'll simply laugh!"

"Let 'em laugh till their faces ache," said McGregor furiously. "My Scotch blood ain't been give to me for nothing. I'm gunna see that there's justice done to the boys here. You understand me? They can holler and they can try bluff. But it won't work. We know what we're worth, and we're gunna have our price or nothing at all! If you don't like the proposition, then you clear out of here and try to get somebody else to handle your dirty work in the hills for you!"

I went gloomily from the house, for I saw that it was perfectly foolish to attempt to bring these ex-brigands to their senses.

"There would never have been any trouble like this if

Holles had remained in charge of that crew of freebooters!" said I to the doctor.

"No," said he, "he was a lad of a different color!"

"Was?" cried I. "Why do you put him in the past tense, Cochrane?"

"Because," said the doctor, "he's a dead man!"

"What!" I cried, stopping short. "Arthur Holles is a dead man?"

"That's it. Don't stare at me!"

"Why, Cochrane," I gasped, utterly sick and amazed, "I knew that he seemed badly done up. But surely, a mere pummeling, even from the hands of a giant like McGregor—has something been broken in the—"

Cochrane held up his hand, and his face was wonderfully stern.

"What I guess at," said he, "I don't know. And I'm going to put my guess to a test before long. In the meantime, I can tell you between us that Arthur Holles is a dead man unless he is taken from that house!"

CHAPTER TWENTY-THREE

I HAVE EVER BEEN ONE TO HATE MYSTERIES. The shadows that fall in cities sent me out West, and under the broader skies and breathing the clearer air of the West, I have felt that I should be able to shake off the old uncleanness, the old sense of taint. And now the horror came back to me.

What was happening to Arthur Holles in that house, surrounded as he was by his friends, his chosen men?

I asked no questions, but as we went down the street of Dorking Hollow, a mangy cur ran out from a shack and barked at us; a savage, useless, ragged creature.

"I'll buy that dog from you, friend," said Cochrane to the man who was idling in the door of the hut.

"Take him," said the man. "Hanged if I don't want him less he wants me. He done the adopting. I didn't!"

Cochrane tied a string around the neck of his new possession and led him down the street with us.

"Have you turned yourself into a dog doctor?" said I. "Are you going to try to cure that case of mange?"

"You never can tell what a new remedy will do," said Cochrane. "I'll have to try something on this poor dog."

When he reached his shack, he asked me to go in with him.

"I have to make my report," said I.

"Very well," said he. "Make your report, then, and afterwards come back here, will you?"

I lingered for a moment, watching him pour something forcibly down the throat of the stray. Then I hurried on to find Lucas and some of the other important miners. I found them awaiting me in some anxiety at the house of Lucas. Their first question was about Holles. I told them frankly that there was something mysterious about his case, and that the doctor would not yet commit himself. Then they asked me about the hunt for bandits under the direction of Christy Munn.

I had more to say on this point. When I told them first that big McGregor had expressed his willingness to come on our side of the fence and fight for us, there was an actual cheer of applause. But then I told them the only terms on which he would come, and a groan followed the cheer.

"He's mad!" said some one.

"No, not mad," replied Lucas, "but he knows his power over us. Because, if we can't have Holles to work for us, what will happen to the mines? What will become of them, I ask you? Has any one an answer?"

No, there was no answer. Some of the men, in their fury, wanted to mass all our forces, armed to the teeth, and attack the shack. But the older among us discouraged such an idea. A dozen repeating rifles firing from that little fort would so sweep the open ground around it that we had little or no chance to approach. At night, to be sure, we might have better fortune if we could steal close with a large body of men. But even then, what would be gained? We would have slaughtered the only men who could really defend us from the men of the woods!

There was some talk, back and forth, but nothing was concluded until finally it was suggested that the best we could do was to try to beat down the terms of these ruffians who had been so inspired by big McGregor.

I was to go back and try to hold them to ten per cent. If not that, I could go to fifteen; and beyond that, in case of desperation, I was even to agree to twenty per cent. But as for the one quarter which McGregor called for, we felt that such a sum was too pure a robbery.

I started back, accordingly, and on my way I stopped in at the shack of Cochrane. I found him seated in his one room staring fixedly into a far corner, and there in the shadows I saw the mangy dog lying as though asleep. I approached it a little closer. The poor creature shuddered violently and turned up its eyes at me, but closed them again at once and moaned faintly.

"What's this, Cochrane?" said I. "Is this the way you cure mange—and kill the dog? Was it only an experiment?"

"Yes," he said slowly. "Only an experiment?"

He stood up and faced me, and his eyes were dark, his

teeth were set.

"The medicine I gave that dog," said he, "seemed to have a good effect at first. Gave it a tremendous lot of life. The poor brute jumped all over the house and seemed beside itself. But afterwards it began to quiet down, and now, unless I'm very much mistaken, it's a sick dog. Very sick. As sick, almost, as young Arthur Holles up the hill!"

"Man, man!" I called at him. "What do you mean by that?"

"I mean," said he, "that the medicine I gave him was the remains of the greenish drink that our friend Holles was taking when we came into the room."

The hair lifted on my head. I was cold with the most miserable fear.

"Cochrane!" I gasped.

He merely nodded gloomily.

"The Indian doctor!" I cried.

"The Indian murderer!" said he.

"And poison—how does the scoundrel dare do it?" I asked, "in that house, where Holles is surrounded by his men—"

"Don't you remember who brought the doctor to him?"

"Yes, McGregor."

"Well, is McGregor a friend to Holles?" I started.

"McGregor would never consent to such a dastardly thing!" said I.

"Consider this," said Cochrane. "If Holles gets well, McGregor will have a fight on his hands, and a real fight. You've told how his duel with Holles went before, and how he seemed to be fighting with a spirit rather than a man. Well, when Holles is on his feet once more, McGregor knows that he, Johnnie McGregor, will

140

be no better than a dead man. He has that firmly in mind, and he isn't ready to die!"

"A fair fight—" I began.

"What fight is fair when Holles is one of the fighters?" asked Cochrane impatiently. "I saw him do this!"

He took from his pocket a silver quarter, badly bent.

"He hit that while it was spinning in the air—hit it with a snap shot from the hip! And McGregor knows what Holles can do with a knife as well as with a gun. No, I tell you that McGregor will never chance another meeting with Holles, and this is his way of avoiding that meeting."

He finished by pointing at the dog in the comer of the room. The poor creature just then rose on shaking legs and dragged itself to a basin of water, from which it lapped a mouthful and slumped down upon the floor again.

"Then Holles is a doomed man!" said I bitterly.

"How he has stood up under the volley of poison that they have been firing into him," said the doctor, "I frankly cannot understand. Of course, the man has a most miraculous constitution, or else every one of those doses which first set him up and then depressed him would have taken his life. Or it may be that the Indian devil varies the strength of his doses. This one which we interrupted was potent enough! But some men have a singular ability to throw off the effect of poisons. Holles must be one of the lucky. He's immune to what would kill half a dozen of us ordinary people. But what can you do to get him away?"

"God knows! But I'll see him first and warn him that he's being poisoned by that drink."

"After which they can poison his food."

"True! What shall we do?"

"I don't know. We've got to get him away from that house!"

"Listen to me, Cochrane. Suppose that I am able to persuade Christy Munn, or one of the others, that McGregor is poisoning Holles?"

"Could you do that?"

"I could try."

"Then take luck with you. It might work."

I left him hurriedly. The day had ended. The evening was thickening rapidly toward night, and from all the houses I could see the yellow shining of lights; and the fragrance of cooking meat and boiling coffee was wafted up to me from all sides. But nothing seemed attractive to me. My mind was filled with the great task that lay before me, and how I could possibly manage to execute it.

I thought of going back to Lucas and the others for further council, but on second thought I guessed that they would have very little to proffer that I had not figured out already. I hurried on to the house on the hill to which we had looked so often with hope when Holles first established himself there, and which had now become more a center of danger than of comfort.

I went up to the door, and at the first rap, I was told to enter and found the men seated around a long, roughly made table, having their supper. What a meal! Holles had employed two men to take care of the house and do the cooking, and they attended to the needs of their masters in the most royal style. I saw venison saddles, and great hams, and large fowl of some sort, and all of those rough fellows devouring the good fare with the most excellent appetite,

Who is responsible for the fallacy that a quiet

142

conscience gives an excellent appetite? Perhaps it does; and then again, what of those men who have no particular conscience to pacify? I looked around that board and decided that conscience was simply a useless word in this assembly.

"Well," said big McGregor, who was sitting at the head of the table, "what's the news?"

"Ten per cent, Johnnie," said I. "We're willing to be robbed to that extent."

"Robbed?" roared McGregor. "My friend, you ain't talking to a fool. And if you came up here with power to offer nothin' more than that, you can go right on back again!"

I looked him in the eye and saw that he meant what he said.

So, instead of bargaining at great length, I said simply: "McGregor, what's the rock-bottom division that you and your men will take?"

"I've named it before,' said McGregor. "I ain't a hog. I might have said half, or forty per cent. But I didn't. I said a quarter. And that's where I stick. A quarter, or nothing! Do you like the game?"

"Is that final?" I asked.

"Absolutely, Loomis."

"Then good night to you," said I, and turned for the door. But before I reached it, a great shout of "Loomis! Hey!" made me turn again.

CHAPTER TWENTY-FOUR

IT WAS CHRISTY MUNN WHO HAD INTERFERED.

"Hello!" said I. "Have you anything to say in this deal, Christy?"

143

He cast an ugly side glance at McGregor, by which I could guess that the giant did not possess over these men quite such an unquestionable authority as Holles had exercised, and then said: "McGregor will talk for us. But take another look at this deal, McGregor, will you?"

McGregor scowled at the last speaker and then—at me.

"He was bluffing—a rank bluff, Munn," said he. "And you had to horn in and spoil everything."

"If you think that I'm really bluffing," said I, "try me out!"

"All right, all right," growled McGregor. "I ain't so unreasonable. It's just a matter of principle with me to see that these boys are not trimmed out of their rights. What's your offer, my friend?"

"I'll make the top one," said I. "Mind you, we all consider it rank robbery. But we're helpless to a certain extent. We'll let you take fifteen per cent of our shipments. And the silver which fails to get through the woods to the river will all be deducted from your share! That's our top offer!"

McGregor blinked.

"Pretty soon," said he, "we'd be your debtors, wouldn't we? That is, if the boys in the hills made a few good stiff raids?"

"I don't know, McGregor," said I. "You're filling the place of Holles, now, and Holles was able to run the rascals ragged. Nothing was lost while he was at the head of things. I've made our highest offer. What do you say to it?"

McGregor favored me with a black look and then said bluntly: "Boys, what do you say?"

"Take it!" clamored several of them. "Before we're

through with this job we'll clean the woods out, and then we can sit pretty and rake in the profits."

"It's against my advice," said McGregor. "It's plumb against my idea of good business. But this here is all on your own heads! You want this here settlement, and I'll make it for you. Do we get a written statement from you, Loomis?"

"If you want it," I agreed.

"No," said McGregor on second thought. "After all, I suppose we don't need anything like that. We got each of us a couple of witnesses on the hip, and they'll speak up for us if we don't get our rights."

He pulled out a heavy Colt and banged the butt of it on the table, until all the dishes jumped and jangled.

"I only want to know if the agreement is satisfactory and binding," said I. "You boys are responsible for our losses, if we have any; otherwise, you collect fifteen per cent?"

"Right," said Munn.

"But first," broke in McGregor hastily, "we want a few days to police the woods before you send out any shipments."

"I'm willing. I'll agree to that. Three days, say?"

"Make it three days. We'll sweep the hills clean. So long, Loomis."

"And how's Holles?" I asked.

"He's dog-gone poorly," put in Christy Munn. "The old boy ain't himself at all!"

"I'd like to see him," said I.

"Leave him be! Leave him be!" said McGregor. "Let the man rest, will you? He's fagged out with all the visiting and the noise that he's had to put up with. The poor kid just needs some peace and some rest!"

I said, inspired for the moment: "There are a lot of

you fellows here, and you're not the quietest bunch in the world. Suppose you let me take Holles and bring him down into the town. We could put him up in the shack of Lucas. You know that's a quiet house, and he'll have the best of care, of course!"

"A good idea," said Munn instantly, nodding.

I liked Munn better every instant that I knew him. Rough handed, ready with his weapons he certainly was, but he was apparently as good hearted as he was rough, and there was a certain flare of honesty about the man that appealed to me immensely. I felt that if these negotiations had been made through Christy alone, we should never have had any trouble.

"Well, then," said I, overjoyed, "I'll bring up a little help and we'll take Holles away at once. I'm sorry that I didn't think of it before."

"Leave him be for a time!" said big McGregor. "Leave him be. Dog-gone me if I ain't surprised at you, Christy! Here's a gent that would send away our pal Mex. And what would they do for him? He's dog-gone weak, is Mex. You see that for yourselves. He needs plenty of attention, and he needs plenty of good care and the right kind of cookin'. Now, where would he get just what he wanted except here?"

"It's true," replied another. "We want old Mex where we can watch him get well. Let him stay here, boys!"

"Where McGregor's own Indian can watch him!" proposed another. "That Gregorio is a wise gent. Better than all the fancy city doctors, Loomis."

"Do you know that for a fact?" said I.

"Don't I?" said the other. "I seen Mike Lacrosse dyin' of a fever and sick as a dog, and the Indian, he dosed him up with some funny-looking stuff and had Mike sitting up and cracking jokes inside of three days!

146

In a week, Mike was sitting in front of his shack and smoking his pipe. That's what I seen Gregorio do!"

I nodded. For that matter, I had often heard that the Indians had a certain skill in the use of herbs, but though Gregorio was able to cure the sick now and then, was it not almost certain that such skill would teach him, also, the cleverest ways of killing them? Arthur Holles was being poisoned; and there was not the slightest doubt in my mind that McGregor had schemed the thing. Cochrane believed it, and so did I. And now it was McGregor again, who prevented us from taking the sick man away from the house. It was maddening to be held back at the very verge of a success. And I raged at McGregor in my heart as I heard him declare that he was only thinking of the welfare of the invalid!

But what could I do?

I merely suggested: "Suppose we put it up to Holles? Let him decide whether he'd rather be here or in the village."

"Another good idea," said Christy Munn, rising.

"Hold on, Christy," put in McGregor, and I could see that he was growing more serious. "Hold on, there. You're always rushin' onto things! The kid was enjoyin' a fine sleep, the last that I seen him, a little while ago. Leave him be, will you? We'll ask him in the morning what he wants to do about moving."

Morning? I knew that if Holles remained in that house all night without a warning of what was threatening his life, he would never see the morning light.

But what was to be done? Already I had insisted so long that I feared McGregor might be suspicious of me. And the first moment he definitely suspected that we guessed the foul play which he was attempting, that

147

moment he would polish off Holles so that all the good work of Gregorio, the poisoner, should not be in vain.

I never have come so close to nervous hysteria in my life, but I took an iron grip on myself. I had Christy Munn behind me, but if I attempted to force the issue, I foresaw that McGregor would be far too strong for us. The gang was fairly under his thumb. They allowed him to do all their bargaining for them—his word was law in that place!

So I bade them good night hastily, and went off down the slope toward the village. Two or three times I turned and looked back at the house, with such a burst of lights shining out of the windows that one would have chosen it from all the town as the place most filled with honest good cheer.

All manner of thoughts revolved in my mind. I thought first of all, of course, of getting Lucas and the rest to give me advice. But on second thought I knew that this was foolish. There was nothing they could do that I had not done. And if they tried to use the force of numbers—well, there was no force in Dorking Hollow to match the trained weapons in that shack.

Then I thought of calling Christy Munn away from the shack and giving him warning in full of what I suspected. But I doubted the wisdom of that proceeding for two reasons. In the first place, it would be very, very difficult to convince Christy that poison was being used, even in spite of the testimony of the doctor. The Indian would simply say that what was fatal to a dog was good for a man. And who was there to prove that he was wrong? Indeed, the dog might not have died!

But even supposing that I convinced Munn, it would take so long to send for him, convince him, and get him back to the shack that McGregor, if I had made him at all suspicious, would have had plenty of opportunity to see that the final and decisive dose of poison was given to his victim.

There was a third reason, about as conclusive as the first two. Even if we got Munn back in time, what could he do? How could he accuse McGregor before the entire gang?

No, I saw that Munn would not do as an agent of deliverance. Neither was there any force in the town capable of delivering Holles from his captivity. Or even of warning him of the horrible danger in which he lay in that house!

I was sick, beaten, and despairing.

First of all I went to the house of Cochrane. He greeted me in silence, and pointed to the mangy dog, which now was in an opposite corner, and lay with its head on its paws, but with its eyes open. Cochrane spoke, and the poor brute wagged its tail.

"It's getting better," said Cochrane, "and it's grateful to me for having put it in such state, I think! That's dog nature—God bless 'em!"

"He's going to live then?" I asked.

"He'll live," Cochrane nodded. "But he had a reasonably close thing of it. A bit more and he would have been gone." He added: "And what about Holles?"

"I couldn't see him."

Cochrane whistled, long and softly.

"Don't ask me," said I, "why I couldn't get into Holles' room. It was simply McGregor. Damn him! Damn the scoundrel!"

"Tell me," said Cochrane. "Have the boys in the shack learned the true story of the fight between Holles and McGregor?"

"Apparently not," said I. "At least, McGregor seems

149

to have them in the hollow of his hand. After all, there are only two witnesses of that fight. Brick and I!"

"Only two witnesses," nodded Cochrane, "and he could talk you down, I suppose?"

"I suppose so."

"And also," said the doctor, "there now remains only one witness."

"Hello! Has Brick closed his place and left camp suddenly?"

"He didn't close his place," said Cochrane, "but he left camp suddenly."

"Ah? Trouble?"

"I don't know. It depends upon the way you look at it. Brick is dead!"

"Dead!" gasped I.

"Dead," nodded Cochrane. And he added with a sudden earnestness: "If I were you, old fellow, I would watch myself rather carefully. You might have an accident with a gun, too!"

"Tell me what happened!" said I, the moisture standing on my forehead.

"News just came to me," said Cochrane. "I'd gone down to get some stuff to mix for this poor mangy cur. And while I was in the store I learned that Brick had been found lying dead on the ground near his shack, with a gun still gripped in his hand. He was shot through the temple. And there was one bullet discharged from his gun."

"Suicide, then!"

"Do you think that a fellow like Brick would ever commit suicide?"

"Why not as well as another?"

"Because he wasn't the hysterical type; neither was he an old Roman."

"You think he didn't fire that gun?"

"No."

"Were two shots heard?"

"No. Only one."

"Why, man, how do you make that out?"

"Old fellow, doesn't it strike you that it would be pretty hard to tell one Colt from another?"

"Well?"

"And another thing: How could a man turn a gun on himself and shoot himself through the temple without bringing the muzzle of the gun so close that his skin would be power-burned. Look!"

He drew his own revolver and turned the long weapon toward his head.

"Ah!" said I. "I understand!"

"Yes," said Cochrane. "Brick was killed. And wouldn't it be a lucky thing for big McGregor if you were to die, also! Then there would be left no more witnesses of the way he fought with Holles, and took a dirty advantage of that maneater! Loomis, look to yourself!"

I stared at the doctor and gripped my own weapons. And then I shrugged my shoulders, vainly striving to get rid of the trouble which had entered my mind to stay there.

Finally I said: "I want a couple of pounds of bread. Can you give it to me?"

I think that any other man in the world would have asked a few questions, given all the attending circumstances. But Cochrane was a rare fellow. He said not a word, but marched to the cupboard, took out a heavy loaf of cornbread—soggy but nutritious—and handed it to me. I put it under my coat and walked out of the house without saying good-by.

151

I could not be bothered by details of good manners just then. I felt that my life was terribly endangered, and, in addition to that, I had made up my mind to undertake a most perilous adventure.

I had determined to go up the hill to the shack of Holles, and there, if Fate gave me luck, to get to him long enough to whisper a warning in his ear!

CHAPTER TWENTY-FIVE

IN THE MEANTIME, I have to explain how a crisis had arisen in the Holles shack which nearly toppled big McGregor from his high place.

After the first trouble between us and the Holles men, there was a good deal of hesitation on their part about leaving their house; but after the proposals were made and accepted for the guardianship of Dorking Hollow by these same warriors, they felt more free. Several of them left the shack, and the last to come back was Lefty Sherburne, a lean, savage little man, blind and squinting in one eye, but sharp as a ferret with the other, and famous for his speed and his surety with a revolver.

Sherburne came into the shack and flung himself down sullenly in a chair. McGregor was at that moment out of the room, and when someone asked Lefty what was wrong, he said: "Wait till Johnnie comes back!"

McGregor returned a moment later and Christy Munn said: "Lefty's got something up his sleeve. He wouldn't talk about it till you came in."

"Come out with it, Sherburne," said their chief.

"It's this," said Lefty gloomily. "They say down in town that we got a damn murderer and a sneak for our leader, Johnnie. You want to hear the rest of what I've heard?"

Of course McGregor must have known what was coming, but he merely nodded, now, as if it were a matter of course.

"I been wondering," he said, "how long it would be before they started to put us against one another. I been wondering that right along! Well, what dodge have they cooked up?"

"A damn queer one," declared Lefty, "because they say that when you fought with Mex you agreed that there wouldn't be no taking of advantage if a gent slipped in the wet grass by the river. You slipped, they say, and Mex just leaned over and slapped you on the back and didn't take no advantage. And then he slipped and you grabbed him while he lay on the grass."

He said this with one hand gripping the butt of his revolver, as though he expected that the giant would refute the report with a bullet, but McGregor merely smiled in a lofty way.

"Kind of amusin'," said he. "Dog-gone me if it ain't amusin'! I would ask you, has Holles said nothing about such a doing?"

"Mex," said Sherburne, "wouldn't be accusing you of nothin' after the way that you had brought him up the hill and back to the shack."

"Ah?" says McGregor. "Is that the way of it? Mex don't say nothing about no such happening. Lemme see. Who is there in town that seen me crook Mex?"

"There was Loomis and Brick."

"Go get Loomis and Brick, then," said McGregor, "and bring 'em up here and ask them what the truth is. I want to have 'em say such a thing to my face!"

It was bold, steady talk, as you'll agree, and it had weight with these men who were beginning to glower at

153

the giant. For they were wonderfully devoted to Mex. He had led them with a dauntless courage and a skill that amazed them. More than that, he had kept them well; he had poured money into their pockets, and in all the period of his leadership he had never made unfair demands of them. They loved Mex for his deeds, and they loved him for himself, and McGregor must have known that if his dastardly conduct in the fight were ever proved, he would be deserted at once. And all those expert guns would be focused upon him.

"You'll never get Brick," said Sherburne. "Because Brick is a dead man!"

"Hello!" cried McGregor. "Dead? Well, after tellin' a lie the size of that one, he may have choked! Who killed the pup?"

"He killed himself," said Sherburne, "which is a doggone amazin' thing. Which, I mean to say, that Brick was the most cheerfullest gent that ever you seen. How come that he would shoot himself through the head?"

"Was he seen doin' it?" asked Christy Munn.

"No, he wasn't seen. But just as good as seen. I mean, they heard one shot, and when they got to the spot, there lay Brick, dead, with a bullet through his temple and one bullet fired out of the gun that he was still grabbing!"

"He got himself," said McGregor sternly, "before I got him! He knew that I would be on his track after that sort of a lie that he had told. But what about Loomis? Did you go find out from him?"

"Sure," said Sherburne, "I went to find out from Loomis, but he wasn't anywhere to be found, y'understand?"

"He's been here time and again," said McGregor.

154

"And as if he would do any business with me if he thought that I was that sort of a skunk!"

"I dunno!" said Sherburne. "I dunno! You tell your story that you got him when he was down!"

"Would I ever have admitted that, if there had been any agreement about not jumping the other gent if he slipped?"

It seemed sound argument. They looked hard at Sherburne, and back at McGregor, because it seemed plain that the giant was in the right; but it also seemed plain that Sherburne, whose intelligence was much respected, was not yet convinced.

He stared back at McGregor for a time, studied the floor, and then suddenly left the shack.

"Poor Lefty!" said McGregor with apparent good humor. "He figures that I'm really a skunk, I see."

He shrugged his vast shoulders.

"Well," he continued, "he's got a right to think what he pleases. This here is the freest part of the freest country in the world. Only"—he went on, his voice swelling in volume—"if any of you gents begin to press me too far and too hard, I'm gonna raise a little hell around here. I'm gonna bust things, and bust 'em proper!"

And snatching up a thick piece of firewood, he burst it between his great hands, flung the pieces on the floor with an oath, and strode out into the night.

The Indian doctor was coming in the door at that moment, but he turned, and went hastily back on the trail of his master. That left the men in the shack alone for the time being to talk over what they had just heard.

"Talk out, Christy," said young Chalmers to Munn. "Talk out and tell us what *you* make of this here wrangle, will you?"

But Christy Munn had picked up the broken fragments of the stick of firewood and was staring at the ends of them most curiously and attentively. "I'm gonna keep these for relics," said Christy, "of the strongest man that ever lived!"

That was his only answer to the question, if answer it could be called. At the least, it put an end to the argument, but it did not put an end to the thinking. McGregor had saved himself by some consummate acting but the question remained open. He would probably hear more of it later.

CHAPTER TWENTY-SIX

IT WAS NOT VERY LONG BEFORE this discussion took place in the Holles house that I left the cabin of Doctor Cochrane with the loaf of bread and the determination to do my cautious and most guarded best in this difficult affair.

What drove me on so hard? Why, I think that it was partly our needs in Dorking Hollow, now that we were being held up by robbers on the outside, protected by other robbers on the inside. And it was more than that, a real affection for Mex. I had seen him half a second and half a thought away from a miserable death by hanging at the hands of our revengeful posse. And I had seen him go free on his word of honor and redeem that word by riding straight into our camp. And, finally, after seeing him rout our enemies from the hills, I had watched him crushed by foul play in a fight where he could thrice have stabbed his enemy to the heart. I felt, indeed, that I had never wanted anything so much as a chance to protect young Mex from the horrible death that now threatened him.

But I had not gone fifty yards before I had reason to forget about Mex and remember myself. I was passing through the broad torrent of lamplight that flowed through the open doorway of a cabin when a hornet darted past my face. No, not a hornet, but the unmistakable buzz of a bullet, followed immediately by the clanging of the report.

I leaped backward into the darkness, and lying prone, I saw a stealthy figure rise from some brush and come toward me. Did he think that my leap had been the convulsed effort of a dying man, and had he come to make sure of me?

I was so furious that I did not wait, as I should have done, until he was close. Instead, I leaped to my feet again and blazed away at him with my revolver. He disappeared at once in the brush, and I heard him crashing away at full speed. His activity told me that my short legs and scanty breath would never take me up with him, and I determined to march straight on toward my task.

All of this gunfire had not so much as brought an inquirer to the door of the shack which had furnished light for this attempt at assassination.

Ah, those were the days of men, in Dorking Hollow!

Then I remembered that Cochrane had said—that Brick had gone first, and that it would be most convenient for McGregor if I were to follow to the land where men tell no more tales of what they have seen and heard on this earth.

This attempt at shooting had come too close on the heels of that warning not to make me feel that Cochrane was right, and that McGregor had had a hand in planning this murder. And I confess that I was weak in

157

the knees as I climbed up the hill toward the shack.

When I got to the edge of the brush, I sat down to examine the lay of the land. All around the shack, as I have said before, the ground was cleared, except for a meager bush or two, and I decided that I would creep along from one to the other of these. Yet I hesitated before going ahead in this fashion.

If I simply walked boldly up to the house and were seen, I could invent some errand that had brought me here. But if I were seen crawling along like a serpent, a bullet would ask all necessary questions of me. And there was an end of the matter!

However, I decided that crafty caution would be best, and I started on my knees along the ground, until I heard a soft step near me. I flattened out beside a bush, not even dragging out my revolver. I was no fighting hero, you must remember, and I was too badly frightened to think fast.

Turning my head toward the sound, I saw a slender, quick-stepping man come past me through the darkness, and something about the gait and proportions of the man made me think that I recognized in him McGregor's Indian doctor.

I breathed more easily after he had gone past me toward the house. There I heard a voice roaring out something, and following the sound, the giant silhouette of McGregor filled the entrance as the door was flung open. The other turned back with him. They came to a stand in the darkness not three strides from my bush. And there they remained, for a moment, talking softly and earnestly in a language which I did not recognize. But it was very guttural, and because the Indian spoke it fluently, and the big man with many halts and pauses, I guessed that it was the native tongue of the Indian.

I cannot tell you how all my suspicion of foul play was strengthened as I lay there listening. It was almost as though I heard the Indian report to his master that he had just made his attempt on me, and promising better luck next time that chance brought me within range of his rifle at night.

And then they moved off still farther down the hill.

At any moment, they might come back closer to my bush and see me. Therefore I gathered courage from necessity and crawled softly on toward the rambling shack. I placed another low clump of brush between me and the pair. And then I gained the corner of the house and could pause a moment to regain my breath after that close call. I knew that the room of Mex was just around the corner, and lighted by one small window.

Through that window I must climb. And now that I stood at last before it my heart quite failed me. In the first place, it was so small that I doubted my ability to squeeze through it. In the second place, suppose that I were caught in the room after gaining my entrance? In that case, they would give me short shrift, for McGregor, I knew, would welcome the first chance now of putting me out of his way.

The window was luckily open. That was my stroke of fortune, and leaning in through it as far as I could, I whispered "Mex!"

I had to repeat the name two or three times, and finally a faint, faint voice answered "Yes?"

"This is Loomis," I whispered. "For God's sake don't make a sound!"

Then I started to climb through the window, and halfway in my hips stuck fast. At the same time, there was a loud roar of laughter from the next room. And, with the sweat starting out on my body, I was sure that

159

they knew all about me and my predicament, and that presently they would saunter in, drag me from my place, —and shoot me full of holes.

The laughter died down a little. I heard the voice of Christy Munn quarreling with another man. And at the same time I managed to free myself and get my hands on the floor of the room.

It squeaked horribly under my weight as I got in from the window but I managed to reach the side of the sick man's bunk.

"Mex!"

"Yes, Loomis."

"How are you, boy?"

"Sick, Loomis. Sick, sick, sick!"

He sighed as he whispered it. And then: "Why are you sneaking in here like a thief, old fellow?"

"Because of your sickness, Mex. I mean, there's dirty work behind this!"

He whistled—no sound—only the thin noise of his breath.

"Ah?" said he.

"They're poisoning you, Mex. That swine of a doctor—"

"No, no, Loomis! You're wrong there. His stuff always makes me feel better!"

"That's it, of course. Makes you feel better for a while and then nearly kills you! Cochrane took that half glass that he stole from you and poured it down the throat of a stray dog in town. And he watched the dog turn happy as a drunken man—and then have a sinking spell that nearly killed it! That dog lay wavering on the point of death, Mex, barely able to roll up its eyes."

There was no word from Mex, and I whispered hurriedly: "Do you hear me?"

160

"Yes, I hear."

"Do you believe me?"

"I can't!"

"It's McGregor, Mex!"

"It can't be, after I had him three times under my knife, and after he crooked me that way!"

"I tell you, Mex, a man hates the fellows whom he has wronged. And that's exactly the case of big Johnnie. He wants you dead. Because when you get back on your feet, you're sure to call him to account, and he knows what that means!"

"Ah!" murmured Mex. "I didn't think of that."

"Think of it now!"

"My head is whirling, Loomis. I can hardly understand all this."

"Only understand this much. From this moment you're to take no more of the doctor's messes. You hear me?"

"I'll drink no more of his stuff. That's straight. Wait till I tell some of the boys——"

"Tell nobody! That would ruin everything. Suppose that the Indian pretends to fly into a passion when you accuse him, and throws a knife into you—or suppose that McGregor stops your mouth with a bullet and—"

"The boys would tear him to pieces. He never would dare!"

"He's getting them in the hollow of his hand. How can you tell what he would dare? Besides, he'd have to! Kill you, or die himself!"

There was a little pause, during which I heard the hurriedly taken breath of the sick man.

"You're right," he said at last, "and I'm neatly trapped. Get me out through that window, old fellow—"

"Can you help yourself a little?"

161

"I don't think that I could walk a step. My nerves are half paralyzed. I have no appetite. I can't eat a thing!"

"It's the dope they've given you. If I tried to get you away while you're helpless, they'd be sure to hear. McGregor and the Indian are outside the house now. I have reason to think that McGregor had Brick murdered. And just now a rifle was fired at me—and missed me by half an inch—"

"You and Brick were the witnesses—I remember," said Holles.

Even sick and drugged with poison as he was, that brain of his was swift enough once it was roused.

"Yes," said I. "The witnesses are to go. And afterward, McGregor can talk down any secondhand evidence. He wants to run this gang. He sees a fortune for himself in it!"

"Of course, and—" began he, when at that moment the door of the room opened, the great form of McGregor stood there, and the light shone full on me, where I crouched beside the bed of the sick man!

CHAPTER TWENTY-SEVEN

AH, THERE WAS A MOMENT strung as tight as a breaking wire!

I could not move. I expected to see a gun flash into the hand of the giant, and then to hear the crash of the revolver. After that, the eternal darkness for me!

But the blessed voice of Christy Munn called something, and McGregor turned a little away.

He had not seen me, then!

The next instant I was stretched under the bunk, my heart deafening me with its pounding.

Then across the floor came a heavy and a softer tread. McGregor and his man of darkness!

"How is he?" asked McGregor, muttering.

A pair of knees appeared on the floor beside me. The Indian was kneeling above his victim.

He murmured something in his own tongue, and McGregor said: "He looks bad—damn bad. Is he asleep, only?"

For it appeared that Holles was playing possum for my sake. Now his own voice answered: "I'm feeling better, though, old-timer!"

"We'll have you cured, kid," said McGregor. "You can be sure of that! Damn my hands! I wish that they didn't have such a grip in the fingers for your sake, Mex."

"Damn my feet," said Mex. "I wish that I had taught them never to slip."

There was a brief pause after this, and I cursed the imprudence of Holles in making such a remark—at such a time and to such an auditor! After that, the voice of McGregor came sharp and hard: "You still hold it pretty much against me, kid?"

"Against you?" said Mex, his voice wonderfully soft and good natured. "No, not a bit. You just lost your head in the pinch. I don't see how I could blame you. And when you saw that I was so done up, you carried me up here where I could get help, instead of simply running away into the woods, as you might have done!"

"That's true. By heaven, it's true!" said McGregor heartily. Still the fiend was tempting Holles to draw himself into danger which already was great enough to satisfy two men—and two heroes, at that.

Said Mex: "Though there are some of the boys who wonder if you carried me up here because Brick and

Loomis would have been witnesses if you had murdered me on the spot. But of course, that's nonsense. I know you, McGregor!"

A consummate actor, that Holles! Born for the stage, I know! But he had said a great deal too much, no matter how guileless he made his weak voice. McGregor answered sharply: "You know me, do you? Well, I hope that you find the book of me good reading, old fellow."

"The best in the world, absolutely!"

"Good! I thank you for saying that, Holles. Now drink off this glass of stuff—I'll hold you up for it—"

I knew perfectly that this was to be the fatal dose. They had delayed as long as they dared. They had at least delayed long enough to make it appear that poor Mex had been withering away under a strange affliction. And now they would strike the final blow.

Every nerve in my body was jumping and I was almost on the verge of crying out a warning, but there was no need. My suspicions were in the mind of Holles, and they would be sure to work there far more surely than in my own mind.

I heard him say: "That stuff has made me feel a little ill today, Johnnie. I think I'll wait till the morning before I take any more of it."

"Don't be a fool, old-timer," said McGregor with a pretended heartiness which was most manifest sham. "Don't say a thing like that. I tell you, you're in a very serious condition, and unless you follow the doctor's orders, who knows what'll happen before the morning comes?"

Serious condition? The trick was that McGregor didn't know how perfectly the patient understood the seriousness of his condition—and his position, too!

"I'll take a chance on that," said Holles. "But now I feel a bit sleepy, and I think that sleep would do me more good than any medicine. So long for this evening, Johnnie. And thanks a lot!"

A dubious pause followed this. I heard McGregor and the Indian whisper softly together, and then: "Holles!" said McGregor.

"Yes, Johnnie?"

"The doc, here, says that it's a matter of life and death. You've got to take this medicine."

"Serious as all that?" asked Holles innocently. "Absolutely as serious as all that! Drink this or you'll never see the morning light!"

"Bah!" said Holles. "I don't believe it. That sea-green stuff has nauseated me, I tell you, and I'll take no more of it until tomorrow."

"Ten thousand damnations!" growled McGregor. He added swiftly: "You don't know what you're saying. You're a sick man, old boy, and you'd throw yourself away, but you can't. We all think too much of you. We'll save you in spite of yourself, Holles!"

That whining hypocrisy made me writhe, but I heard Holles say weakly but angrily: "Take your hand away from my head, Johnnie. Hang it, I won't be bullied! Get out of here and let me sleep, will you?"

So the thing had come to a violent crisis.

I trembled, and wondered what would come next. For that matter, the giant could hold the patient helpless while the doctor poured the poison down his throat. But after a word or two to his companion, McGregor said finally: "Well, you're too sick to be forced, Holles. Have your own way, and God knows that I hope for the best! Look here, I think that you'd be better off in that other room. It's bigger and brighter, a lot. I'm going to

165

carry you in there, Arthur!"

I heard the rustling of the blankets as he started to gather Holles in his arms.

And once those blankets were raised I would be plainly seen lying like a foolish eavesdropper on the floor; the whole extent of the knowledge of Holles would be revealed at the same time, and death for both of us would follow swiftly, I could be sure.

Then I heard Holles exclaiming: "Damnation, man, will you leave me alone? Will you get out of here? I want to sleep—here—in this bunk. Let me be!"

There was enough force in this threat to make even McGregor back up suddenly. The awe which surrounded the name of Holles had not yet lost all its original force.

McGregor withdrew a little, growling: "You fool, Mex! You fool! Gunna cut your own throat, are you?"

"Let me be!" repeated Holles. "I want to be alone. Confound you, isn't this the very first time I've had a chance for a sleep that I really wanted?"

Back to the doorway went McGregor, and there he conferred for a time with the doctor. Apparently they were in some doubt. The Indian argued for something with a great deal of vehemence and force; but McGregor as constantly resisted. I have no doubt that the redskin was suggesting that the black deed be consummated at once, even though force would have to be used, but McGregor overbore him. He called, presently: "Good night, Arthur. Happy dreams, old fellow!"

"So long, old man," said Holles. "So long, doc. Excuse me. But that stuff went against the grain, today. I'll drink a gallon of it for you tomorrow!"

The pair went out, and after a moment, I gathered

166

enough strength and courage to drag myself out of the place beneath the bunk where I had lain for so many seconds within reach of the beckoning finger of death.

Luck was with me on that terrible night!

I found that Holles was lying back in the bunk, trembling violently, and breathing hard and fast.

I waited a moment, and finally he said: "The curs!"

"Aye," I agreed. "The unspeakable curs! Will you listen a little more?"

"Yes, of course. Loomis, you're giving me my life the second time."

"There's no time for pretty speeches, Arthur. You know that you can't drink that so-called medicine any more?"

"Yes, I know that!"

"Besides, you must not touch any of the food that's cooked in this house."

"Shall I have to lie here and starve to death, then?"

"Certainly not. I've brought you a lot of good cornbread. There's no poison in this. Take nothing but plain, pure water. The instant that there's a shade of bitter or sour in the taste of the water that they give you, and the instant that it has even a slightly cloudy look, you must refuse to take it."

"I understand. I'll do exactly what you tell me to do."

"Eat this bread; drink the water. You'll probably find that by tomorrow night your nerves will begin to straighten out and that some of that paralyzed feeling will be disappearing. At any rate, tomorrow night I'm going to come back for you. Holles, if you can possibly drag yourself to this window when we come, do so. Then we can lift you through and try to get away with you. But I dread the noise that we might make by entering the room! If they heard us—"

167

"I understand. I'll follow everything that you direct, old-timer, to the letter. When you come to the window—God bless you—I'll manage to drag myself out of bed and come to you. You can pull me through and walk me off down the hill. But I'm pretty weak, Loomis. I'm as weak as running water. I can't raise my own Colt."

He said it rather with wonder than with sadness or with fear.

"I've said all that I can think of. Good-by, old fellow."

"Good-by, Loomis. This is the second time!"

He could put a world of meaning into a whisper.

For my part, the instant I turned away from his bed, I was too filled with terror on my own account to pay any attention to Holles.

I had come into this cursed house by stealth and done my work here. But how should I be able to get away unheard? For the noise of talk in the next room had died down. McGregor was in there telling a story, apparently, very slowly, and in the intervals I could hear even the crackling of the fire. How easily they would be able to hear any sound that I made here.

I think it took me ten minutes to steal to the window. Through it I thrust my head and shoulders, and then inch by inch I worked my way through until my hands touched the earth outside. My exit was strangely easy, compared with my incoming. I passed out noiselessly, and found the sweet, fresh, open air of the night around me.

Already my heart breathed more freely, though I still had not crossed the clearing. But I dropped to my hands and knees and began to worm myself cautiously along, just as I had originally come to the shack of Holles that night.

Halfway out, I saw but did not hear the Indian as he circled the shack with a ceaseless vigilance. And while I detested him I could not help wondering what made him the obsequious slave of the scoundrel McGregor.

For life or death, he was the tool of the giant. There was something pitiful in the thought. And something terrible, as you can well imagine, for one in my position.

I waited now until he had passed to the farther side of the house, then I crept on, gained the outer brush, reached the trees and then stood up and fled like a boy afraid of the night.

I fled till I came to the house of Cochrane and when I entered, a look at my face made him slam the door shut behind me, and then reach for his guns.

"Who've you murdered, man, in heaven's name?" said he.

CHAPTER TWENTY-EIGHT

WHEN A LITTLE MORE QUIET RETURNED TO MY NERVES, I started to tell Cochrane what had happened to me; but suddenly I stopped talking.

"Have you turned dumb, man?" said Cochrane. "You were saying that you had gone on toward the place a little way, and as you were crossing a shaft of light from an open door—well?"

I stopped and stared at him.

"Cochrane," I said at last, "what I have to say is a lot better unheard."

He seemed much moved by this, growing hot in the face and asking me noisily if I distrusted him. I told him

169

that I did not, which was true; but that I distrusted the very air that stirred through Dorking Hollow, now, since it might overhear my words and betray me.

"Betray you to whom?" asked Cochrane. "At least, tell me that and I'll patch up the rest of the story with a little guessing on my own account!"

"I've talked enough," I said to him. "But—give me a drink out of that black bottle, and then I'll leave you!"

He had turned dour and dark owing to my lack of confidence in him, but he passed me the whisky bottle, and I took a long drag of it. Not for the taste, but simply because I needed a little extra courage and strength just then!

Then I went on from Cochrane's house, leaving him very displeased. But I had to chance that, for it was better to have him even hate me than it was to allow Johnnie McGregor and his terrible "doctor" to so much as suspect me of being hostile to them. Indeed, I knew that they had a shrewd suspicion already, and therefore it behooved me to keep very quiet concerning what I knew and what I guessed at of the house on the hill.

As I left Cochrane, I told him simply that his own life would probably pay the forfeit if he talked of what he knew. I left him staring grimly after me, and slipped back to my own house as quietly as I could. I was tolerably sure, now, that between the rest of Dorking Hollow and the men of McGregor, there could never be any lasting peace.

All my hopes for myself and for the town rested with that young and terrible gunman, Mex. Without him Dorking Hollow was the most unpeaceable, the most danger-racked and tormented of all mining towns. But with him, it was the safest, and most profitable and jolly community that I had ever been in! Dangerous and wild our King Stork had been, but we had no wish for any other king than he.

These were the thoughts which occupied my mind as I lay for a long time on my bunk that night, staring at the blackness above me. Now that I was away from the shack on the hill, it seemed very wonderful that I had ever dared to enter the place on such an errand, or that I had lain within reaching distance of the terrible hand of Johnnie McGregor. I closed my eyes, sick and faint, when I thought of the vengeance that he would have worked upon me if he had found me then and there!

At last I slept, and when the morning came, I learned that Johnnie McGregor and most of his men had ridden out of Dorking Hollow between midnight and dawn, with no warning given to a soul. On what secret summons they went, we could not guess, but our hopes began to rise a little.

Fifteen per cent was a great deal to pay, but after all, the mines were so very easily worked, and the flood of the precious metal poured out so fast, that we could afford to pay the penalty so long as we really needed Johnnie McGregor. That might not be for many weeks.

So that all the nerve tension in the camp was relaxed for a few hours, while we waited to learn what had happened during the cruise of the giant and his men through the forest. Some one had got up to freshen a camp fire that was dying, and they reported having seen a stalking figure, almost larger than human, moving down across the hill, with a train of horsemen behind him.

Tradition declared that McGregor could move almost as fast as a horse—at least, over rough country such as this—so that he was not apt to hold them back very greatly on their marches.

171

In the meantime, I formed great hopes that during the absence of the leader I might be able to get Holles from the house. I thought first of enlisting the help of Lucas and a few others, but afterward I decided that I would go up to the place myself and see how the land lay. Afterward, I could tell how much help I needed.

As I neared the house my heart sank, for I heard a rousing camp song raised in the interior from three or four voices. When I knocked at the door, it was presently opened by the Indian doctor himself.

It gave me a queer shock of anger and of fear combined to see this fellow who, as I well knew, had tried to take my life the night before, and who had probably killed poor Brick, also. But I controlled my emotion as well as I could. I was playing with marked cards, and so was he. It was a game in which secrecy and silence carried heavy rewards, of course.

The Indian said: "Johnnie McGregor not here." And he closed the door in my face.

My temper got away with me, then. I seized the latch and flung the door open for myself.

"What the devil does this mean, you red-skinned hound?" I asked the doctor.

He simply folded his arms and looked at me with a stony eye, but I had another answer from one of three men who sat at cards at the table.

"Back up, Loomis," said he. "The big boss ain't at home, and the house is closed."

"I don't understand," said I.

"The store's closed. Shades are down. It's Sunday," he explained. "So back up, old-timer, because you can't come in. Chuck, it's your deal!" And he tossed the cards across the table to another of the trio.

I ran my eye over them carefully. They had their

weapons with them, and besides the revolvers which they carried in their holsters there were enough shotguns and repeating rifles to have stocked a company of soldiers and turned that house into a perfect fort.

"I'd like to see how Holles is," I said.

"You would? Why, that's reasonable—" began one of them.

"Nobody's to come into the house," said the first speaker, whose name I have forgotten. "Johnnie was firm on that, and we'd better be firm, too!"

I saw that argument would be foolish. At least, from what they said it was plain that Holles still lived; and if that was the case it meant that the Indian doctor had not been able to introduce any more poison into his food or drink. For the next dose, I was perfectly sure, would be the last, and the death of the sick man.

I went back from the shack toward Dorking Hollow, my head humming with many conjectures. There were only four men in that shack—outside of the two cooks, who probably would be of little use in a fight—and those four might be borne down by the weight of the fighting men of the town. But my heart misgave me when I thought of the number of gallant fellows who must fall before the shack could be taken. Aye, and before it was taken, suppose that big Johnnie McGregor and his troop came back to Dorking Hollow? How they would crash through us with flaming guns!

No, I decided that I would keep my council once more and say nothing to a soul; then, when the night came, I would try to get into the house as I had done before, and bring Mex away with me for the future salvation of Dorking Hollow.

Ah, but my head was heavy that day as I wandered about my mine and watched the workers toiling, and

173

heard the sound of the shots in the neighboring claims boom deep and hollow when noon and night fell!

But in the late afternoon, we had a disturbance which called all hands from the mines, for there was a sound of firearms from the town; and when we flocked down in haste, we found a party of veritable madmen celebrating in Dorking Hollow.

Big Johnnie McGregor had found the enemy and smashed them in a great victory which promised to shake the robbers to the very ground. He had left, so report said, seven dead bandits on the floor of the woodland; he had brought in eight prisoners whom I saw with my own eyes. And he had lost from his own troop only one man killed and two wounded. These were results as great as those of Holles. Mex had taught a lesson which had been well learned by others, and these followers of his were capable of carrying on the good work under the guidance and inspiration of big McGregor.

There was a difference, however, and that was in the celebration which followed the work. Holles had kept his men sternly in hand in the shack. But McGregor let them roam through the town as if they owned it. He had liberally enlisted new recruits, and raised the number of the band higher than it ever had been under the rule of Holles. But whether new recruits or old veterns in this work, all were celebrating with equal violence. And as I came down the hill into the town, I saw two wild riders careen down the street, each with a pair of Colts, shooting at windows as they flew along, and making the quiet air of Dorking Hollow ring with their Indian yells.

"Hell has started!" said Avery Lucas. "Let's hold together if we can, or they'll have us by the throat!"

I can't say, however, that every one in the Hollow

was displeased by these things. Some of us, older and soberer than the rest, were partly frightened and partly disgusted by what we saw and heard; but there were many of the youngsters who knew the license which prevails in most mining camps, and who were glad to see the new rule take possession of the town.

On the whole, Dorking Hollow went on vacation that evening. Lucas and half a dozen of the rest of us remained in his shack, armed and ready for trouble only if it came to find us, while up and down the length of the town we heard the noise of the riot. I watched my time and listened to the furor reach a crisis. Then I thought that the moment had come when I must make my attempt upon the shack of Holles and bring him away.

CHAPTER TWENTY-NINE

AND AGAIN I FELT THAT IT WOULD BE BETTER to move alone. To be sure, I would need two or three strong and reliable men, if possible, to help me carry poor Holles from his death cell. But how was I to manage the secret approach of such a number when I alone had barely been able to reach the house on the night before in spite of my utmost precautions.

As I left the shack of Avery Lucas, giving no explanation of where or why I was going, I was sick at heart. I walked up the hill in a most dreamy humor—but all the while keenly noting every shadow that stirred before me among the trees. And so I came safely at last to the edge of the clearing in which stood the Holles shack.

How little did he own it now! And, at that moment, as

I was steeling myself to cross the open space, creeping softly from bush to bush, I heard a crashing of horses through the brush, and half a dozen riders stormed into view. They drew up at the door of the shack and streamed into it, shouting, laughing. They owned Dorking Hollow. They showed the joy of new possession in their manner!

My heart sank at that. I decided that it would be madness for me to make my attempt on this evening. And I was about to turn back through the trees when I suddenly remembered my promise given to poor Holles the night before. How had he been during this long day? How had he managed to refuse all food, and all medicine? What suspicions had he awakened? Were either the Indian doctor or big McGregor once really alarmed with suspicion, a knife would end Holles' fight for life.

So, unwillingly I started forward, stealing with trembling limbs toward the wild hubbub which had broken out in the house. A dozen times I paused and looked around me, and a dozen times I saw nothing moving in the darkness of the night. Still, it would almost have been better if I had had an actual living danger to face. Imagination was giving me many a bridge of dreary length to cross.

I gained the corner of the shack again after a nightmare passage. There I crouched a moment to regain strength and assurance, gripping the edge of a corner log as if it had been the hand of a friend in time of need. And so onward once more until I had reached the window of Holles' room.

I stood up and looked inside, revolver in hand. There was deep blackness within. What if they had moved him? I turned cold with the thought!

"Mex!" I whispered.

God bless the instant answer: "Loomis?"

"Aye, Loomis!" said I, and then I laid hold on the edge of the window and fell to shaking like a hysterical girl.

As I was about to lean inward, something, I thought, stirred behind me. I whirled. Merciful heaven, a dark and slender shape stood just behind me, and there was a naked gleam of steel in a rising hand.

I had not forethought enough to turn my revolver in my hand and shoot. I merely struck out blindly toward the knife thrust, and it happened by the grace of fortune that the hand with which I struck was armed with the heavy Colt. The barrel clipped hard against the skull of the man. He fell with a slight gasp—and no other sound. And I found myself looking down on a prostrate form.

Still I remained there for a moment, though the anxious whisper of Mex sounded within the room: "Loomis! Oh, Loomis!"

I kneeled and fumbled at the head of the man. It was the Indian doctor, of course, that secret and malignant ally of big McGregor. My fingers found the place where I had struck him. It was hot and wet with oozing blood. I fumbled next for his heart. I felt no motion. A dead man!

I felt no shame or remorse. I merely thanked God that I did not have to strike to the heart—with his own knife—an unconscious figure. For if I had thought that the man was not dead, I should certainly have murdered him in cold blood in spite of his helplessness. I could not afford to leave a living witness behind me when I entered that fatal room.

Then I leaned through the window: "Here I am, Mex. Can you get to me?"

177

"I'll try—I'm trying!"

But then came a gasped: "It's no good. I can't handle myself!"

I slipped through that window with a snaky ease, now. I cannot tell you the hot triumph and the sense of victory that I felt since I had felled the Indian—God forgive me for it! And now I found Mex lying sprawled along the floor. I raised him in my arms and carried him back to the window and looked out.

Ah, what a moment that was, as I stood inside the prison looking out toward the freedom which I hoped to win for Holles and saw that on the ground the dark form of the Indian no longer lay!

I craned my neck still farther out. No, he was not to be seen! Already, perhaps, he had rounded the corner of the house and was bursting into the noisy assemblage in the next room to tell them

"Mex," I gasped, "God help us! They know what we're doing. Help me as much as you can!" And I pushed him forward, while he strove to draw himself on with his hands. Those hands which had been so swift and sure, but which now were cold lead, and trembled with feebleness and uncertain nerves!

Then I heard a door slammed, followed by a sudden silence among the celebrants in the next room.

The Indian had come—now he would speak!

Then I heard the shout of the great voice of McGregor: "By heaven, who's killed my man? Who did it? Speak, man!"—

Then, as I frantically thrust Holles before me and prayed with closed eyes, I heard another say: "Give him a moment! Here—here's brandy. Take this."

And McGregor cried again: "Who did it? Who did it?"

178

The thundering voice rang and boomed through the house and washed through the thin partition which separated us just like water through sand.

I thrust Holles through the window by this time, and he fell limp on the outside. And as I wriggled through in turn I heard another voice saying: "Wait—quiet—he's surely trying to speak—"

And then McGregor yelling: "Didn't he say Loomis? Didn't he say Loomis? Where, man? Where did Loomis do it? Where's Loomis? I'll burn him alive—I'll—"

I was through the window by this time breathing: "Mex! Come on!"

I caught hold of him and raised him a little. He slipped through my fingers a limp weight. He had fainted! At that, darkness spun before my eyes. I remembered that death was behind me, and leaped away; but in two steps I turned and rushed back and caught Holles.

What a light weight he was! The terrible Mex, the magnificent Arthur Holles, man queller, was hardly more than a child in my arms. Or did hysteria give me wonderful power on that night? Perhaps it was that.

With Holles thrown loosely over my shoulder—very much as his unconscious body had been thrown over the shoulder of big McGregor on that other day—I stumbled and ran across the clearing. I gained the edge of the trees at the same moment that I heard a terrible shout from the shack: "He's gone! Holles is gone! Get him, if you have to tear hell apart!"

And, almost instantly the door of the shack opened, and lanterns flashed, and men rushed out.

I had gained the edge of the trees, as I have said, but there the false strength which had supported me for the great effort suddenly gave way. I sank down on the ground, holding Mex loosely. My heart was thundering. My nerves were jumping. And gradually I felt the body of Holles gather life and strength, and heard him groan.

I muttered: "Quiet, Mex. Quiet, for heaven's sake!"

He pushed himself up to a sitting posture on his shaking hands, while behind us we heard the voice of McGregor bellowing: "Some of you range around in circles through the woods. Have your guns ready. If you find 'em shoot, and I'll tell you afterward why they have to die! Some more of you ride for the house of that hound, Loomis. Meet him there with your guns! I'll have blood for blood—the sneaking—" And his voice burst into a wonderful volley of curses.

Then the quiet murmur of Holles said: "I'm better now. Sorry I passed out on your hands. We'd better go on!"

I got up, spurred by fear. He drew himself up without help, and now he managed his own legs, with one arm thrown for support around my shoulders.

We hobbled through a thick grove of trees.

"Loomis," said Holles, "they'll kill you if they ever find you. And you're entirely too good a man to die for me!"

"Don't—talk!" I gasped. And we blundered ahead.

We made enough noise to have attracted the attention of a thousand searchers, except that those who were rushing through the woods behind us made racket enough to drown our footfalls on the crackling brush. For one thing, the night was black as pitch, and they had brought out lanterns which filled the woods before them with swaying, shifting shadows of the trunks of trees.

Suddenly guns boomed. "We've got them!" we heard distant voices shouting.

But they did not rush toward us. What caused that

180

false alarm I never was to know, but I did know that it drew the pursuit in exactly the wrong direction. We gained precious yardage and moments then, working our way steadily through the woods. Twice Holles' head rolled weakly back on my shoulder. But I heard the gritting of his teeth, and with wonderful courage he kept his legs moving. I did not have to drag his full weight a single step of the distance after he recovered his senses. Then, behind us, we saw the lights coming again. And the swaying tossing shadows filled the woods before us. We gained a clump of shrubbery and sank into it; Mex had fainted again, and I was so spent that I hardly cared whether we lived or died. And the lanterns bore straight down upon us!

CHAPTER THIRTY

THE DARK MAY BE TERRIBLE, when your imagination fills it with danger. But it is nothing compared with the terror that follows lights in the hands of an enemy. I cowered in the brush and heard the whisper of the dauntless Holles: "Steady, old fellow! We'll play the devil with them yet!"

He actually drew one of my revolvers from its holster and, too weak to hold himself erect, leaned far back and grasped the butt of the gun with both hands, so that I knew surely he would sell his life dearly when the final pinch came. Far more dearly would they pay for him than they would have to pay for me! He had barely the strength to lift the weight of the weapon, but his weak hands were steady as rocks. One or two shots he would fire; and each bullet would take a life.

When I made sure of this, I realized my own

contemptible weakness more than ever. And yet it was a comfort to know that we could not die ignominiously so long as we were together.

The lights swept on. And, worse still, we heard the booming voice of big McGregor directing the search. They poured around us in a wild torrent, here and there they crashed through the underbrush, and then: "Sherburne, search that clump!" thundered McGregor. Footfalls broke in upon us, and the slender, active form of Sherburne stood above us—and looked straight down into the mouths of our revolvers.

Not an instant did he hesitate, but in a clear and ringing voice he called: "Nothing here!"

"Damn them! We'll get them soon. Who would have thought that Holles would double-cross us!" shouted McGregor, and away burst the pursuit toward another part of the woods, leaving Sherburne with us.

They had no sooner gone, than I made Sherburne, at the point of my revolver, raise Holles and support him out of the brush and deeper into the trees. I had taken the weapons from the gunman, now that he was helpless, and he submitted without a word of protest.

Only he said, as we finally paused for a breathing space: "Arthur, why are you chucking us for this gent?"

I wondered what Holles would say, but I was surprised when he merely answered: "You'll all find out, one of these days. It's no use talking, Sherburne."

That was all that was said, and then we pushed ahead again, and forged steadily through the woods. At last, Holles said that Sherburne need not accompany us any farther.

"And what shall we do with him, Loomis?" he asked me.

I stared at the arrow face and the shifting, bright eyes

of the gunfighter, and shook my head.

"Holles," said I, at last, growing desperate, "if we turn him loose, he'll have the flock of them at our heels in no time."

"You mean that dead men don't talk?" said Mex.

"What else can we do?" said I.

"No," he replied, after a moment of thought. "I think that we can trust Sherburne. He's a white man. Sherburne, you're free. Give him back his guns, Loomis. Otherwise, questions would be asked when he got to the shack!"

I was amazed, but the strangely overbearing force of this youngster's mind made it impossible for me to resist him. I gave the weapons back to Sherburne. The latter seemed benumbed.

"My hands are free, Mex?" he said finally.

"You see that."

"I don't get a bullet in the back when I'm going off?"

"Did I ever shoot a man in the back?"

"And—you don't even make me give you my word that I won't bring the gang back on you?"

"You're a man of honor, Sherburne, I don't have to speak to you about that."

Sherburne turned on his heel without further talk and went slowly back in the direction of the shack, while young Holles nearly fainted again—collapsing so that he almost fell to the ground. I steadied him until he could hold up his head again, and then he insisted that we march on while his strength endured.

"I know a place near here," he murmured. "Around the edge of that next hill. We'll be almost safe there!"

I helped him as strongly as I could in the direction he had indicated, panting: "Sherburne won't come back at us?"

"Sherburne's a treacherous snake," said Holles. "But I couldn't murder him! And the only other thing was to appeal to his few scraps of honor. Maybe he'll betray us. Maybe he won't!"

After that he spoke no more. He was entirely spent, and the last couple of rods I carried him, my knees sagging under the burden.

Finally I found what he meant—a little black hole in the face of the cliff, and I crawled in, dragging him behind me. Inside it was dry, and the air was fresh, and the narrow hole opened out into what I saw, by lighting a match, was a considerably large cave.

I remained there for a moment, exhausted and weak, and when my strength returned a little, and my nerves steadied—for fear had tired me more than the great labor of carrying the sick man—I got water from a little stream which I heard trickling through the deeper reaches of the cave and with it washed the face of Holles. He revived at that, and said that he would soon be better.

So I left him and went out into the woods. There I cut a quantity of tender young fir branches and brought them back in great armloads until I had built up two big beds, one for my invalid and one for myself.

I got Holles comfortably on one of these, and presently I knew by his deep and regular breathing that he was asleep. That left me in the dark to meditate.

I went to the mouth of the cave and watched the stars. They were quiet and calm enough, but by this time, I knew that a storm of exceeding might had burst through Dorking Hollow. The fury of McGregor at the wound— or the death—of his Indian doctor, and the double rage and fear he must feel at the escape of Holles, would drive the giant to almost any limits.

What would he feel with the terrible Mex at large? He must know that Mex suspected everything concerning the dastardly plot to take his life. And if that were the case, then as soon as Holles regained his shattered health, death would come swiftly and surely upon McGregor.

For that reason he was sure to sweep the countryside with a comprehensive search, and if he could not find us, he would go half mad with terror. And what is to be feared so much as a frightened bully?

I dared not go back to Dorking Hollow for the present, even to scout about for information.

In the meantime we must have food. But there was little difficulty in providing that. The moon was rising, and by its light, I arranged a dozen little snares such as poachers used on the rabbit runs which I found among the trees and the open meadows. An hour after I had set them, I made the circuit of my snares and found that two little cottontails and three big, fat rabbits were taken.

I found a natural circle of rocks, and with these to cut off the red rays of the fire, I soon had a blaze going in the midst of the circle, and, after cleaning the rabbits, I roasted them to the queen's taste.

Then, with those prizes, I returned into the cave with the first pink of the dawn just beginning.

Holles was not asleep, but he was shivering with the cold and the dampness, so I took off my coat and put it as well as some lighter branches of the evergreens over him. That done, I felt that he would sleep quite warmly. As for me, my own health and comfort did not matter. It was the recovery of this young tiger that I must work toward. I dropped onto my bed, so completely exhausted that I was soon asleep, and did not waken again until the slant rays of the sun beat into the mouth of the cave in the midmorning.

I found Holles sitting braced on his pile of boughs, eating cold rabbit, and nodding and grinning at me. He had replaced my coat on me as I slept!

"Hello, Mex," said I, "you're much better!"

"A thousand times," said he. "I'm almost a well man; all I need is a bit of strength. That will come soon enough! What's happening in Dorking Hollow?"

"I don't know."

"You haven't been there?" he exclaimed.

"Why, man," said I, "big McGregor will be raging and ramping through the place trying to find either of us, and I value a sound skin more than that!"

He blinked at me, much amazed.

"You would have gone in scouting, of course," said I, "but I don't know your tricks, and I haven't your grit. My job is to get you back on your feet, and if I can do that—why, I'm contented."

CHAPTER THIRTY-ONE

No one ever had a more pleasing smile than did Mex when he cared to use it, and he used it now, broadly and well.

"You're hero enough, Loomis," said he. "But—let Dorking Hollow go. What good will it do me to know about the way things are running there so long as I can't lift a hand to take care of the boys?"

I was very curious to find out what this pantherlike youth had in mind.

So I said: "McGregor will be raising the devil, Mex."

"No doubt," said Mex, and set his teeth. "I'll tell you the worst thing that a man can do in this world—and that's to show any mercy to a hound dog of a man—"

He paused. I could fill in the blank for myself, for it was plain that he cursed the day that had made him show any mercy to big McGregor.

"McGregor will have a band of wild men at his back," said I. "He'll be able to do pretty much as he pleases in Dorking Hollow!"

Mex groaned in disgust and in wrath.

"He'll spoil all our work, Loomis," said he.

"Ah, but he's already started to run out the crooks," said I.

Holles shook his head.

"He's run out the crooks who won't join his camp— that's all. He'll have fifty men around him. A regular gang of bandits. They'll make hell howl in Dorking Hollow, you can bet on them. They'll take the place of the vigilance committee!"

He smiled sadly as he said that.

"But what can be done, Mex?" I asked him.

"Break them in bits!" he said through his teeth. And he added suddenly: "It was all working as smooth as oil, old-timer. Think how we'd straightened things out! The crooks were hot-footing it east and west and south and north. They wanted nothing from Dorking Hollow except distance. Everything worked like a charm. The folks were easy in the town. The mule trains went through the hills without the slightest trouble. The mines were working full blast. And now look at the picture as it stands today! All ruined, all the good work undone, and big Johnnie McGregor with his pack of thugs running the town—"

He broke off with another groan, and, turning white, lay back on his bed of branches.

That alarmed me. Yet I was delighted to see the

current that was carrying his thoughts along. He wanted to continue his constructive work in Dorking Hollow. No doubt, he had never realized how delightful that work was until his hand was pushed from the helm of our little ship of state.

"Take things easy, Mex," said I. "You can't do a thing now except to get well. Take your mind off the trouble in Dorking Hollow!"

"You're wrong," he said. "Because the longer I think of it, the quicker I'll get well. It can't do me any harm to know that I'm needed!"

I could believe that, and I said no more about his worries. They were the same that I had, for that matter.

I wondered where he could take hold.

"Suppose you were back on your feet with your full strength, Mex. Where would you begin—against such numbers as they can muster against you? Because now McGregor will turn even your own men against you, and he'll swear that you've run away to betray them."

Mex nodded.

"I'll cross every bridge when I come to it," said he. "All I know is that McGregor is the knot of this problem. And a knot may be hard to unravel, but it can always be cut!"

With a bullet he meant, of course. And I had no doubt that with Johnnie McGregor out of the way, the rest of the rough elements in the town could be kept in hand fairly well.

I talked no more with him for some time, but went out to obliterate all the traces which we had left when we entered the cave during the night. I moved with the greatest caution, because I never could tell when a face might appear among the trees. And then both of us would be lost. They could smoke us out of that little

188

cave just exactly as Holles himself had smoked out big McGregor.

However, there was much in the philosophy of Holles, and we must cross our bridges as we came to them.

When I returned to' the cave, Mex was asleep once more, and I was glad of it. I leaned over him and listened to his breathing. It was fairly deep and regular. He smiled as he slept. His mind was at rest, now that he was out of his prison. And when the mind is at ease, the body must soon be well.

I had every hope. If only the invalid could regain his strength before Dorking Hollow was utterly ruined! And I trusted that the recovery would be most rapid. After all, the sickness had not lasted very many days, and his constitution could hardly be seriously shattered.

When he wakened, he was hungry again, and ate wolfishly, then demanded a cigarette, rolled it with lightning fingers, and lay back on his bed, drawing every breath of the smoke to the bottom of his lungs. He made a most luxurious picture—for a sick man.

"Tell me what happened today in the shack, Mex," said I. "Did you have to fight hard to keep away from the dope?"

"No." said Mex. "The Indian brought in my cup of poison this morning. I couldn't look at it without shuddering, and he took it away at once. Afterward, he brought me in a big breakfast with his own hands—the skunk! But I told him that I had not the slightest appetite and that I would get on without further food this morning. Even that didn't seem to bother him. He told me that I should rest easily and not worry about anything, and then maybe I would be able to get well without taking any more medicine."

"That's queer," said I.

"Not a bit queer," said Mex. "When he said that I fairly shivered. I never have been so frightened. Because I knew they understood that I was suspicious, and that the first thing I knew they would have a knife slipped into me.

"However, they had business on their hands today. Mc Gregor, you know, rode out before dawn. And while he was away, he evidently told the Indian to keep his hands off me. No one was allowed to talk with me, though. I was desperate and called to one of the boys, but the Indian wouldn't let him come in and said that it would upset me if I did any talking whatever.

"There was something in the smile of that red-skinned viper that made me know that he understood perfectly what was going on in my mind, and I felt very sick again, you may be sure. Well, I got through this day with my nerves frayed almost to pieces; and when the darkness of the evening began, I was sure that it would be the finish for me, as big McGregor came thundering back to the Hollow all covered over with glory.

"When I saw that, I had a hope that he would be too busy celebrating the whole night through to bother about murdering me before the morning. Still, my hopes weren't actually very strong, and I've never been so glad of anything as I was of your voice when you leaned through the window of my room and whispered to me. And—tell me, old fellow—did you smash the skull of the Indian?"

"I hope I did," said I, "but I'm afraid that it was merely a glancing blow. I really hit him more by accident than by design."

"Ah," murmured he, closing his eyes. "When my turn comes to hit him—"

He left the sentence unfinished, but it was an incompleteness which I could fill in for myself very effectively. I could not help smiling with a savage satisfaction when I pictured the future meeting between big McGregor and the Indian and his agile young destroyer.

Night came again on the long day. I waited until moonrise, and then ventured out to snare rabbits again. By this time Holles was so far recovered that he could creep to the mouth of the cave and lie in the moonshine, looking about him on the forest with his bright eyes. When I brought in the game which I had caught—for the hills were simply alive with rabbits—I found Holles sitting cross-legged in the mouth of the cave, handling a pair of revolvers with what seemed to me a wonderful lightness and agility. Even in his weakness his fine craft made those guns like feathers in his hands.

It was a most hopeful sign. We had a cheerful supper there by moonshine, and then to bed and to sleep.

And the last words of my young tiger were: "God help Dorking Hollow—till we can get back to her!"

Day and night, you see, his thoughts were only on what terrible damage big McGregor might be doing to "his" town. It rather amused me to hear the possessive tone in which Holles spoke of the town which, on a time, had been so supremely anxious to hang him up by the neck. Yes, which had come so perilously close to doing so! However, all was for the best.

The next morning Holles began to grow extremely restless, and he was a little irritable for the first time. The rabbit meat, he said, disgusted him. He was going to go out to get some venison.

"Man, man!" I protested. "Don't you know that the hills must still be filled with the searchers of McGregor?

191

And if they hear the explosion of a gun—"

"I know," said he, "but they'll never catch me. I'm a lucky man, old fellow. And besides, just lately I've had enough misfortune to last me for years. Stay here, if you want. I'm going out to get a deer!"

I finally dissuaded him from doing any shooting, but out for a walk through the trees he certainly would go. And out for a walk he went.

He managed his legs in a fumbling, uncertain fashion, and I begged him not to overdo; but after the first five or ten minutes I noticed that he walked more lightly and easily, and that he carried himself more erect. After all, his instinct had been right, and what he needed was a little exercise, and a sight of something other than the walls of the cave.

When dusk came on, his nervousness increased to a frantic point, and finally, he shoved his revolvers into his belt and declared that he was going.

"Where?" said I.

"To Dorking Hollow."

"For God's sake, Mex, don't undo all our good work!"

"I'll go mad," said he, "unless I know what's happening!"

"Wait till the morning!"

"No—but now, now! My instinct tells me to go now, before it's too late!"

"You're weak as a child!"

"No, I can handle guns as well as ever I could. I'm a bit weak on my pins, but a little walking will soon strengthen them!"

"Then stay here, Mex, and I'll go and do the scouting for you! Will you make that exchange?"

He must have realized that, after all, he was still far

from fit. For he sighed and suddenly shrugged his shoulders.

"Very well," said he. "Go on to the Hollow. But take care of yourself. McGregor would like to kill me out of policy. But he would like to kill you out of sheer hate!"

CHAPTER THIRTY-TWO

NO MAN'S HEART WAS EVER MORE FILLED with gloomy forebodings than was mine as I began that walk across the hills toward Dorking Hollow, and when I had covered the few miles that separated us from the hills overlooking the town, I paused at the edge of the trees and looked down into the Hollow with amazement. The moon was not yet up, so that I could not see clearly what was on the floor of the little valley, but I saw no lights from the entire southern half of the village. It was as though the creek had risen and washed half the place away!

I rubbed my eyes, stared again, and finally circled around on the hill ridge until I came to the northern edge of the Hollow. Then I began a cautious descent into the place.

I could see the long, low outline of Jackson's place in the distance, twice as garishly lighted as ever before, and that made me augur ill for what had happened since I was last a member of the community. When I came closer down the slope, I had further proof, in a sudden outbreak of wild voices from the nearest house. And, a moment later, there was a rapid chattering of revolvers, quickly ending, and leaving the hills ringing with deep echoes.

This was not the Dorking Hollow to which I had

grown accustomed. I feared the worst, and went on with an increasing caution. I have no doubt that no spy ever went into a hostile town with more care than I went into that mining camp.

I scouted from shack to shack until I came to the rear of Avery Lucas' hut. It was pitch dark, though the night was very young, and since Avery was generally up quite late, and since he never went to the gambling hall, I was more troubled than ever.

I decided that I would enter the shack to learn whether or not it was inhabited, and how long it had been left vacant, for I was quite sure that Avery had been the victim of foul play. I tried the rear door, found the latch not caught, and walked in.

Suddenly a voice called sharply out of the darkness: "Stand fast! Don't move! I've got you covered!"

The voice of Avery Lucas, hard and sharp with determination and fear.

"Avery!" said I. "Avery, you're here, thank God!"

"It's Loomis, by all that's wonderful," said he. "Man, man, they didn't murder you, after all!"

"Did they say that they had?" said I.

"They've called you a sneak, a renegade, and a traitor," said he. "And they've taken your mines and they're working them—for the public good, they say. Which of course means for their own pockets!"

I cursed softly.

"They haven't dared to do that!" I groaned.

"But they have, though."

"You mean McGregor and his crew?"

"Just that lot. Who else?"

"They have the town?"

"Aye, what's left of it."

"What do you mean by that?"

"Man, haven't you seen with your own eyes?"

"I've sneaked out of the woods and down into the Hollow. I haven't seen a thing of the Hollow except the lights. I noticed that there were no lights in the southern half of the town!"

"It's gone!" said he.

"Gone?" cried I, amazed.

"It happened yesterday morning," said he. "But you really know nothing?"

"Not a thing since that night."

"The night before last, Tucker Grey was tackled by one of McGregor's bullies and killed the man—pure case of self-defense. I saw it with my own eyes and could testify in any court. The next morning, what happens? The vigilance committee calls on Tucker and—"

"Why did you do that," said I, "if you knew that he hadn't been guilty of—"

"I? I had nothing to do with it."

"But you said the vigilance committee?"

"I'm no longer a member. Resignation requested."

"At the point of a gun?"

"Yes. You understand how it is? I should have refused. But I'm not a hero or a Spartan. I resigned. The other vigilance committee has all the prime scoundrels in the camp enlisted in its membership, and the great Johnnie McGregor is the leader and the chairman, of course! McGregor, then, went with his gang to the house of Tucker Grey. Tucker, like a brave man, refused to talk to them except with a leveled rifle. They bored his house through and through with at least five hundred shots. But still he fired back at them, and managed to wound two of the rascals. It sounded like the roar of a pitched battle, so many rifles were working. Finally, in a rage, they set fire to the grass in front of his shack, the hut caught, and Tucker was shot down and killed as he ran from the flames—"

"Tucker Grey!" I cried. "As decent a man as there was in the camp!"

"His kind are not wanted here now!" said Lucas bitterly.

"Go on! Then what? Nothing was done to McGregor for the murder?"

"Not a thing. But the fire spread. The wind drove it down on the rest of the town, and we were barely able to save the upper half of Dorking Hollow."

"One half wiped out!" I gasped. "My shack among the rest?"

"Yes, they burned you out. They set fire to your house on purpose as soon as the flames were under way. But finally they were frightened and they all turned in at last to help save a remnant of the place."

"And nothing's done against McGregor for such conduct?"

"What can be done? Half of the decent men in the town have left. The rest of us are thinking of leaving."

"The mines are closed down, then?"

"No, they're being worked as they never were worked before!"

"Ah?"

"And two thirds of the proceeds pass into the pockets of McGregor and company. Their shack is filled with the metal. They're rich men, every one. They're literally gutting the mines, old man."

I groaned with rage and grief.

"Can't we send for help?"

"We've tried to do that. No doubt, the military will hear about it in due time, but it will be a couple of

196

months before troops can get here. And before that time the ruin will be complete! We used to call Holles, King Stork. I called him that myself. But, ah, Loomis, how we want King Stork back now! Because the devil has come to be king in his place!"

"Could he do anything now?" said I.

"No," said Lucas. "Even if he were brought back to life, he couldn't do a thing. Every one of the thugs are devoted to McGregor and they have their reasons. He fills the pockets of those pirates with money."

"No more thieves in the woods?"

"Not a one. Why should there be? McGregor has invited the worst and the cleverest of them to join his band. And the rest have been run off and chased clear away from the hills."

"Then all the evil's concentrated right here in the Hollow?"

"Yes," said Lucas. "You've no idea what a hell they've brought onto this section of the earth. They've made every man who has the slightest claim to be decent live as I live—with never a light showing. Because if a light shows, it's sure to be shot out. Not an evening passes that doesn't bring a few volleys fired at this shack of mine. They have me labeled for murder, and sooner or later they'll get me!"

"But you won't leave?"

"I try to leave. I make up my mind to leave every evening, but when the morning comes, I change my resolution again. I can't go, old fellow! I have the wealth of a very rich man staked out here in the Hollow. I can't turn it over to these scoundrels!"

I waited, turning slowly through my mind the long catalogue of disasters which I had just heard.

And suddenly I exclaimed: "Holles was right. He

197

knew. He prophesied it!"

"Holles? Holles?" said Lucas. "Why do you mention him? If we had had him in time, he could have saved us from this. But they knew, and that's why they murdered him!"

"Lucas," I told him suddenly, "Mex is not dead."

"What!"

"Soft, soft," said I. "If the thugs should learn what I have to tell you, they'd burn me alive. They would any way, if they could find me."

"It's true," said Lucas. "There's a standing reward of ten thousand dollars offered by the vigilance committee for the man who gives information that will cause you to be apprehended, dead or alive. Preferably dead, I suppose. But Holles—is it possible that he's living?"

"It is possible. It's a fact. I've left him alive and well back in the hills, and burning hot to get here to Dorking Hollow and undo the work of that devil McGregor!"

"Holles! Arthur Holles! Mex!" repeated Lucas over and over, as if the name were a talisman which might mysteriously deliver us from evil.

He added: "And well? *Well*, do you say?"

"Where's Doc Cochrane?" I asked suddenly.

"Murdered, perhaps. At any rate, he's not been seen in the village for some time."

"And he's not talked to you?"

"No, not before he left."

"Lucas, Cochrane knew what I knew—that Holles was being slowly poisoned by the Indian doctor of McGregor in the shack on the hill. That was why I went there the other night, and I managed to bring Holles away with me when he was too weak to walk. It seems a miracle, when I look back on it—but the fact is that I have him in the hills, and practically a well man this

198

very night. He's merely recovering a little strength. His nerves are as steady as ever!"

"Heaven be praised!" said Lucas.

"Hush!" said I. "Was that something passing the door?"

"Look at the rear of the house. I'll look in the front. I shouldn't be surprised. They're continually spying on me. Nothing would please them more than to have a chance to string me up—that vigilance committee!"

I went to the rear of the shack and opened the door and peered out, but all was quiet. The late moon was rising through the eastern trees, and from far off whoops and singing floated to me across the night.

CHAPTER THIRTY-THREE

WHATEVER DANGER THERE WAS seemed reasonably far away. But how could I tell what people were lurking in the brush near the shack?

I went back inside and said to my friend: "I think that we're safe enough."

"Aye," said Lucas, "I think that we may be. I feel that this is my lucky night. And we can talk, old fellow. Tell me whatever is in your mind."

I could not help smiling.

"You mean," said I, "to tell you what's in the mind of Arthur Holles?"

He laughed in turn. It was strange to see how rapidly his spirits were rising, now that he knew that Holles was a possible rescuer of our town.

"As you please," said he. "And what has the great Holles to say? What's his plan?"

"He has none."

199

"Hello!" murmured Lucas. "No plan, did you say?"

"No plan at all."

"Then what will the strange rascal do?"

"I don't know. As a matter of fact, he doesn't know himself; but when the time comes, he'll wait for an inspiration."

"Why, perhaps that's the best way. Holles is free and safe and well. By the Lord, five minutes ago I thought that nothing in this world could make me smile! But now I begin to see that life may be worth living, after all! Holles is free! Confound them, he'll make them pay through the nose for the deviltry which they've been working in this town. Loomis, I've always felt that no big man could be capable of really fiendish malice. But I've been wrong, because this man McGregor is a fiend incarnate."

"More a fiend now," I explained, "because he's in mortal fear lest Holles should come back at any time. He knows that Holles is alive, and, knowing that, he's simply waiting for the time when that slender youngster will rise like a ghost in his path. God help McGregor on that day, because there's blood in the eye of Mex!"

"I remember," said Lucas, "the day when you first brought him into the camp and how entirely skeptical about him I was. I was sure that the camp would go to the dogs at once. But it hasn't gone. Confound it, it's still buzzing in my mind! How could he have turned out so well? How can he be the man to save us all?"

I had asked myself the same question so many times that now it was merely enough to make me laugh.

"God works in mysterious ways," said I, rather pompously. "We can't pretend to understand such people as Holles. But since Holles won't lay down a plan himself, you and I had better have some sort of a working basis prepared!"

"That's natural, and that's what we must do, even if Holles refuses to use our prepared ideas. In the first place, how long will it be before Holles will be able to take his part?"

"If it were any other man," said I, "that had just been through a course of poisoning, more or less thorough, besides being mauled beforehand by great McGregor, I would say that a month's rest might bring him back to normal. But as for Holles, whether he's really fit or not, I know that it won't be more than three days before he's in the thick of some sort of action. He really looks on us as his people, and this as his town," I explained.

"He'll come, then, inside of three days, you think?"

"I think so."

"And he has not worked out any plan?"

"None whatever, I know."

"Do you suppose that he may underestimate the strength of McGregor, and McGregor's grip upon the gun fighters in the town?"

"I don't know. I really feel that Holles understands those ruffians better than you or I ever could. It was Holles who in the first place started using them, you know."

Lucas admitted that.

"A few of them," I suggested, "are so devoted to Holles that they'll probably go over to him as soon as he shows himself. I think, for instance, that Christy Munn—"

"As great a ruffian and rascal," cried Lucas hotly, "as any of the entire pack!"

"That may be," I broke in, "but at the same time he's an excellent fighting man, and the important thing is that I think Holles could win Munn over to his side."

"Ah, that would be worth while!"

"Yes. it certainly would! Very well, there would probably be two or three others—enough to make a nucleus."

"A nucleus against a storm wind!" groaned Lucas. "I suppose that McGregor has fifty trained gun fighters behind him, and in addition to that he has the solid support of such rascals in the town as Jackson, and all of Jackson's dishonorable crew."

"Very well," said I; "they may muster a great gang. Suppose that they bring out a hundred or even two hundred men—battles aren't always won by odds, when one side has a Napoleon! But the first thing for us to do is to organize a small group of fellows in whom we can trust. Men like Cochrane, for instance, if we could only have him back with us! Men like Chalmers, Van Zant, Pieters, and Chisholm!"

"Not one of the lot you've mentioned," said Lucas bitterly, "would have the slightest chance in the world in a fight against the least skillful of the gun fighters."

"No, individually we may not amount to much," said I, "but when we have a group, it means the beginning of a faction which may bring others over from the side of McGregor. He's heavy-handed. He's sure to have offended a good many people. They'll be glad to leave him. And besides, a hundred of us, even if we can't shoot as straight as McGregor's ruffians, may be willing to stay shoulder to shoulder longer than his men, and fight with better discipline. That counts! At least, it's the best suggestion that I can make."

"A good suggestion, of course. But how'll we get these men together?"

"We can't, because we don't know when young Holles will come. But we could have everything ready for a given signal of some sort, to bring all our side together at a crisis."

"Yes," murmured Lucas. "That sounds hopeful. What sort of a signal?"

I cast my thoughts vaguely around.

"I don't know," said I. "Suppose that I said—the lighting of your house? It's on a rather high place here. If it burned, every one could see it, day or night."

"Certainly," said Lucas without a moment's question. "If our fight didn't succeed, I wouldn't need a house afterward! And if it succeeds," he added grimly, "there will be plenty of vacant places after the battle. We could agree on that as the signal, in fact. When we want to rally, I'll send my shanty up in flames. And, in the meantime, we have to pass the word around cautiously to all our friends, and swear them to the most perfect secrecy. Is that correct?"

"Exactly!"

"Confound it, Loomis, don't you see what a lost and hopeless cause this is?"

"Perhaps so. But it's better to try to fight like this than to give up without another struggle!"

"Yes," said he. "Yes, better to fight it out. But if ever I get free of this tangle, I can promise you that the wide free West will never see me again! I'll be through with it forever!"

So said Lucas, very bitterly, and I agreed with him with all my heart.

"How many men can we think of?" said I. "I can mention about a dozen."

"Wait a moment. Yes, I can make it fifteen. If we have fifteen as a nucleus, each of them may be able to bring in one or two more. It doesn't sound like a great army. But if thirty or forty well-armed and desperately determined men turned up in the middle of the town here, prepared to fight the battle out, and with Mex to lead us—why, who can tell?"

I felt as he did. It was our last great and desperate gambling venture to save the relics of our fortunes and to save Dorking Hollow from complete destruction.

I sat for some time longer, listening to the tales which poor Lucas told me of the tyranny of big Johnnie McGregor, and of the manner in which his bullies overrode the decent folk of the place. He said that none of McGregor's men dared to interfere very decidedly with his will and his way. He was a complete and perfect tryant, and the rest of the crew held back and let him select the evil which they were to accomplish at his bidding.

Lucas told me how the mines were being sacked and ruined; the most valuable property being rifled rapidly, and two thirds of the best ore blocked away because these legalized bandits knew that their lease of power might be rather brief.

"Do they expect to be rushed out at any moment?" I asked Lucas.

"No," said Lucas. "So far as I can gather, they are not rushing too frantically. They seem to feel that they may have at least two months to complete the sack of the town, and by the end of that time, as a matter of fact, I don't think that there will be much worth while in Dorking Hollow to be picked over."

We were both silent for a time. Then I said: "Shall I start back now?"

"Go back now," said he. "Take whatever you want with you."

"Bacon and flour and salt. We can get everything else—no, tobacco and coffee also!"

"Here, I'll give you what you want. Have no fear of that. I can load you down with such stuff. God knows, I would go with you, and bend my back double to cart the stuff to Holles if I thought that it would get him well any more quickly! But, as a matter of fact, if you have him in a safe and undiscovered place, it's as well to leave him where he is. Safety and secrecy for Holles. Then, afterward, our revenge. Think, Loomis, how like a pillar of fire he'll burn in the eyes of McGregor and his crew!"

Lucas was getting together his store of edibles as he said this, and presently he gave them to me in a stout canvas bag. I slung it over my shoulder and wrung the hand of my friend. Then I stepped out into the light of the stars and paused a moment to take stock of all that was around me, noises near and far, and the lights in the adjacent houses. And, as I paused, a vast shadow stepped around the corner of the house.

I saw it; screamed, I think, like a frightened woman. I dropped the sack and tugged out my Colt, but at that instant the vast shadow leaped on me. A hand of iron clutched my gun arm and the voice of McGregor said: "Give up, you little fool, or I'll break you in pieces!"

CHAPTER THIRTY-FOUR

I LOOKED UP INTO HIS FACE and I thought that his eyes were burning like the phosphorescent eyes of a great cat in the dark of the night. To resist him would perhaps have been possible to another man. I might have used my free left hand to snatch a knife and bury it in the breast of the giant. But I was completely overwhelmed, more by the surprise than by his mere might, though that was great enough.

He had mastered me in a moment. On my wrist he snapped a pair of handcuffs which he took out of his pocket, calling at the same time: "Get Lucas, too! We have two of the birds! Get Lucas! Five hundred to you boys for getting him here safe and sound—no shooting of him!"

I wondered, even at that moment, why he wanted Lucas safe and sound instead of asking for him dead or alive.

At the same time, I saw half a dozen men leap from the brush and start for the house, paying no heed to the door near which the giant was standing with me, but rushing around to the far side of the shanty.

The giant, revolver in hand, commanded that doorway, and yet straight out at McGregor sprang Lucas, now. He came with a shrill cry far different from his usual tone of voice. I suppose that it was the screech of a desperate, hunted beast rather than the voice of a man. He came with a leap and a rush and fired a pistol straight at the face of McGregor.

McGregor, with a curse, threw one arm around his head and sank to the ground, but his other arm retained its grip on me and dragged me to the ground with him as he fell. I struggled with all my might to get clear, but what was my might compared even with the force in his single hand?

And at the same time I remember feeling a vast wave of hot satisfaction. It burned the fear out of me. It left me clear-headed with rejoicing, for I felt sure that McGregor had received a mortal wound.

I saw the pursuers dart out of the house and past us, and down the path which twisted away among the shrubbery, along which Lucas had fled. He was out of

206

sight, and the others disappeared in turn, except two who came at the heels of the rest.

They left the leaders to go on with the chase. They paused by McGregor and I felt that I was a lost man.

Then McGregor stumbled to his feet and, lifting me with both hands, he hurled me like a stone at the feet of the other two.

"Take this hound!" said he. "I think Lucas has murdered me. Sam, hold a light here!"

The companion of Sam thrust a gun into the small of my back as I got to my feet, dizzy and stunned by my fall, but I paid little heed to that; I was too keenly interested to discover what had actually happened to the giant in this encounter.

As the match flared close to his face, I saw a red streak of blood and nearly shouted with a savage joy. But then I heard Sam say: "It's only a grazing wound, Johnnie. Thank God for that!"

The devil should have been thanked instead.

"They've put a mark on me, though!" cried McGregor, his voice huge and broken with his fury. "But I'll set my mark on a hundred of them in exchange! I'll teach them whether or not the vigilance committee is the law in Dorking Hollow!"

Law? I nearly laughed as I heard that word come from that mouth. Law! However, it was a shrewd lesson to me. For those improvised forms of law on the early frontier were apt to burn the hands which used them like wildfire!

"It's nothing bad," said Sam comfortingly. "We'll have that blood washed away in a jiffy. It's stopped bleeding already. But a quarter of an inch more, and you would be dead as dead, old fellow!"

"Bring Loomis along," ordered McGregor. "It really

don't matter so much about Lucas, except that it would be a pleasure to stretch his neck for him. But bring along this—"

And he embarked on a dreadful stream of curses.

Strangely enough, my situation hardly troubled me. After that first shock of finding myself in the hands of the monster, I cared for nothing that followed. The worst had happened. I had suffered worse pangs than death in that instant of dread and suffering. And now I walked calmly along between my two guards, with great McGregor stalking on in front.

Now that I had time to think it over, I wondered what could have been overheard of the conversation between Lucas and me. As for Lucas himself, if he escaped from the pursuit—and it seemed most unlikely that he could have the speed or the luck to get away from those swiftfooted youngsters who had taken after him—he did not possess the vital secret, the place in which Holles was hiding.

But these lurking spies who had served their gigantic master so well might have heard our murmuring voices when we discussed our plans for the rising against McGregor. That would be a serious blow to us. For some plan of concerted action was, of course, vital to our success.

Let Lucas escape from them, and let him have a chance to give the word to even a single one of the men we knew and could trust, and then the plan of revolt might grow and come to a head quite without any services of mine.

It would be a vast comfort to me. I felt, as I walked up the street, that I would die without much great regret if I knew that McGregor would die not long after. And by the hand of our Achilles, Arthur Holles!

A little crowd gathered around us as we walked. And by the time that we passed the house of Jackson, the gambler, I think there were three hundred people boiling around us and streaming behind us in an odd procession. Shouting, laughing, congratulating McGregor on this capture, or else sympathizing with him because of his wound, I was astonished to see many of the people whom I had considered the most reliable workers in the town now forming a part of McGregor's rabble. An old miner who had worked for me for many weeks, came up and shook his fist in my face and would have struck me, except that one of my guards pushed me ahead, with a laugh. And I think that a dozen of the ruffians promised to fill me full of lead if, by any chance, the vigilance committee failed to make an end of me.

And the most complimentary term that I was called was traitor!

What had I betrayed? To whom had I failed to be true? It hardly mattered. There are certain terms that come to the lips of men almost as readily as curses in order that they may express their violent hate. Traitor is the readiest word of all. And therefore I was a traitor. Above all, I had taken Holles away from them. On account of me, Holles now lurked somewhere among the hills, perhaps, ready to fall upon them like a lightning blast.

That was the profound reason for their hatred of me. I was the archvillain. I had prepared a thunderbolt which might drop upon their heads, and out of a clear sky!

I was taken around to the rear of Jackson's place and put in a small room and guarded still by three armed men. McGregor disappeared, and a little later I heard loud cheering through the gaming rooms.

"Why are they yelling?" I asked the guard. "Is it

because they've managed to capture the great gun fighter and desperado, Loomis?"

The guards grinned at this bit of irony.

"It ain't you, Loomis," said one of them. "But now that we've got you, we'll soon get the other one."

"What other one?"

"Well, man, what other one can there be that's giving us all bad dreams? I mean that streak of hellfire, Mex!"

"You'll soon have him, eh?" said I.

"You'll see," said he, and he peered at me with a cold-blooded cruelty that started me thinking.

They would try to make me confess what I knew about Holles and his whereabouts, of course. Well, I set my teeth and swore to myself that even if they shot me full of holes, they would never get a word about Holles from my lips.

I was fortifying myself with that resolution when an order came to take me out; and I was led into a larger room where I found a semicircle of half a dozen men lounging on boxes and benches and with them was McGregor himself, with a bandage around his head.

"You boys make yourselves comfortable," said McGregor to my guards, and he pointed to a bottle as he spoke. "There's some cigars, too. Set down and make yourselves to home. Maybe we won't have to keep you long. Now, Loomis, you see where you are?"

I was silent. It wasn't the sort of question that needs much answering.

"You're in here," said he, "before the law!"

"Law?" I asked, smiling a little, as I surveyed those grim, bearded faces.

"Yes," he thundered back at me, "you're here before the vigilance committee of Dorking Hollow!"

"Good!" said I, still grinning. "Then I'm sure to get

good treatment from you fellows. You know that I'm an old vigilante myself!"

At this one of the men leaned forward with infinite malice in his face and said bitterly: "You was, and you ain't gunna be forgot. Not by me. I'm Hugh Minnerode!"

I searched my memory, and as he saw my face a blank he added: "You're murdered so many in your day that you don't even remember the name, eh? Well, you hanged my brother one fine day. And now, old-timer, I'm gunna have my fun with you. I'm gunna have the pleasure of seein' you stretch your neck, and the last thing that you hear will be me laughing!"

"Hold on!" said the giant. "This ain't the right way. We got to try this here gent before we can hang him."

"Try him!" cried Minnerode furiously. "Don't every body know what he is? He's a traitor. The worst traitor in Dorking Hollow. If he ain't guilty, then hell is full of angels! Why waste time judging him? Hanging him is all that needs to bother us!"

"Are you all agreeing to that?" asked McGregor.

"No," said another. "Hanging is too good for that skunk! String him up over a slow fire and toast him a bit first, I'd say!"

That brought a hoarse shout of approval from Minnerode. And suddenly McGregor broke in: "All right, boys. I understand. If you think that he's safe in my hands, leave him with me for a while, will you? I got things to say to him!"

CHAPTER THIRTY-FIVE

THEY LEFT THE ROOM WILLINGLY ENOUGH to find the bar. But they promised to be back in time for the "fun." After them, McGregor sent the guards. Indeed, it amazed me to see what perfect control he exercised over these ruffians.

When we were alone, he leaned comfortably back against the wall and folded his arms together over his chest.

"You see how it is?" said he.

I nodded.

"It's all mine," he went on, his grin broadening. "All the work that you gents put in to build up Dorking Hollow—it's all work that was done for me. And all the trouble of them that first discovered the mines here— why, they was simply taking all of that trouble for me, unbeknownst to them! And all the smartness of Holles in combing the thugs out of the woods—why, that trouble was all taken for me, too!"

He paused. I was filled with such swelling bitterness that it was difficult for me to reply.

I said finally: "Perhaps you're right."

"Oh, I'm right," said he, twisting his fingers into his thick, square-cut beard. "I'm right about it. The proof of the pudding is the eating. And I'm doing the eating, old-timer. And I'm gunna be able to digest it, too. Even if it is a silver pudding."

He put back his great head and laughed hugely at me and at all that concerned me.

"You understand, eh?" said he.

"I suppose that I understand."

"These other gents," said he more seriously, "they got no education nor nothing. They ain't able to see that what they're doing is all for me. But you, Loomis, you can understand. You can see that I'm the winner. You can see that I'm going to come out on the top of the heap, and you'll be able to guess on what side your bread is buttered!"

I wondered what he could mean by this, but he went on very glibly: "You see where I'm fixed. Matter of fact, I'm gunna clean up a couple of millions out of this job, Loomis. I ain't no piker, though, and them that help me through are gunna get their cut. Part of my job is to get the stuff, and part of my job is going to be to settle down peaceable afterward. Now, for all that sort of work, there ain't nothing so good as a smart lawyer, and I know that you're a bang-up dog-gone good one. So it sort of seemed to me, since you been out here where you've seen me work and so know all of the facts, that you might want to throw in with me, Loomis. What about it?"

I was too amazed to answer him for a moment, and before that amazement ended my thoughts were coming so fast that I had no words to speak.

It appeared, on the surface, that this arch scoundrel desired to settle down after he had made his clean-up at Dorking Hollow, and he was willing to recompense me liberally if I would agree to help him over the rough places. Rough places there would be, and that in great numbers, of course. Because the past life of the great McGregor was notorious, and he was not the man to put on a disguise and adopt a new name because he adopted new ways of living.

It required an effrontery as colossal as that of McGregor to make such a proposition to me, but I have

213

noticed that many criminals are totally unable to understand the manner in which the mind of a fairly honest man works. I decided that it would be much the best thing to draw this fellow out a bit and find all that was in his mind, and therefore I said: "Look here, McGregor, why not be aboveboard with me? Why don't you come out and tell me just exactly what you have in your mind?"

"You've mostly guessed it already, I think," said he. "I want to get a chance to spend what I've made, Loomis. I want to step out of this sort of life and settle down some place back East. I'm a Connecticut man, Loomis. I've got a little land back there still. I'd like to go back to it, and build a big house, and a great, red barn, and set out a fine orchard, and I'd like to buy up some of the other places around there and make myself a fine big farm. You understand? I remember that the church in the old town was nearly falling down. Well, I'd build them another church to take its place. That would fix me up in their eyes. They'd think that I was a pretty fine sort of a gent then, wouldn't they? And suppose that somebody come along and said that I had been a crook out West, why, the folks in that village would simply laugh and they would say that I was the best sort of a gent that ever stepped. Ain't that right?"

I looked back into my own knowledge of Connecticut and saw in my imagination a little hollow among the rolling, beautiful hills, and in the hollow a village, with the slender white spire of a church pricking the pale blue sky. And all around the town old farmhouses sprawled in comfortable places under the lee of hills. And then I looked at Johnnie McGregor, and roused myself as though from a dream. Johnnie McGregor, prisoner, gun fighter, murderer, thief; Johnnie to

214

become the quiet mainstay of a village church and the great and good man of a town; why, it was partly amazing that such an ambition had ever formed in his mind, and it was partly shocking. Yet I suppose that such men have been before.

There was a thrifty streak underlying the prodigal villainies of this giant. And now he wished to retire with his spoils as a lion retires to his den with his prey.

"You could manage these here things for me, you being a right smart lawyer, Loomis. I would set you aside something handsome. Say even a couple of hundred thousand dollars, if things turn out here as well as I hope that they'll turn out!"

"Suppose that I were to agree to work with you, McGregor," said I, "just what would I have to do?"

"Why," said he, his eye gleaming as he felt me falling in with his proposal, "in the first place, we'd have to work things out in Dorking Hollow. That would be only natural, of course. We'd want to get this here town all cleaned up. Makes a lot of difference. We want to get our share of the silver shipped, old fellow, don't we? And we want to keep our hands on the wheel? We want to scrape together what we can here, and we've got to work fast. Maybe we've got six weeks. Maybe we've got three months. But we'll have to plan on three weeks and get what we can in that time, and have it shipped out, and get the certificates of deposit in our pockets. And, of course, there's one great thing that has to be worked out before we ever can feel safe with what we have."

"Well?" said I, enchanted by this fairy tale of villainy.

"Well," said he, "there's that slippery hound, that Holles. Of course, we've got to put him where he ain't going to bother us no more. There's a lot of men here in

215

Dorking Hollow that would call you the best fellow in the world if you gave us a chance to bring Holles to justice! And besides that you and me would specially have to do it because Holles would be the main monkey wrench that's liable to be thrown into our machinery and wreck our plan."

"Oh, well," said I, "we could dodge him for a while. He's only one man. I wouldn't want to betray him, McGregor."

"Don't you go making no such terrible mistake," said McGregor, his voice husky with earnestness. "He's the most important gent that you've ever had any dealings with in your whole life!"

"Is he?"

"Absolutely! Slippery, sneaking, cunning as a fox. Never done with his tricks. Always up to something new and something smarter than the last thing that he's tried. You never seen such a man, I tell you! Never in your born days! Oh, man, that Holles is a caution! Murder is his middle name. And he'll still be killing with one hand when the other hand is gone. And he'll still be shooting as long as there's a spark of life in his heart. And every one of his bullets, they'll find a life. I know him. Damn him, I know him well!"

He spoke with an almost poetic enthusiasm, and I knew that Mex, for one, would have been heartily glad to know that he was so cordially detested by this rank scoundrel.

"We've got to kill him," said McGregor. "We've got to kill him! The whole town knows that. You see how hot the boys were to string you up? What they got against you? Nothing except that you've been associating with that poison skunk Holles! And they'd downright love you if you give 'em a chance to beat

216

Holles! I'd answer for that. You wouldn't need no bodyguard. You'd be the most popular man in the whole town, Loomis."

I smiled at him, and I said nothing.

"What do you mean by that grin?" snapped McGregor, suddenly suspicious. "Are you laughing at me?"

"I'm laughing at you, McGregor," said I.

"By heavens," said he, "I really think you are."

"Oh, don't make any mistake. I really am!"

"Then, what do you mean by it? Are you clean dippy?"

"No, I never had my senses more about me!"

"You mean that you've just been stringing me along to find out what I would say?"

"Perhaps," said I.

I thought that he might leap from his bench and strangle me. His hands were working convulsively and the great veins stood away out on his forehead.

"Suppose that the boys here in Dorking Hollow were to know how you plan to double-cross them," said I.

"Bah! Would they take your word against mine?"

"They might, McGregor. A good many of them don't love you!"

"Love? What do I care for love? But they fear me. Yes, they'll show their teeth, but they're mighty careful that the teeth are showed behind my back! Oh, I understand 'em right enough!"

He strode over and stood above me.

"You ain't gunna be such a fool, Loomis," said he. "You got brains. You see that I'm offering you a chance to get in on the ground floor of a great thing. You see that I'm offering to make you rich."

"I see that," said I slowly.

217

"And you ain't gunna turn down the chance, man!"

"I'd rather be strung up, McGregor," I told him at last, "than have anything to do with you—unless it were your hanging!"

He raised a vast fist that would have smashed my skull like an eggshell, if it had descended. Then he controlled himself.

"You swine!" said he through his teeth.

Then he went to the door, kicked it open and called loudly. In ten seconds the ruffian vigilance committee had trooped back into the room.

CHAPTER THIRTY-SIX

"I'VE TRIED REASON ON HIM," said McGregor, pointing to me, "and it won't work. I might have knowed that before. You got to take a whip with you when you talk to a dog! I was gunna treat him fine. But he won't have fine treatment. So it's up to you to handle him. You, Minnerode, you got something to suggest, maybe?"

I looked expectantly to Minnerode. He had spoken with so much venom before that I expected some terrible suggestion of torture from him now; but I was amazed when he said quietly: "The fact is, Johnnie, we've been thinkin' it over, and it seems to me like we can't blot this gent out none too quick. Blot him out, and how'll we have any information about Holles?"

"How do we know that there *is* any Holles?" said McGregor.

"Eh?"

"He's dead," said McGregor fiercely. "He's dead. I got the word of a smart man for that. He must be dead— unless he's got ten devils inside of him!"

I saw in a sudden flash what he meant. The Indian doctor felt that enough poison had been given to young Holles to insure his death, and that explained why McGregor and the poisoner had not been more violent in the shack in insisting that their patient continue their "treatment."

"He grinned when you said that Holles was dead," said Minnerode. And he thrust a forefinger at me.

"Loomis, man," said McGregor, "tell me true, will you? Is Holles dead or is he living? If he's living and well, he would have come in with you. If he was living but sick, you'd still be with him. If he was dead, though, then you'd come back from him. Tell the truth and shame the devil. Holles is dead!"

There was a certain amount of actual entreaty in his voice. As if I could give him this great good of making Holles dead by merely assenting to his own suggestion.

"Or suppose," put in Minnerode, "that Holles was about well, but not quite, and sent in Loomis to find out how things was coming!"

That made McGregor wince.

"I'm not talking," said I. For I had decided that it would be better to take my chance with what they might have in store for me rather than to talk too frankly.

"He won't talk," said McGregor. "He knows that Holles would be a card up his sleeve, and he ain't going to admit that he knows where Holles is!"

"Ain't there ways of making him talk?" said Minnerode. "Ain't there ways, though?"

"How?"

"Give 'im to me," said Minnerode savagely, "and I'll make him chatter like a parrot. I'll get out of him anything that you want!"

"Have you got some kind of magic?" asked

219

McGregor, drawing out this conversation, and from time to time glancing at me to see how I took it.

"Sure," said Minnerode. "No, not magic. I'm a musician, if you want to know. And I can play a tune with a piece of rope, or a gun, or a knife, or splinters of wood, even. Dog-gone me if I ain't seen fine music made just with splinters of wood. And I can do a pretty clean job even with only a common riding whip. But, of course, you need fire for the best work. You got to soften a gent before you can shape him. Gimme a bit of fire. No, just some twists of paper and a few matches, or even the matches without the paper, and I'll find out anything that's inside the head of this here gent!"

As he made this devilish proposal, I glanced swiftly around at the faces of the others, watching for some tokens of horror or disgust, but I could see none. They merely grinned at the suggestions of Minnerode, and then they looked with much interest on me—with the same sort of interest, indeed, that is in the eyes of a cow-puncher when he picks out a calf for branding.

I remained silent until McGregor turned on me and said: "You hear what's being suggested, Loomis? It ain't me. But the boys see that they got to know what you know!"

Still I was silent.

"Take him, then," said McGregor. "Take him and do what you please to him, Minnerode. And find out what he knows about Holles. Where he died, if he died. And where he is now, if he ain't dead. And whether he's got enough strength to put up a fight, even if we was to find him!"

He bellowed out these words, working himself into a fury.

"You've done it to yourself," said he. "You've done it
220

to yourself, and God help you, I say! I been giving you a white man's chance to come clean to us and tell us what you know. And then we would let you go. We'd give you a free pass out of the camp. We'd do more than that. We'd even let you have a chance to work your damned mines again. But nothin' will do. It ain't no matter how generous we are to you. You don't see the way things stand. You're gunna play the fool, and get yourself tortured! Minnerode, go and give him all the music that you can think of!"

He strode away from me and stood with his back turned.

"You can stay and watch," said Minnerode, coming slowly up to me, and feasting his eyes on me as a cat might feast its eyes on a helpless rat. "You can stay and watch the fun; or else, you can stay outside, and just listen to it. Because I've been promising you a bit of music, ain't I? And by the look of him, I'd say that it's gunna be a regular concert."

I suppose that he meant by that my white face and my trembling. Because I could hardly keep from fainting at the thought of passing helplessly into the hands of this black scoundrel, to be tormented as he pleased. For what crimes his brother had been hanged by the vigilantes, I could not remember. But I guessed from the face of Minnerode that his family must be a worthy one for the rope all around.

I scanned all the resources of my mind swiftly. And finally my eyes rested upon the turned back and the slightly bowed head of McGregor, who had now started rapidly for the door, calling out as he went: "It's your own doing, Loomis! You've brung this right onto your own head!"

That tenseness in McGregor seemed, I thought, the

221

promise that he did not like this sort of thing. He was big and brutal. He was even capable of having a helpless man poisoned. But still, perhaps his nerves were not of the order which can enjoy the infliction of actual torment.

I called suddenly to him: "McGregor!"

He stopped short but did not turn.

"You needn't shout at me!" he said. "It ain't me that's gunna manhandle you. It's Minnerode. It's him, and you can make your bargain with him. Damn you, didn't I offer you a way out of this job?"

"I'm not shouting at you, McGregor," said I. "I'm only telling you not to be a fool!"

"Ah," said McGregor, "I'm a fool, am I?"

"A fool, man, and a plain fool!" said I. "And all the rest of you are playing a foolish part, too!"

"You can explain that when you got time," he drawled. "I ain't gunna wait while you talk like a crazy man!"

"Do I talk like a crazy man?" I called to him furiously. "You'll change your mind about that when Holles is riding through Dorking Hollow like Death on a Horse!"

McGregor spun around on his heel, and, pointing his great arm at me, he shouted: "It's true, then! It's true! Holles is alive! Holles is alive! By heavens, that slippery snake ain't dead yet!"

The rest were silent. McGregor himself became quiet, and then began to pace up and down the floor nervously.

"Look here, man," he broke out at last, "you ain't lying to us to make an effect for yourself?"

I shrugged my shoulders.

"I've told you the truth," said I. "You know that

Holles is not an easy man to handle. But if the time comes that he has to fight against you in Dorking Hollow, then God help you if you have the murder or the torture of me on your heads in addition to what you've done already against him!"

"It's a lie!" cried Minnerode. "He's scared mostly to death, and he's trying to back us out of our chance at him! What difference does it make? Don't we know that Holles hates all of us, and that he'll do for us all, if he can?"

"Aye, aye, we know that!" said the others in hearty chorus. "What difference does it make what more we do agin' him?"

"This difference," I told them, my nerves getting a little steadier as I saw that there was at least a ghost of a chance of talking them out of their devilish purpose against me. "This difference—that now he's simply coming back to drive you out of Dorking Hollow. But if he finds that you've consented to torturing me, he'll not stop with Dorking Hollow, but he'll trail you across the world. You know Holles, and you know what he can do on the trail—and when he finds his quarry. Now, think for yourselves!"

It made a great impression upon them. There could be no doubt of that. They stared at me and then looked anxiously at one another. I, staring back at them, thought that I had never before seen such a formidable collection of warriors, not even the hand-picked men who had been assembled by Holles for his posse work. And yet all these heroes were frightened almost to death because of one slender youth who was now a sick man among the hills!

To me, who had never been a great fighter, Holles seemed a wonderful warrior. But the impression which

223

he made upon me was nothing at all compared with the impression which he made upon these ruffians. To them he was a miracle—a bolt right out of the blue.

"Wait a minute," said Minnerode, seeing that his fiendish opportunity was likely to slip through his hands, "how do we know that Mex is so set on this gent? Loomis ain't any brother to Mex, so far as I know!"

But another said instantly: "It was Loomis that caught Mex, and then give him a second chance for his life. It was Loomis that backed Mex up in town. It was Loomis, too, that persuaded Mex to leave the shack and go away from McGregor. We all know that. It sort of shows that he's got a pretty strong hold over Holles!"

"Hold on," put in McGregor. "I never was gunna let you go through with this thing, Minnerode. But I figured that maybe we could bluff Loomis out. Since we can't do that, we'll talk to him in another way. Boys, gimme another chance at him, will you? Scatter out of here, and take him along and jail him. In the morning I'll have another talk with him."

Jail?

I wondered dimly what sort of a place they had as a jail. But my wonder was not very strong. I was sick and faint with relief, because I had passed through the most horrible peril that ever confronted me.

CHAPTER THIRTY-SEVEN

AS I HAD HOPED, they had used the building that Mex himself had used as a jail. It was no more formidable as a lockup than it had been in those days when we trusted not to the strength of the wood of which it was made but

224

to the vigilance with which we guarded the prisoners. That being the case, I hoped devoutly that I might have some sort of a chance to get away.

But that chance vanished at once.

Minnerode himself, whose hatred of me seemed to be increased by my escape from the torment earlier in the night, now mounted guard with three companions. And all the night they watched me. There were no other prisoners in the place, and therefore their attention was given entirely to me.

What troubled Minnerode most, apparently, was not so much my present safety as the fear lest I should consider my security for the moment as a guarantee for the future; and half a dozen times during the night he wakened me out of a sound sleep to ask me if I knew that I'd hang the next day.

"Let me hang, then," I cried out impatiently at last. "I shall hang if I have to. Why trouble me about that now?"

"Because I know the kind of a gent you are," said Minnerode. "I know that you got a soul, and that you spend a lot of time worrying about it, and taking care of it, and I figgered that maybe you would want to stay awake all night so's to confess your sins and ask God to pardon you. But I forgot. You ain't got no sins, so you don't have to ask no pardon!"

At that I said to him: "You're a cruel devil, Minnerode. But you can't bother me now."

And I would turn my back on him and fall asleep again. For I had been thoroughly exhausted by all the trials and nerve strains leading up to the final delivery of Mex from the shack, and above all by the care of him after we left the place of the poisoner. However, again and yet again Minnerode would come to waken me and

225

tell me that I was an hour or so nearer to hanging by the neck and kicking the thin air. I submitted to this because I could do nothing else, but as a matter of fact fatigue had reached such a point that I was numb to fear, and I wakened the next morning only half rested.

I had finished any breakfast and was filling a pipe when a soft footfall made me look up, and there I saw the Indian doctor. I though it was his ghost, at first, but then I was aware of a broad, thick bandage encircling his head. He stared in at me, and made not a sign of a word or a glance to betoken that I was other than a lifeless curiosity in a glass case, so far as he was concerned. But I knew very well that he had come to satisfy his malice.

I called out suddenly to Minnerode, who was sitting sleepily in a corner, but still fighting off sleep until the next guard came on: "Minnerode, did this fellow cook my breakfast?"

I pointed at the Indian, a sort of deadly qualm coming over me at once, but Minnerode shook his head with a growl. The Indian, it seemed, had had nothing to do with my rations.

And then, after a moment, I breathed more easily. If big McGregor desired my death, it would be too simple for him to use the engine of the camp law to get me out of the way. He would not have to waste time and trouble to get me out of the way with secret poison.

Just before noon there was a rushing of hoofs through the street, a triumphant clamor, and then into the jail came none other than Avery Lucas, closely guarded, McGregor and others in attendance. McGregor was hugely triumphant.

"You see," he cried gleefully, "I run you gents down at last. It may take me a little time, but in the finish, I always get you. You're in the hollow of my hand, Loomis. You understand me? And when you realize it yourself and want to talk to me, I'll be ready to talk back. Only, your time is short. You have your mind made up by noon."

I understood what he meant, of course.

He gave me till noon to decide whether I preferred to live and tell the whereabouts of Holles, or to die this same day. However, after Lucas was left in the cell next to mine, I went over to the bars and questioned him eagerly.

He took his capture and his imprisonment as calmly as he took all things. That man had no excess of nerves to worry him. He was as methodical and lethargic as a machine. And now he settled down to a pipe and, lifting his head, he regarded the roof with a mild criticism.

"When we built that jail, we certainly roughed in the roof, Loomis."

I glanced upward, also, at the gaping cracks. Then I said half angrily: "That's not what I want to hear from you!"

"There's time," said he. "You want to know how they caught me."

"I want to know how you got away."

"By using my legs as I never used them before," said he. "I managed to get clear of them, and when I'd come clear, I ducked into the brush and remained there for almost two hours. They almost walked in my face as they hunted for me, but luck helped me out. And finally I had a chance to get clean away from them. I drifted off up the hill and found Cliff Burgess camping out for the night in his little mine. He has that big raw vein exposed, you know, and if he didn't guard the hole, the thugs would be there in no time to spoon the stuff out."

227

"You talked to Burgess?" I gasped, full of eagerness.

He puffed at his pipe and then nodded.

"Good! Good!" said I. "Then we still have some ghost of a chance, old fellow?"

"A ghost of a chance? I don't know! Perhaps so! But only a ghost! Only a ghost! Well, I talked to Burgess, and he was interested. Oh, yes, very interested! He agreed that if Mex came back in strength and health, something might be done under his leadership. Burgess swore that he would make a member of the posse to fight against these thugs who have control now. Then I left Burgess, after he'd suggested two or three of his friends to whom he'd give the good news. He went one way, and I went another. I think I saw about a dozen men before the morning came, and I gave them all the message, and most of them declared that they had two or three friends that they could ask in, and all swore that they would keep the thing a dead secret. So that, on the whole, I think we could fairly count on more than the fifty men you seemed to think would be our limit against McGregor."

"And now that you planned that out, what signal did you hit on?"

"I couldn't hit on a better signal than the one that I'd agreed upon with you. Some of the boys thought that it would be rather foolish to burn a house in the middle of the town, but I told them when the crowd comes together to watch the flames there'll be a natural reason furnished for our men to be there; and if those men draw together and make ready to fight their way through the game—as young Holles may choose—then it will be a simple matter for them to form up and deal their first blow in the most telling fashion. Who has Holles' horse?" Lucas added suddenly.

228

I wondered why he asked such a question, and he said he thought that if Holles could have that horse he would be three times as formidable, because he was still more than half an invalid, and Lou, the white mare, carried him without friction. He said that he had hunted for her, and while he was hunting he had been seen by one of McGregor's scouts, pursued, run down, and captured.

"I didn't fight back," said Lucas simply. "I knew that I didn't have a chance against them. Besides, I had done almost enough for the plot. But, Loomis, tell me, how will the signal be given?"

That was the crucial point. Lucas had gone up and down the length of the valley and had invited all the good and true men of Dorking Hollow to respond day or night to a signal which would be the burning of the Lucas shack. But who was to take the responsibility? To whom would young Holles reveal himself? If to the right man, then he would learn of the plot which we had been making as a frame for his arrival.

But, as Lucas said, the main thing was now not the plot, but how we should keep our own precious lives until the next two or three days had elapsed? How long would the fears and the patience of McGregor balance one against the other? How long would it be before that patience snapped short and he ordered our execution?

I agreed with him on this, of course, and all that day we waited with a growing tension for the coming of big Mc Gregor.

To our utter amazement, he neither came nor sent for us; but in the middle of the afternoon, Minnerode, out of his undying malice, gave us the clew to the secret.

He leaned against the bars of my cell and snarled at me: "D'you think that Johnnie has forgot you? No, he's just warming himself up with booze. Though why the

229

snaking-in of two swine like the pair of you should make any gent want to celebrate, let alone a he-man like big McGregor—"

When I had a chance I murmured to Lucas: "Did you hear?"

"Aye," he nodded. "Perhaps McGregor feels that now that he has scooped us both into his net, he's killed the head of the enterprise against him. And perhaps he will take more time, now. Do you think that?"

I hardly dared to think so! If only he would take a day or two longer, then surely young Holles would come down to find out what had become of me when I started scouting to Dorking Hollow. He would come, and he would not come in vain!

So I thought. I cannot tell you how implicit was my faith in that slender, dark-eyed youngster!

At any rate, the important matter for us was that all that vital day passed without the coming of McGregor to an inquisition, though every time the door of the jail creaked on its rusty hinges, we assured ourselves that this must be McGregor, or a messenger from him, at the least.

But that dragging day passed. The windows turned black, and then held the thin yellow image of the single lantern which burned inside the cell. And still no word from McGregor.

We heard the rattling of pans in the prison kitchen, and knew that supper was being prepared; and then, softly above us, we heard a voice saying: "Loomis! Loomis! Look up!"

Spirits?

No, not a ghost. It was the voice of Holles!

CHAPTER THIRTY-EIGHT

WHEN I LOOKED UP, I could see nothing above me except the shadows.

But the voice said again: "Loomis, it's Mex! Do you recognize me?"

"Not so loud, for the Lord's sake," said I.

No, no, too late!

There was a harsh snarl from the corner, and Minnerode rushed to the door of my cell.

"Are you going batty?" he demanded. "What d'you mean by talkin' to the air like this?"

I felt my face turn cold as the blood left it. The rescue had come so close—so close! And now it was beaten back from us! For a single wild instant I wondered if that young worker of miracles would not shoot down Minnerode through a crack in the roof such as the one through which he was speaking, and then tear the roof itself asunder to get us out. But no, that was madness to hope!

I glanced aside to Lucas. He was as white as I, no doubt. I have never seen a sicker or more despairing face.

Minnerode bellowed: "Will you answer me? What're you lookin' at Lucas for? Does he know the answer, too? I ain't gunna have the pair of you foxes kenneled here side by side! No, damn you, I'll have you apart— hello!"

He whirled about, his ready pair of revolvers leaping into his hands. For the door of the jail had been dashed open.

Holles! Holles dashing in to rescue us despite the

perils on the way! So cried my heart, when it heard the sudden screech of that heavy door swinging back.

No, it was, instead, the least—welcome form in the world. It was great Johnnie McGregor, a little uncertain in his footing, but otherwise steady enough, and apparently rapidly being sobered by the force of some recent shock.

We learned the nature of that shock at once, for he bellowed: "Minnerode!"

"Well, Johnnie? All's well here!"

"You lie!" roared McGregor. "There ain't nothing well no place! Hell's loose!"

"My God," cried Minnerode. "You mean, you mean—"

"I mean Holles, yes!"

"He aint' come in to—"

"He's come to raise hell, of course."

While they talked, half paralyzed with fear, I saw that my last small chance was given to me of sending the vital message to Holles. If that tigercat were still on the roof of the jail, peering down at us, hungering with all his heart for a chance to drive a bullet right down through the heart of McGregor—

No, he would not do that, for all responsible legend declared that Holles had never fired at a man who could not see his face fairly.

I took a letter from my pocket, and spread it out. It was a big sheet, unfolded to the full. Then I took from my pocket a carpenter's pencil with a great, broad, soft lead and I swiftly printed on the paper in huge characters:

SIGNAL IS BURNING OF LUCAS
SHACK. QUICK!!!!

I risked a little precious time to throw in that final word and the few exclamation points. It had to stand for a long message which I could not write. It had to stand for some such message as this: "If you will burn the shack of Lucas, in the crowd that assembles, there will be a number of men pledged to fight at your back, no matter where you may decide to lead them."

But there was not room on the paper to send any such message. Even as it was, I felt that the letters were far too small and the lines not thick and black enough to be read by the dim lantern light and from the distance of the roof.

Swiftly, then, I went over the words once more, rubbing the lines a treble thickness and blackness with my carpenter's pencil. The lead was worn short. I could not wait to sharpen it with a knife, but simply tore the shell of wood away with my teeth and worked on. How long before they would notice what I was doing?

And all the while I worked, I could hear their voices calling loudly to one another: "You ain't really seen him, old-timer?" Minnerode had been saying, his accents thick with fear.

Ah, how they all dreaded that thunderbolt—that Holles!

"His white mare was seen. I tell you, man, she was seen!"

"Ah," cried Minnerode, "but wait a minute! She might be with—"

"You mean that somebody else might be riding her? Why, man, did you ever see anybody ride her? Did you see Sam Purchass when he tried to ride her?"

"Aye, I seen him pretty near broke in bits! But was there anybody on her back tonight?"

"I'll tell you all that I know—what's the matter with

Loomis? Is the fool losin' his wits and started to writin' on the floor?"

My heart stopped.

No, they were too occupied with their own affairs, and rushed on with the tale, after that glance at me and my strange occupation.

"I know that there was danger that way. The mare was a trap. I figgered that Holles would aim for her. And you know I kept that pair of Texas outlaws down there to guard the place."

"I know. I know. They dodged Salt Creek by coming out here, that bunch."

"They were handy with their gats. I gave them plenty of money. I knew that they'd stick on the job. They called me their second father, seemed ready to die for me, and swore that they'd let nobody ever get to the mare."

"Go on! What in—"

"Well, they *did* die for me. They was found dead beside that corral. And the white mare was gone!"

"Dead? Dead?" said Minnerode, throwing a sudden glance over his shoulder.

"Aye, I mean just that."

"Shot?"

"Knifed. The pair of them. Knifed so quick and smart that neither of them had so much as a good chance to yell out. And the mare was gone. Does that look like the work of Holles or of some other devil?"

"It's Mex!" said the other hollowly. "It's Mex, and no mistake! Lord forgive us for fools if he's got back inside of this here town, McGregor!"

"Don't talk through your hat. This here town is my town, Minnerode. And you and me alone would be enough to meet and beat that kid. Why, he's just got the boys buffaloed with a few sleight-of-hand tricks."

I was finishing the last of my message. I moved it now where the light would fall more clearly upon it, closer to the bars of my little cell, and as I did so, I smiled a little to myself, grimly. For what an absurdity this was, this blankly boastful speech of great Johnnie McGregor, that Holles had charmed the ruffians of that town into fear of him through a few sleight-of-hand tricks! He and Minnerode would face the young destroyer alone? No, no! Not half a dozen like them could turn the trick. Their hearts were already beating at fever speed at the mere thought of encountering Mex. Their hands would be trembling and weak. A mere child could have beaten them with the guns when they were in such condition.

"What's that fool Loomis got there? Go out the back way and see if there's any one hanging around there, will you old fellow? And call Chuck and Les Hanson— hey, Loomis, what's that?"

I had displayed my message as long as I dared. Now I must destroy it if I could before it was read. I crumpled the paper.

"Nothing but an old letter, McGregor," said I, truthfully enough.

"Lemme see that old letter," said he.

"No," said I, "I want to make a torch out of it to see if—"

"Loomis, gimme that—"

I had already lighted a match and touched it to a corner of the paper.

"Drop that!" shouted McGregor. "Put out that fire— it's a message, Minnerode!"

I did not drop it, but I held the paper upside down so that the flame would catch more quickly; and at the same instant there was the crash of a gun, and a bullet sang just past my face. I dropped the paper then and leaped back, fearful for my life.

McGregor did not pause to unlock the door of the cell. He simply laid his incredible hands on the bars, and' plucked them away as you or I might pluck away dead reeds.

He gave his shoulder to a third bar and smashed it in, then leaped into the cell and stamped out the fire which was burning the half-consumed paper.

After that, with a grim look at me, he picked the paper up and spread it out.

" 'We were glad to learn that you've built yourself a new house,' " he read aloud, " 'and that you've decided to board the floor. I should think that you would have to do that to keep out the damps. And when I speak of damps, dear Paul, I do hope that you are keeping to warm woolen underwear, because otherwise rheumatism and'—why, what's this bunk?" roared the giant.

I merely smiled at him, though the smile was rather faint.

"It was just a personal letter, McGregor," said I. "I didn't want you to read it because the old woman who wrote it was—"

"Bah!" he snarled. "You're a sneak. There's nothing but trouble comes out of you. But I got my eye on you now, Loomis!"

I held out my hand for the letter, but his temper was up and raging as high as his fears. He crumbled the letter and threw it on the floor at my feet.

My heart beat more freely again. I leaned to pick up the letter and as I did so, I heard the devil that lived in the wits of big Minnerode and inspired him cry out: "There was something wrote on the other side of that paper. What was it, McGregor?"

236

CHAPTER THIRTY-NINE

NO, STILL NOT SAVED, still far, far from saved! With a thrust of his hand, McGregor sent me staggering back against the wall of my cell. There I stood miserably, wondering what would happen to me if the truth could be guessed. What remained of the message? Surely the fire had consumed part of the words. What part? Perhaps all of them.

Signal is burning of Lucas shack. Quick!!!!

Signal for what? To whom? Surely, even if they had the message intact, they would not be able to make head or tail of it, and in the meantime, precious seconds were slipping past.

If Holles had seen the message and made it out even dimly, surely he would do what it suggested.

If only he could get to the shack of Lucas to set it on fire. But how could he do that? The whole town had been alarmed. I could hear horses pouring up and down the street outside. I could hear many voices and shouts. There were even a few shots in the distance—no doubt they were simply the guns of high-spirited youngsters who were delighted to turn out for this occasion.

No, McGregor had started his muster at the first alarm. His portion of the men of Dorking Hollow would be ready for trouble if any came!

And yet Holles—who could tell? That youngster was capable of great and strange things. There was no telling what was the limit of his cleverness. Where another man would simply throw up his hands and despair, Holles would probably be devising cunning schemes. He had done so before. And perhaps in spite of the throng he would be able to make his way to the shack of Lucas

237

and by kindling it bring the mob about it.

Aye, but that done, how would he know whom to rally? How dare he then to show himself to the crowd in order to gather the right men about him! I reached that point of my despairing reflection, and then my thoughts were called back from Holles and the possible action of which he might be capable to my own predicament, which was none too simple.

The men had spread the paper out, and Minnerode, standing at the shoulder of the giant, spelled out the words: "Of Lucas shack. Quick."

I thanked God again! This, at least, could tell them nothing.

"The Lucas shack? The Lucas shack?" they repeated, staring at one another.

Then McGregor whirled on me.

"What does it mean?" he roared.

I was simply dumb. Explanation was not possible.

"Scared to death," said Minnerode, striding up to me, "but still poisonous. He's been usin' his wits. These lawyers have always got their wits working, damn them! Look at him shaking! McGregor, I tell you that this is something important. I thought he was crazy, too, before you come in!"

"Go on!" said McGregor, scowling and fingering the butt of a Colt impatiently. "What made you think that?"

"I seen him with his head cocked back, talkin' to the ceiling."

"To the ceiling?" echoed McGregor, bending back his head and staring upward. "Now what the devil could he have in mind by doing that?"

"Batty, I guess."

"Batty? No! He meant something. But what?"

He spread out the paper again and stared at the

writing.

"What made him make the letters so big and black, Minnerode?"

"Lord knows, old-timer, unless he *is* turned kind of crazy!"

"Stop talking crazy. It ain't sense to talk that way. He had a meaning. You guessed that yourself. But what could it be? By gum, I'd give a good deal to know what the meaning of that writing is."

"Aye, or of what has been burned away," said Minnerode.

McGregor started a little.

"Sure," said he, "and like a fool, I hadn't thought of that. But look here, Minnerode!"

"Aye?"

I had to stand by, watching their fear-sharpened brains fumble at my little riddle!

"Minnerode, it's done like a telegram, sort of. 'Of Lucas shack. Quick!!!!' Look at those exclamation points! He wants something done, and he wants it done in a hurry. Something that has to do with the shack of Lucas—that skunk in the other cell here at our hand."

"Aye, that's true enough."

"What could it be?"

"Lord knows. It makes my head kind of spin around to try to think it out, even."

McGregor groaned with impatience and beat a hand against his forehead. "It says: 'Quick!' And something's happening, while we stand here and wonder what it is. The lightning is getting ready to strike us, while we try to work out that riddle!"

"The lightning would be Holles."

"Aye, any fool can see that!"

"I dunno, old-timer!"

"Then leave me alone to do the thinking. Don't talk. Wait a minute. He was talkin' to the roof?"

"Yes."

"And then—"

"I bellered at him. Then you come busting in—"

"And he began to write on this here paper."

"Yes, that's true."

"Why, man, he was talking to somebody that was on the roof."

"Hey, that ain't reasonable!"

"We ain't talking about reason. We're talkin' about Holles."

"Aye, there's a difference there!"

"There is, and a grand one, at that."

"But who could have been on the roof. Holles himself?"

"Lord knows!"

They looked up in horror at the high ceiling, until McGregor, with a shudder, said: "No, he would shoot us through a crack like that. He's promising himself the pleasure of letting me see him stand in front of me, his two guns working on me. Damn him, but I'll beat him yet! One man can't beat Dorking Hollow!"

"No, nor the tenth part of Dorking Hollow," said the other, but jumped violently as a door slammed. "What was that?" they gasped.

"Nothing! The wind!" said McGregor, recovering himself more quickly than his companion. "But I say, this here bunch of words was just a part of a message that was sent off by this Loomis to somebody. Look here! Why would these letters be made so big—and so black—except that somebody at a distance was to read 'em? How big a distance? Well, what's the distance from here to a fellow on the roof?"

And suddenly he shouted. "Minnerode! Get outside! Guard the roof! He's there, I tell you! He's on the roof! Holles! That devil Holles himself is up there!"

It made my blood curdle, and it took my breath. They had got to the bottom of my secret. They had got there with dizzying speed. And yet, when I look back over the thing, I hardly see how they could have reasoned it out so well. Neither of them was a peculiarly brilliant man, as you have seen. But I suppose that fear had supplied their wits on this occasion.

I saw Minnerode flash one white-faced look of venom at me as he turned toward the door.

"McGregor, we'll not leave this skunk living behind us, will we?"

"No, no, damn him! We'll—"

"I'll finish him for you!"

The gun had glittered in the hand of Minnerode. At the same instant, as I saw that I was about to be murdered, my body turned limp. I pitched for the floor as the shot rang, and I heard the hiss of the bullet tearing past my head. The second bullet that had missed me by an inch or two in the last few minutes!

"Go on!" shouted McGregor.

"He was falling before my gun was out!" barked the other.

"You fool, I seen the bullet dust him before and behind! Go on! Have we got so much time on our hands?"

They charged for the rear of the jail, their feet thundering over the floor, while I lay still and dazed, unheeding the low-voiced cry of Lucas: "Loomis! Loomis! Oh, he's dead! He's dead!"

I remember that I felt a great wonder as I lay there. Not wonder that my life had been spared so narrowly, but wonder that Lucas should feel such actual emotion about my fall, for he was as cold-blooded a fellow as ever lived, I assure you!

And then, from the door of the jail, I heard a wild cry from the throat of McGregor: "Look, Minnerode! Look! Where's that fire?"

"I think—why, down the hill."

"Is it Chalmer's house?"

"No, Chalmer's house has the tall poplars right behind it."

"Then it's the Lucas shack!"

"By heaven, I think it is!"

"The message, Minnerode, the message—'the Lucas shack. Quick!' That fire has something to do with it! Minnerode, it's a signal, and these clever devils have tricked us and beaten us!"

"Ten thousand damnations!" groaned Minnerode. "McGregor, let's climb on to our horses and ride for it!"

"Wait—wait!" cried McGregor, steadying himself a little. "Not yet. Look at those men! They're all mine! They're all mine. Every man jack of them. Leave Dorking Hollow? Leave all these fine fellows that are ready to fight for me and die for me? No, by heaven, but I'll stay here and fight it out at their sides! If Holles finds me, he'll never live to tell about it tomorrow! Minnerode, here, come on with me!"

"I will," shouted Minnerode, "and you're right! We'll smash them right off the face of the earth!"

They cheered together. Other voices from the street answered them, and then from outside the jail, I could hear the thundering accents of big Johnnie McGregor as he rallied his chosen men about him and urged them forward at full gallop for the shack of Lucas.

I ventured to raise my head. Lucas cried out joyously.

And then my eyes followed the direction of his hand, and beyond the door of the jail, far off down the hollow, I saw the narrow, rising plume of a fire which waved like a magic hand, disappeared, and sprang up again greater than ever.

CHAPTER FORTY

I HAVE TO TAKE YOU FROM THE JAIL where I had spent some of the grimmest and wildest moments of my life and carry you away to things that had been happening elsewhere before and after those moments. I have the history from the, most unimpeachable onlookers, or from the chief performer himself. Go back with me, then, to the time when I left young Holles to embark on my almost fatal scouting trip to Dorking Hollow.

He waited for me through that night. I don't mean to say that he remained awake, for he didn't; he was sound asleep on his bed of evergreen boughs five minutes after I left, and he didn't open his eyes again until the morning light was glimmering through the cave.

Then, wakening, he called out: "Hey, Loomis, is it time for breakfast?" For his appetite was raging, as the appetites of most convalescents are.

Then he looked around him and saw that I was not in the cave, and in a moment he remembered that I had gone off on the scouting expedition the day before. It was barely possible that I might have slept in the cave, having returned long before from my hunting expedition, and that I had just gone out rabbit hunting. He felt my own pile of boughs. It was damp and cold. No sign of warmth in it.

Then, again it was possible that I was even now

returning for the dawn was still pink in the sky. He waited in the mouth of the cave for my return. I did not come. Patient as an Indian he watched until the sun stood in the center of the sky.

Then he decided that I had met foul play of some kind and he swore to himself that he would rescue me, if I were still alive, or failing, die in the attempt.

And what did he do? Draw up his belt, seize weapons, and start after me toward the Hollow?

No, no!

He first snared a rabbit, deliberately roasted the flesh, ate, and then lay down and slept for an entire hour. After that, he wakened and felt that almost his full strength had returned to him. Now he looked to his guns, saw to the edge of his big knife—a favorite tool with him, it seemed—and finally, he stood in the entrance to the cave prepared to leave, with the sun turning crimson in the lower western sky.

He then started rapidly through the woods, with a strange sense of lightness and of power in his body and in his limbs. The last vestige of the poison was now either out of his system or else assimilated by it, and he strode along rejoicing in his old self, now restored to him.

He felt some gratitude, as he went, to me. For he knew that without my clumsy help he would have died under the hands of the Indian doctor and McGregor. But now that was behind him. He was well, he had almost his full power in his hands again, and he was armed as he desired to be armed, except that he had no rifle.

However, for night work and quick hand-to-hand fighting, revolver practice would probably be more to his liking.

So, with the sun still half up above the western

244

horizon, he gained the hills which overlooked the Hollow, and to make sure of what lay before him, he climbed a two-hundred-foot pine to the top, and hung there, panting in the swaying tip of the giant tree while he looked down to Dorking Hollow in the dying light of day.

He saw the black streak, dappled with the white of ashes which had not yet blown away, and he knew then that one half of Dorking Hollow had been eaten up by flame.

Rage took him by the throat as he saw that. For it was now his town. Dorking Hollow he looked upon as a child would look, say, upon a favorite doll's house. It was his possession, because he had rescued it from ruin and given it secure prosperity once more.

Now all his labors had been undone, and he blessed himself that he had been permitted to come back and resume those labors where he had left off. They should hear of him, and that before the morning, he vowed as he hung there in the top of the tree, looking down upon the hollow in the fainting light of the sunset.

Where should he begin? That he had not the slightest way of guessing! But while he stared across the village, he saw one thing that caught his hawk eye instantly, and that was a glint of white behind a barn. Yes, a flash as of silver—a horse!

He knew even at that distance that it was his famous mare. And he vowed that he would begin with her. So, as the evening shadows gathered to a little more secure depth, he slipped across the edge of the hill and came down into Dorking Hollow.

Often I have smiled rather fiercely to myself, imagining how Arthur Holles came out of the forest and descended upon Dorking Hollow, not like a frightened fugitive, but like a prowling man-eater, secure in his own powers, and merely hunting for prey. I can see him, in my mind's eye, pausing from time to time, and looking swiftly first to one side, and then to the other, and swinging forward, once more, with a swift, soft, panther-like stride!

Ah, if the rough and bold men of Dorking Hollow could have guessed at that shadowy destroyer coming down upon them, softly, secretly, but more terrible than the mountain avalanche, more sudden and more deadly!

They could not guess. And down he came, not crawling miserably from brush to brush as I had done, but walking boldly along. He can afford to be bold whose footfall makes no sound. And so it was with Holles.

He skirted the edge of the town, and then he turned in behind the corral in which he had seen the white mare. Lying in the edge of a thicket, he looked forth upon her. He could see her, a faintly glimmering form through the twilight. And then he could make out the forms of two men walking up and down near the fence. And finally, he heard them break into a rollicking melody that swung richly through the night.

Poor devils! They were a wicked—enough pair, as I had heard big McGregor himself say, and he should have known. And yet it was dreadful to think that their singing should have furnished the noise under cover of which stark death slid down behind them.

Not creeping upon his hands and knees, but striding lightly though boldly came Holles.

"Friend!" called one of the guards, seeing the stranger approach, and instantly went on with his singing.

Another stride and Holles was close enough.

"Guard yourselves!" he called to them, and leaped.

I close my eyes when I come to this point in my thoughts. But after all, the hand of Holles was not my hand, and why should I shudder, knowing that he struck in a good cause that evening?

Twice that dreadful, subtle knife flashed. And two death cries were choked with death itself. Two men lay dead beside the corral, while Holles, crouching close to the bars, wiped his blade on the grass and called softly to his mare.

She came with a whinny of delight. He fondled her for an instant; then glided into the shed, found the saddle and bridle which were his, thrust into the rifle holster a Winchester which he found leaning against the wall—arms of all kinds were as common as the dirt underfoot in Dorking Hollow—and so equipped, he went back to the corral, saddled the mare, and, throwing off the top bar, jumped her across the rest.

He would have had her into the brush and safe among the shadows, where she knew how to move as secretly as a serpent—or the mysterious elephant—but the mare was wild with joy and insisted on bucking and snorting and playing tricks to welcome back her master. And as she bucked and danced, Holles heard an exclamation from the side, and knew that he had been seen.

He ducked the mare into covert promptly enough at that, and hoped that his appearance would be laid down to the passing of a ghost. But he was a little nervous and very depressed by this happening. He felt guilty, too, in that he had first of all looked to the welfare and the secure possession of his mare instead of going directly upon the trail of his companion who had been lost in the Hollow. So he remained for a moment in the brush, gritting his teeth impatiently. Finally, he lodged the mare in a very dense thicket, and started out to pick up

247

my trail, if he could.

Luck favored him most miraculously. Or, perhaps, it was not so very miraculous after all, since most of the men of the Hollow would naturally be talking on this evening, of the double capture of King Log and Loomis. At any rate, as Holles came out of the brush, he heard a by-passer say to another some word about Loomis and the jail.

That was enough. Fast as running quicksilver, Holles glided through the town, crossing the narrow street in a spot of dense darkness, and so coming up to the jail, where guards marched or stood within or without!

The cellar? There was no cellar to try! There remained the roof, and in ten seconds he had slipped through the slowly pacing sentinel line and was perched on the top of the jail.

You know somewhat of the things that followed. Of how he spoke to me as soon as he saw me, with Lucas in the cell next to mine; and of how I looked up and started to answer when Minnerode broke in so rudely.

Then, lying anxiously on the roof of the jail, he watched through a conveniently large crack all that followed, saw the arrival of big McGregor, heard the words between him and Minnerode. And all the while, as he lay there, he heard the forces of McGregor mustering up and down the Hollow.

I think of the iron nerve of that youngster as he lay there on the jail roof, with enemies gathering thick as flies around him—no, thick as wasps, and ever wasp capable of a mortal sting! But there he remained, until he saw beneath him that I was writing large on a piece of paper—knew at once that it must be a message for him, and strained his eyes with despair to make out the writing.

Not one syllable could he make out before I retraced and reblackened all the letters. But then he read, and instantly he knew that he must fire the Lucas shack. What would that signal mean? Well, on such a night as this, it was almost too dangerous to think very far ahead!

CHAPTER FORTY-ONE

FOLLOW HIM, THEN, AS HE SLIDES DOWN to the edge of the roof and supports himself there, watching. People swarm beneath him. But it is not a long drop, and when no one is immediately beneath, he drops suddenly from the edge of the roof and walks away.

"Hello!" calls someone behind him. "Did that fellow jump up out of the ground?"

"Ask him," said another. "If he kin do that, maybe he's Holles, or some other devil!"

That apt remark only brought a greeting of laughter, and Holles hurried on, not anxious to draw any further comment. When he regained the shelter of the brush, he took the white mare farther down, until he was opposite the spot where the Lucas shack stood. Then he tethered the mare, and once more slipped forward.

His going was far more difficult now. He had no hat. The least gleam of light on his face would cause him to be recognized by the crowds that were surging up and down the street. And every window and door had a light in it, by this time.

Certainly no man could have stood in much greater peril. But Holles thought not of how he should go back, but merely of how he should go forward. It was not a question with him of what he should do, but simply of how he should do it.

Oh, gallant Arthur Holles! There have been better men, but never one so noble in action!

How did he cross that street, seething with people who had responded to the alarm sent out by McGregor. "Holles is loose! Holles is here!"

And every rascal in the crowd trembled. They would fight not so much for the sake of McGregor, their leader, as for the sake of their own skins! And every eye was alert, and every eye searched every face that passed, no doubt.

Yet Holles was among them, crossing that very road!

He picked a dark streak of shadow between two houses, and waited until a considerable group came past in a single cluster, he slipped out, joined them, worked through them deftly, and as they moved on, they left him behind in front of the house of Lucas.

He had reached the spot! And now to give the signal!

Back there in the jail, he knew that McGregor would be apt to tear a certain amount of critical information from me, and therefore he wanted to act quickly. But, as he mused inside the door of the Lucas shack, he wondered how he should possibly be able to tell friend from foe in the crowd that would rush to view the flames. Dorking Hollow was thoroughly afraid of fire since half of it had been wiped out in the last big conflagration, and there would undoubtedly be a fierce rush of men with buckets of water.

He must make sure that the flames should not only catch, but also gather such headway that nothing could put them out. Luckily, he found some oil in a two-gallon tin, and this he used to soak a corner of the shack. In the corner he dropped his lighted match, and then stepped outdoors by the back way to see what would happen in the exciting moments which were to follow.

He had barely reached the brush when the inside of the cabin was aglow. And, a moment later, the shout of *Fire!* went up and down the street.

A score of men charged on the shack; they were driven back from the doorway by a sheet of flame billowing in their faces. And now the fire gathered head with great speed, and began to show a wagging arm like a veritable human signal above the top of the roof.

All was going well, when with a rush and a bellowing of orders, down came big McGregor to the scene, with Minnerode behind him, bent on extinguishing the fire at once. Under the orders of McGregor, a bucket line was quickly formed, and steady streams of water were flung into the little house.

But it was not such easy work as might have been thought to put out the fire. On the side of the door and the windows, the fire rolled out and threw up such a vast wall of heat that the men in the bucket line dared not come close enough to fling in their water with any degree of accuracy. So on the other side, with axes, they broke open an entrance and through this poured in the water.

The minutes went rapidly. A rumor went through the crowd that there was treasure in this shack, for otherwise, McGregor surely would not be working so frantically to put the fire out.

However, he stopped as abruptly as he had begun, and, with a curse, he announced that the house could burn and be damned, for all of him. He rushed off through the crowd, bent on another purpose. Straight back toward the jail went McGregor, filled with haste.

But here I must break off to tell what had been happening in that jail. For, after I found myself left for

251

dead and with the way out of my cell opened to me, I would gladly have bolted for freedom, but of course I could not abandon poor Lucas. He had done a great deal for our cause. And now that the signal fire was burning in his own shack, how could I leave him behind?

We tried our united strength on the bars of his cell. Certainly those bars were no more securely nailed on than the ones which McGregor had peeled off the side of my cell with such ease. But between us, though we struggled desperately, we could not budge them. There was no time to cut through one of the bars and let Lucas try to slide out through the opening, and therefore we looked around for another means. One of the great splintered fragments which McGregor had left on the floor caught my eye, and catching that up I used it as a lever and threw my whole force into the work. I had the luck to budge one of the bars at the first strain. At the second, I pulled it loose at the bottom. Then Lucas took the lever inside his cell and tried it on the bottom on the next bar. This proved a harder fight, but finally we loosened the bar and now there was nothing to do except to pull the two bars out.

Even that was quite a task, and we were dizzy with labor and gasping for breath when at last Lucas stumbled out on to the floor of the jail, a free man!

No, not quite free, and even as he wrung my hand in gratitude, our eyes were darting toward the jail door. We would not be free, actually, until we were past that boundary line.

Like two boys out from school, we darted for that door to our prison, and we were at it when, against the distant flames of the Lucas house, we saw the giant body of McGregor rising suddenly and just before us!

He had come back, with the terrible Minnerode at his

252

shoulder. And I think that it was not fear which I felt so much at that moment as it was an agony of rage and despair that we should be stopped at the very gate of safety. I heard Lucas groan: "You've ruined yourself for me, Loomis!

I hardly heard that. In despair, I had hurled myself into the face of the giant and his leveled gun.

He did not fire. I still hear in my ears his scornful laugh as he met my charge with a wave of his hand. That light gesture met me and stopped and crushed me. I sank gasping to the floor, bruised and stunned. Minnerode already had his Colt stuck into the side of Lucas, profanely promising to blow his heart out if he didn't obey orders.

But Lucas was no man to play the fool. He simply stood with his hands raised obediently over his head and waited for what might come next. There are different kinds of courage. Sometimes I think that the passive type, such as Lucas had, is as lofty as the sort of heroism that walks on tight ropes, or charges in the battle line.

There was a vast satisfaction in McGregor, now that he had us.

"By heaven," he said to Minnerode, "this here Loomis has got as many lives as a cat! You only killed one of 'em, old-timer!"

"Lemme try him with the rest o' the bullets in these here gats," said Minnerode. "I'd like to test him out— but I told you that he started falling—before I shot at him. The coward begun to sink the minute that there was any danger looking him in the eye. And you said that you seen my bullet dust him before and behind!"

Meaning, of course, that the slug of lead had knocked the dust from me as it entered and as it left my body and my clothes.

"I must have dreamed it, then," said McGregor. "But no matter for that. The main thing is that he didn't die, and I'm glad of it!"

"Is that a joke?" snarled Minnerode.

"This is a fine time for joking, ain't it?" answered McGregor with most murderous violence. "Don't talk like a fool, man! No, but I say that now we'll put the screws on the pair of these gents, and we'll tear out of them the information that they got, if we have to tear 'em to pieces."

"Damn me," said Minnerode, with a grin, "you say that pretty near like a real man, Johnnie!"

"Stand up!" said McGregor, and without waiting he leaned and caught me by the hair of my head and jerked me to my feet. I felt as though my scalp had been ripped from my head. Minnerode burst into a huge laugh as he saw my grimace of pain.

"Now, you rat!" said McGregor, his hand working with a beastly fury as he threatened to take me by the throat and wring my neck, "I'm going to know what you know, and I'm going to know it pronto. Or else, I'll polish you off now, my son! Wait a minute, though. Lucas come in last! He would know a lot more than Loomis. No matter what they've got up their sleeves, Lucas is the most likely one of the two to pump. Give him to me!"

I'm ashamed with all my heart to say that I felt relief when the torturing hands of that monster threw me to one side and reached out for Lucas. The vast power that lay in the grip of McGregor had turned him into more brute than human. He laid hold upon the sturdy body of Lucas.

"Now, Lucas," he said, "whatever you know, come

254

out with it—and quick! I'm needed another place, and I've got no time to waste."

"Do you know where that other place is?" asked Lucas, perfectly calm.

"Where I'm needed? No!"

"In hell," said Lucas, and looked him in the eye.

McGregor lifted his great fist, but held it hung in the air, as though realizing that if he indulged his desire and struck this man, Lucas would be entirely incapable of speech forever.

"The rat's talkin' to me!" said the big man furiously.

"You're too late," said Lucas. "You're not too late to murder me, but you're too late to save your own hide. Listen!"

And as he spoke, there was a sudden clattering of rifle shots and an outbreak of excited voices from the direction of the still flaming shack of Lucas.

We knew that the battle had commenced. Heaven give it the right conclusion!

CHAPTER FORTY-TWO

I HAVE TO DODGE AWAY FROM THE JAIL and back to the main scene, where, as the flames rose rapidly from the little shack, and then the columns of smoke soared up when the water was flung into it, the crowd grew steadily more dense.

Many, under the shouted orders of big McGregor, had been struggling with the fire in the bucket lines; but after he disappeared all attempt to fight the fire had ended, and the mob did nothing but stand around and gloomily watch the fire and the rising smoke.

Then the roof fell in with a crash, and many a man in

255

that crowd started and looked sullenly from one face to another. In the meantime, to one side of the watchers a small group of men collected who were not distinguishable from the others. They had toiled just as hard as any to put out the fire, and they had obeyed the orders of McGregor as willingly. But now they drew back, and presently others joined them. The big form of Burgess was conspicuous in this assembly. And others began to come in, suddenly pushing their way through the rest of the bystanders and coming up to that body of which Burgess was the rallying point.

They looked hard at one another, staring each other full in the face, and then ranged themselves in a solid little phalanx. Some of these men were mine owners, and rich. Others were laborers in the mines or muleteers. But there was one peculiarity about them. They were all armed to the teeth, for whereas most of the men in the crowd carried revolvers only, these with Burgess were armed with rifles also. They kept silence. They did nothing to attract newcomers, and yet newcomers were constantly pressing into their ranks. Thirty, then forty men were gathered there, and others gradually drifted toward them. They could not help being noticed, after a time.

And Christy Munn suddenly rode up on a pinto and called out: "Burgess, what are you doing here? What are you doing with all these men?"

"Watching the fire," said Burgess calmly.

Christy Munn narrowed his eyes.

"I'll believe that," he said. "But I'll believe that you're here for something else, too. What is it?"

"Nothing," said Burgess.

Suddenly Christy dismounted and came close.

"Burgess, I guess at something. If you want me, I'm

256

with you!"

Want him? Why, there was not a more formidable man in Dorking Hollow, outside of McGregor and Holles. Burgess wrung his hand.

"Stand here with us."

"Well, I'll do that. Now what am I to expect?"

"God knows, Munn! All that any of us knows is that we've come here in answer to a signal. And something may happen, now, to tumble McGregor into the dirt."

Christy Munn whistled.

"That was the thing I guessed at, and that's the thing that I want," said he. "Murder ain't a line of business that I like, old-timer!"

"Christy, you'll never regret standing with us, I think," said Burgess.

And as he said it, there was a wild shout from some one, taken up and echoed with a veritable scream of fear by many others: "Mex! Holles is here! Holles!"

And then was seen the flash of a white horse; and there was Holles on the back of his mare, guiding her with knees and voice, his hands occupied entirely by a pair of Colts, his head bare, his long hair blowing in the night wind—a spectacle to daunt all who knew him!

He whirled through the crowd, and suddenly men heard him shouting: "Who's for the old order? Who's for me against McGregor? Sing out, boys! Sing out!"

They sang out lustily. In a deep-throated roar Burgess and his fellows called: "This way, Mex! This way! We're all for you!"

And that phalanx moved suddenly toward him.

"There's ten thousand for the man that drops Holles!" yelled an adherent of McGregor. "Are we all sleepin'!"

No, they were not sleeping. Guns flashed in every hand. Straight before Holles, death glittered against his

257

eyes; and Burgess told me afterward that he fired four times faster than a man could count, and four men were writhing on the roadway before him.

Other guns spoke in answer to his, for he made a prominent target on his horse. But the crowd was pouring this way and that. There was little chance for anything but a snap shot, and now the phalanx of those who stood for the old order charged ahead.

They asked no questions. They had their rifles at the ready, firing again and again.

There was a twisting and rushing in the crowd ahead of them. There was a volley of shots, shouts, screams and curses, and then the street was cleared, and the compact body surged ahead.

It had grown in size. Men dared not join it from in front, but many swung in on its rear—those who really wished well to the old order and who hated McGregor, and many others who saw in this bold, mysterious move a strength which would win. So they shifted readily to the winning side!

What had become of the desperadoes, the gun experts, the hired warriors of McGregor? They were not all beaten. They took refuge in houses here and there. And they opened a spitting fire with their guns as the crowd went by. But they had no organization behind them, and against them there was a well-knit unit.

Pete O'Rourke, bad man by profession, retreated with his cousin, Champ Smith, into the Smith shack, and fired from door and window. And though ordinarily they could have counted on checking any charge by this direct gunfire, they could not count on that now. A blast of rifle bullets combed through and through the shack. A blast of small bullets from shotguns drove the defendants from door and window and dropped Champ on the floor with a slug in his brain. Then the door was beaten in with gun butts. There was a swift tramping of many feet. A man screamed in fear and then groaned in agony, and that posse swept out into the street again and went on.

It had been resisted. It had put forth an arm, and in two seconds the work had been done. Two of its men lay behind in the dirt of the road, but they were unheeded. The blood of the crowd was up. I have heard men talk much about the hysteria of a crowd of rioters, but the anger of a crowd of rascals is literally nothing compared with the anger of a crowd of honest men, burning with just indignation and bent on a common cause.

Chiswick and young Boots Lafferty and Silent Jim Baynes, together with two unknown men, made a fortress of a shack a little farther up the street, but they were crushed with the same murderous discharge of buckshot that had driven the last pair of gunmen from window and door and loophole. And then the doors were beaten in, and five men died suddenly in that shambles.

That was the end of the fighting from house to house. The news went like magic ahead of them that this crowd meant business and could not be stopped. Its might grew. It had for a cutting edge Christy Munn and Mex. Mex and his white horse were the entering point of the wedge. Behind that entering point came a growing weight of numbers, for every weak-hearted man in the town now made up his mind that McGregor was beaten and threw in his lot with the winners. On they went until they came to Jackson's gaming house, and there they had to pause.

The place was bristling with capable defenders, the

hired gunmen of Jackson, quite capable of standing a siege from all the force of Dorking Hollow.

And Burgess told me that when he saw that place, and the closed doors and the lights all extinguished, his heart sank. For he saw the attack split and scattered on this rock. He saw McGregor, in the distance, gathering a relieving force of ruffians. He saw a counter attack sweep the forces of law and order into the creek and give Dorking Hollow to massacre and tyranny!

Then he heard Jackson calling from behind a darkened window: "Boys, you don't come in here! Pass on, and we ain't gunna harm you. But if you try to break in, we'll blow you to hell. We can do it, and we will do it!"

It made the crowd rumble with anger, but it made the crowd halt, and then the clear voice of Holles rang out: "Jackson! Jackson!"

"Who's that calling?" returned Jackson.

"Have you forgotten the grave you dug that other night?" called Holles. "Open that front door in thirty seconds, or you'll have to dig another grave tonight, and this time it'll be for yourself!"

The crowd waited, and heard voices of anguish and wrath raised inside the gambling hall, then: "Holles! What terms would you make with me?"

"No terms!" said Holles. "No terms, except life, and that's all. What terms do you expect us to give to rats?"

He added: "You have ten seconds left."

There was a despairing cry from Jackson, as he saw his months of corruption and labor in Dorking Hollow swept away by the swift, dark rising of this tide of vengeance; but in another moment the front door of the gaming house faltered and then swung slowly open. The mere voice of Holles had had the strength to open for the crowd its most dangerous nest of enemies.

Into the gaming hall went the arm of vengeance. There was a brief scene of wreckage, but not a drop of blood was spilled; for, as the men streamed in, Holles at the door was giving caution: "I'll see the man that uses a gun in this place! No killing! No killing!"

And no killing there was, for, much as they loved their vengeance, they dreaded Mex more than they loved revenge.

And he pushed on with his gathered men behind him, a hundred and fifty strong by this time; nearly all with rifles, so maddened with confidence in themselves and in the magic of their leader that they would have stormed a rock wall if Holles had given them the signal!

Up the street, now, in a swift tide; some of the more joyously energetic rushing even ahead of Holles, until a word from him turned them back!

And from a window of that jail, four men were watching—two of them were helpless prisoners, and the other two were Minnerode and the great McGregor himself! And we saw, all four of us, the dark front of that crowd, streaked with the glistening barrels of rifles, and in the van, the silver form of the beautiful mare, with her wild rider on her back!

Ah, what a picture that was! How it burned into my brain then, and how it leaps out in my thought now!

Why did not great McGregor rush out of the jail when he first heard the guns and the babble of the distant voices at the Lucas house?

I often ask myself that. Often I have talked the matter over with Lucas. Lucas, calm and intelligent man that he is, vows always that there was a mysterious magic in the thing, and that Heaven had a hand in it. For, if

261

McGregor had entered the fight at the right moment—if he had come up, for instance, in time to meet the forces of honesty as they reached the gaming house of Jackson—Dorking Hollow would never have been won back to law and order.

He and Minnerode seemed about to leave the jail at once. Minnerode caught me by the back of the neck and whirled his revolver up to dash my brains out with the butt of it, when McGregor reached out and knocked his descending arm away.

"Don't do it, Minnerode!" said he, in a broken voice.

"For God's sake," said Minnerode, "let's get out of here and do something, will you?"

"What can we do?"

"Fight like hell—after we've finished off this pair!"

"If we murder 'em in cold blood, what if they should get us, later. I mean, the rest?"

"McGregor, you're thinkin' too far ahead."

"Shut up, man, and listen!"

And, out of the distance in a wild wail of triumph, they heard the voice of the crowd screaming: "Holles! Holles!"

They were both silent. As for me, I could have dropped on my knees and given thanks in an outburst of gratitude to God, though I'm no religious man. I looked at Lucas. That grave and stern man was weeping like a child with joy, with relief, and with excitement!

I was amazed at the sight of the great tears flowing down his face, but I'm afraid that I was perilously close to weeping, myself. My nerves were gone.

Then I heard McGregor saying: "It ain't possible! It ain't possible! It ain't no ways possible!"

"Man, man," shouted Minnerode to him, "don't you hear 'em with your own ears? It's Mex! It's Holles!

262

Come on out and help the boys to fight him!"

McGregor rushed to the rear door with a savage shout, but when he reached that point, the mysterious force of dread—or I know not what—stopped him there, and he retreated again.

"Johnnie, have you lost your nerve?" yelled Minnerode, wild with uncertainty and fear himself, but still willing to fight it out.

"No, no! You talk like a fool," rumbled McGregor. "But there's a sort of fate in it. It's here where I'm to meet him. Fate means it to be here."

"You're giving up the fight!"

"No, no. Listen! The boys will be drove back this way. We'll take them into the jail. We got a fort here, you see? Perfect? Walls too thick to shoot through—what could be more easy? Understand?"

Minnerode started to answer, but at that moment there was a savage roar of triumph mixed with explosions of guns. And Minnerode with a shudder stopped speaking. His own nerve was gone. He was only too willing to wait.

And wait they did, in the jail, while their fighting forces were scattered to one side and to the other, and while Jackson's place itself went down before the enchanted voice of our leader!

And so, at the last, all four of us stared out of the one window that looked down the street and saw that the friends of McGregor would not appear at all. They had been scattered to the four winds, and there remained only this battle front of danger!

"I'll get him now!" groaned great McGregor, and he jerked up his revolver and fired at a target big enough and hardly fifty yards away.

He missed! And I saw in reply a rapid jetting of fire from the muzzle of the revolvers of Holles. A storm of lead crashed through that window, and Minnerode staggered back with a great cry and fell on his face.

Over him crouched McGregor, and I heard him saying in a broken voice: "He's dead! He's dead! And I'm left alone! I'm all alone!"

Why, it was like the whimpering of a child!

And then all further sound inside the jail was lost to me in the rushing of infuriated men outside, except the sudden voice of Lucas at my ear: "McGregor has turned coward. He'll give up like a beaten dog!"

No, he was wrong; for at that moment the front door of the jail was dashed open, and McGregor, with a tremendous shout, rushed out upon his enemies, his long hair blowing over his shoulders. In his last fury, he had forgotten all about guns, and by instinct he had caught up a heavy chair by way of a club, and this was brandished above his head as he leaped down from the steps toward the faces of the crowd.

He was received upon the fire of a hundred guns. We saw him outlined against a red flare. And then he disappeared.

EPILOGUE

I AM GLAD, FOR MY PART, that big McGregor at the last found the courage in his heart to die like a man. I am glad, too, that he did not die by the single hand of terrible Holles. Because there would have been something dreadful in the thought of so great a giant falling before such a slender boy! No, he died as he had lived, in the face of great odds, fighting heroically. For even in his death struggle, as he fell down on the crowd, he dashed out the brains of one man with his chair, and crushed the life out of another with the last convulsive effort of his hands.

So died McGregor. So died disorder in Dorking Hollow. There was not so much as a whisper of trouble from that time forward. For one week, Holles remained with us, ordering matters. And there was no sign of a robber in the woods. There was no sign of disorder in the streets of Dorking Hollow. Men hardly dared to raise their voices. The loot which the thugs had taken under the direction of McGregor was largely recovered, because the big man had not allowed the greater part of it to be carted out of the town. So that dream of evil ended for us all, and we were restored to good cheer.

What did we do for Holles?

Well, we spent a good deal of time discussing the matter. Some were for a cash reward. But my suggestion was that we donate to him three very rich claims whose owners were willing to surrender them— one of mine being on the list. And then Holles would be a rich man for life—as he deserved to be.

We reached that decision at a night meeting, but the next morning there was no Holles to receive our reward.

There was only a brief note from him for me:

DEAR LOOMIS:

I have just received word that the Indian is heading for Mexico. It isn't too late for me to cut him off. When I've done that, and prevented him from bringing his deviltry into any new parts of the world, I'm going to come back to you. Forgive me for starting so abruptly, but I can't wait. The trail is burning in me!

Affectionately yours,
A.H.

But he never came back.

We waited. Then we started to work the claims for him. But Arthur Holles never came back. Neither did I ever hear of him again from that day to this.

What became of him? God alone can tell. It may be that the wiles of the poisoner overcame him on his last trail of vengeance. And it may be that after killing the Indian, he went on to take up a new life in a new land.

But what seems to me most likely is that, having killed the Indian, he closed the wilder chapters of his life and turned his face again toward the East. There he entered upon his rightful position in society.

I trust that it is a high one, that all honor and joy have entered his life, and that God has returned to him some of the joy and the good that he did for me and for many another yonder in Dorking Hollow, when he ruled us as King Stork.

But there was this difference, that while the frogs in the old fable prayed that King Stork might be taken away from them again, we in Dorking Hollow never ceased lamenting that he left us.

We hope that you enjoyed reading this
Sagebrush Large Print Western.
If you would like to read more Sagebrush titles,
ask your librarian or contact the Publishers:

Isis Publishing Ltd
7 Centremead
Osney Mead
Oxford
OX2 0ES
UK
+44 (0)1865 250333